NOW
SHE'S
DEAD

NOW SHE'S

DEAD

ROSELYN CLARKE

sourcebooks
fire

Published by Sourcebooks Fire, an imprint of Sourcebooks
P.O. Box 4410, Naperville, Illinois 60567–4410
(630) 961-3900
sourcebooks.com

Cataloging-in-Publication Data is on file with the Library of Congress.

Printed and bound in Canada.
MBP 10 9 8 7 6 5 4 3 2 1

For Aunt Marie, who was an inspiration to many and showed me this dream was possible.

1

NOW

SATURDAY AFTERNOON. ONE YEAR AFTER.

Finally arrived at Highmark! So freakin' ready to ~~endure~~ enjoy some vacay time with my family ~~who I've barely spoken to in months~~. Two weeks at the lake resort where ~~I killed a girl last year~~ we've gone every summer since I was twelve! ~~As long as I don't think about what happened on that night~~, this place is seriously amazing. ~~And I'm seriously screwed.~~ Yay!

I hit the delete button a little too hard on all the parts I can't share. Anddddd post. Post it. Post the photo, Mandy. It doesn't matter that most people won't pause their scrolling long enough to read. Not the girl I made out with last week at a party, or the boy from my dorm who insists I'm amazing but doesn't really know me. My roommate Em insisted I take pics, so they'll care, but they'll never know that it took me twenty minutes of typing and deleting to produce a fake smile and an even faker caption.

My sweaty finger smudges the screen. I have to leave this sauna of a car before I melt straight into the seat. With each passing minute, the smell of formerly iced coffee gets thicker, and the amount of pastel-blue hair sticking to my neck increases at an alarming rate. Disgusting.

I'm disgusting.

Coward.

My shoulders curl. Stalling is ridiculous, but I need a few more minutes to collect myself. I'm fine. I'll be fine. This is fine. I toss the phone onto the passenger seat and grip the steering wheel.

I'm going to spend the next two weeks at Highmark Inn & Resort.

Where a girl—

Where Sara—

Where someone—

Where *I* killed my friend.

Stop it. But I *can't* stop seeing her face. I bite down on the scream, knuckles going white around the wheel. Daffodils, dandelions, dahlias, crap need another that starts with *D*, daisies uhhhh nope, don't think about Sara, keep thinking about flowers, okay carnations, calendulas—

"Shit," I whisper to the empty car.

My gaze flicks to the rearview mirror, where the wood-paneled walls of the main lodge loom behind me, partially hidden by a line of trees. We both have so much to hide. Me, and this place where rustic charm lies like a bad filter over couples that "don't fight in public" and kids who treat consequences like fairy-tale villains.

Sara and I were those kids too.

My chest aches, and my hands fall to my lap, balled into fists. I have to get it together. Mom's been "checking in" too much lately. The insinuations are impossible to miss.

"Come to Highmark with us, Mandy. If it's too much for you, we'll work something else out." Her voice was so gentle, so reasonable on the phone that day, but her meaning was crystal clear.

Show us how well you're doing. Prove we made the right decision letting you start college early.

The annual summer vacation is a test this year, and if I fail, I'm screwed. Mom and Dad are going to yank me out of school in Virginia. And maybe they'd be right to do it, but then what? Eighteen years old with no skills besides breathing through a panic attack and keeping my eyes open during an art history class after only three hours of sleep. Move home and go to community college? That would be a nightmare with Mom hovering every step of the way and Dad watching me like he wants to say the right thing, but has no framework for navigating this new version of his daughter.

And Kelsey. I have to face Kelsey too.

God, I hope my sister doesn't hate me. Fifteen-year-olds hate a lot of things, but an older sister who ignored any and all texts for the better part of a year has to be pretty high on the list.

My sigh comes out high-pitched and thready, more like a wheeze. I haven't made it out of the car, and I'm already a mess.

I slip my fingers beneath my round black-framed glasses and rub my eyes. A lash falls out and pokes me in the eyeball. I hiss, reaching for the visor and ignoring the way my hand shakes.

In the small hazy mirror, bloodshot lines splinter through the whites of my eyes, making the brown irises look muddy and tired. And *goddamn* am I already tired. Ah, there! My nails are cut so brutally short that it's easy to run my finger back and forth over the cornea. Gotcha.

I replace the glasses and blink until the eye isn't watery anymore. I force a warped smile in the mirror. Highmark's main lodge lurks just over my shoulder, and I can't quite ignore the too-fast beat of my heart. Everyone here will remind me of the gap between now and how things were last year, and I'll continue to smile, exactly like this. Lips curled. Eyes crinkled. Screaming inside.

Screaming

Screaming

Screaming

Stop. Peonies, poppies, pansies…think…think of nothing, think, petunias, periwinkles.

I'm okay. I just need a little more time to forget. This will be difficult, not impossible. I give myself a quick shake and half-heartedly brush at the flaky orange crumbs littering my lap. In the passenger seat, the crumpled empty Cheez-It bag is a foil tribute to the only food I've consumed since driving seven hours straight from school. The knot in my throat grows.

Here, Mom will insist I *eat more than just junk,* because-*chips and coffee aren't a meal.* Dad will touch his fingers to the line of silver stud earrings running up both sides of my ears, and he'll say, *Those are new,* but he'll look at me sidelong for a while after. Kelsey will—

I don't know what Kelsey will do, but I know the most important part.

I know Sara Ellis is dead because of me.

2
NOW

SATURDAY AFTERNOON. ONE YEAR AFTER.

The path from the parking lot to our cottage suite wasn't this long last year. There are the same number of slate slabs, and it hugs the front side of the main lodge as it always has, but the path is longer today. It must be, because otherwise, time is working wrong.

But then, why shouldn't it be? Everything else is wrong.

I walk faster, careful to mind my step and avoid the spot where an underground root shoves the slate upward. Just like last year, and probably just like the next. Highmark is all subtly frayed edges clinging to appearances for dear life.

My own edges are fraying rapidly.

Every window fronting the single-room accommodations on the second story is a pair of potential eyes watching me. The wraparound porch buzzes with guests. If I look too closely, I might make accidental eye contact, and I don't want that. Would I see recognition, and if I did, what else would

I find? Pity? Curiosity? Blame? I scowl. I'm overreacting. No one's watching me, because I'm not special. She's dead because of me though, which makes me a monster, which is kind of special.

Knowing that if I'd been seen that night, someone would've come forward by now is a pitifully small comfort. Surely the time for grand revelations is long past.

My suitcase wheels bang over the uneven walkway, and I grit my teeth against every rattle and roll. It's too loud. The tension between my shoulder blades pinches tighter until it feels like there's a large fishhook lodged in my back.

"Welcome!" a paisley-clad Mrs. Miller calls from the porch. Her perfect honey-blond highlights gleam where the sun hits.

So much for not being recognized. She and her husband watch their regular guests arrive from their rocking chair thrones, just like they do every year. Has *anything* changed?

One thing, for sure. No more Sara.

Mrs. Miller—or the Replacement, if the adults are whispering behind her back—waves, iced tea in hand. Mr. Miller does the same, and the softly wrinkled lines of his face stretch as he flashes a crooked smile. It's safe to assume Leigh isn't around. Mr. Miller's seventeen-year-old daughter will be steering clear of anywhere her stepmom is, if she came at all this year.

Lips tight and chin stubbornly tipped down, I return the wave and keep moving. Back then, the cops said it was a tragic firework accident, and Sara was an unlucky drunk teen, but I'd bet the iced tea in Mrs. Miller's hand that she and her husband still blamed me for police swarming their dignified resort. After all, I was with her; then I left her out in those woods, and now she's dead. They don't need to know the whole story to know I screwed up.

Please God, don't let them recognize me.

And they don't. Because Mandy Jenkins doesn't have choppy blue hair or wear frayed shorts with her leather boots. Mandy Jenkins wears her sun-streaked brown hair long around tanned shoulders, with cute jeans and sandals. She sticks to contacts instead of glasses.

Or, she did before—

Soaked jeans clinging to my legs, dirt beneath my fingernails.

A little girl shrieks as she bolts across the rolling stretch of lawn to my right. I flinch. Get to the cottage. Get to my room and put my stuff down and just *chill.*

To my left, a perfectly manicured patch of grass sits between the main lodge and a row of cottages running the length of the river as it curves around to the lake. The water surrounded by oak and pine-covered mountains is picture-perfect, and when I inhale, the air tastes like sunshine and childhood, but there's something distinctly rotten about the nostalgia worming its way through my chest. I look away.

She died out there, tucked beneath those trees, with the water gently lapping at her blood.

"Mandy?"

The voice is uncertain. Deeper than I remember too.

"Alex," I breathe. I lied for him and he lied for me, but facing each other, now, feels painfully honest.

It's not, though.

I've forgotten how to be honest.

His dark brown hair, burnished with coppery highlights, is pushed back from his face, as if he's just run his hand through the waves. A whistle hangs around his neck, swinging in the center of a T-shirt that looks like he's tugged it on and off too many times. Red swim trunks cut across his thighs, and when he walks, the pale, untanned skin flashes as the shorts shift upward.

Alex is as stunning as ever, maybe more, and as terrible as it is given, well, what happened, my cheeks warm. Quick, say something. Anything. Literally anything at all.

"You're here." Not that.

His brows dip over blue eyes—my *God*, and those lashes—and he retreats a half step. "So are you."

Shit. We're off to a great start. Fresh sweat trickles down my spine.

"You're lifeguarding again this summer?" I ask, which earns me a hesitant smile.

He smells like sunscreen and coconut. I bet his skin is warm.

"Exclusively. No more splitting time between the stand and shifts in the Shack."

"That's great. Con-congratulations." I don't quite get the last word out smooth. It feels obscene to be congratulating him on a summer job when the last time we talked, we were deciding to lie to the cops about our whereabouts. "I figured you probably wouldn't be back, what with…"

His jaw clenches, and I instantly regret having said anything. It's weird that he's here, but it's weird that I'm here too.

"Alex!" someone calls from the opposite end of the lawn. She sounds annoyed.

I glance toward the voice and find Hannah waving Alex over. She's dressed in her staff uniform, with khakis and a forest-green polo, and her thick brown hair swings from a high ponytail.

I raise a hand to wave, but she completely ignores me, which is…~~weird~~ interesting, since Hannah and I were sort of friends. I frown. We were at least friend*ly*. What's her deal?

I swallow. I guess none of us ended on exactly great terms, last summer.

"I've got to get to the lake. I'll see you around," Alex says, but the words feel dull, like he's saying them out of obligation and has absolutely no desire to *actually* "see me around."

~~I'm sorry. Sorry for the way things played out and the way I used you and~~ "See you later."

3

THEN

SATURDAY AFTERNOON. FOUR DAYS BEFORE.

Sara stretched, and sweat rolled from her belly button over the curve of her pale hip as she let out a noise somewhere between a squeal and a sigh. Sunlight flashed off the silver heart charm sitting high on her neck. I scowled and looked away, squinting into the bright sky.

"So?" she asked.

I blinked. I'd missed something.

Sara reached across the space between our plastic lounge chairs and gave my forearm a quick pinch. "Mandy. Pay attention."

"Sorry, what did you say?"

She tucked her elbows beneath her to prop herself up and skewered me with a look that pretended to be patience, but was really frustration. "I said Nathan is still texting me. But I shouldn't lead him on, right? It's not like I'm going to get back with him, so should I text him back and tell him to get over me, or should I ignore him?"

I groaned before realizing my mistake and turning the sound into a "hmmm."

Sara had been talking about dumping her loser boyfriend all day, ever since her family arrived three hours after mine. Was it really my fault I'd tuned out?

Then again…at least Sara got to be the one doing the dumping. *I like you, I really do. But I just don't think I love you, and I don't want to start my freshman year in a relationship that's doesn't have a future. I'm really sorry.* I'd worked my ass off, packed my schedule with the necessary classes, all to be able to graduate early and follow Dan up to school in Virginia. We'd been together since I was a sophomore, and one month before graduation he decides I'm not good enough to waste any more time on.

My chest constricted. Maybe I should've been paying better attention to Sara's ramblings. She knew how to be someone worth loving. Someone who never got left behind or abandoned for something—some*one*—better.

People didn't abandon girls like Sara.

"Don't text him?" I offered, but it came out more like a question. How was I supposed to know the right answer to relationship questions? Clearly, I was clueless.

Sara pulled the heart charm to her lips and popped the whole thing in her mouth. The thin chain bit gently into the sides of her neck, her cheeks, her lips. Her teeth clicked softly on the metal as she considered my answer.

Stop chewing on my necklace! I clamped my jaw tight to keep the words from escaping. I gave it to her years ago. It shouldn't bother me anymore, and yet somehow, the wanting, the *needing* to snatch it back seemed to get worse every time I saw her.

Too bad. She could do whatever she wanted with her necklace. Hers. Not mine.

She spat the charm out, the thin chain dropping to nestle between her collarbones. "I won't text him." Her voice was lazy. Cool. Just like the wind that rolled across the lake, carrying the smell of shadowed pine and muddy shores. God, to be that unbothered. If I could've figured out a non-embarrassing way to ask her how to manage that, I would've.

"Sara?"

"Hm?"

I hadn't been able to bring myself to tell her about Dan, but she was going to figure it out soon enough. The one silver lining of getting dumped by my first real boyfriend was that I was finally free to see if there was anything between Alex and me.

Highmark had two main docks: the smaller one that we were on, nearest the lodge, and a larger one attached to the Snack Shack on the other side of the man-made beach. Alex perched atop the lifeguard stand on the larger dock. He'd spent the last two summers stuck in the Shack. At least now he was getting a few shifts out in the sun, and it *really* agreed with him.

"Dan broke up with me," I said, spitting the words out quick and quiet.

Sara gasped.

"Oh my God! Why didn't you say anything sooner? I just rambled for *hours* about Nathan. Why didn't you stop me? What happened?"

I shrugged, unable to hold her worried gaze.

"It's okay. I don't really want to talk about it," I mumbled.

Sara nodded, but not like she was convinced. Her brows shot up.

"Wait, does this mean you're not going to William and Mary anymore? Mandy! Ahh!" She made a strangled, excited noise, and I tensed. I knew what was coming. "Wait a year for me, and we can be roommates at Appalachian State like we always planned."

Oh, she was *not* going to like this.

"Sara, I'm still going to William and Mary."

Her brows snapped together and her mouth wilted. After an awkward silence, she asked, "*Why?*"

It was a good question. If I went to William & Mary, there was a good chance Sara wouldn't be able to follow me, even a year later. Could she pull her GPA up enough in time for applications? I chewed my lip. I'd dreamed of sharing a dorm room with Sara—staying up late watching movies on a laptop, going to parties together, hanging string lights above our beds—for so long. With Dan out of the picture, why couldn't I go back to that again?

Because college was a month and a half away. I'd already done the shopping trips with Mom. I'd found a roommate in the forums; their name was Em and they seemed really chill. More importantly I'd sworn up and down to my parents that I didn't want to graduate early "just to be with my boyfriend." What was I supposed to do now?

"Because I'm already done with high school. My parents won't let me just sit around home for a year."

"Have you asked them?"

"No, but..."

"Come on. Tell them you changed your mind and you're not ready. They're not going to *make* you go. I bet your mom will be happy, even."

I snorted. She might have a point.

"So you'll ask?"

"Fiiine, I'll ask them." I was lying, but I pushed the guilt down. It's not like my parents would say yes, anyway.

Sara squealed. "Yay! Oh, Mandy, I'm so sorry about Dan, but *yay*." A small grin pulled the corner of her mouth up, pink and perfect beneath the splash of pale brown freckles. I'd missed that smile. Sporadic texts and hearts exchanged on posts throughout the year just weren't the same.

"This summer's going to be so much fun," she said, half to herself.

I loved her enthusiasm, but still, my insides squirmed. Sara's idea of fun and my idea of fun didn't always fit together quite right. They overlapped, but not perfectly. She never seemed worried about what-ifs. Her parents and mine might be mostly oblivious while we were here—they were usually too busy catching up and golfing and drinking wine—but I hated pushing our luck. Sara didn't.

Embrace it, Mandy. Summer vacation should be perfect. *I* could be perfect, if I tried hard enough. What would Sara do, if she'd been dumped? How would she move on?

I pushed sticky strands of hair off my neck and smiled back at her. "Since I'm suddenly single," I said, expertly and not-at-all-obviously changing the subject, "want to help me hook up with Alex? Can you get Finn to stop being such a jerk and invite us to hang out with them more this year?"

Sara snorted and my smile slipped. Why had she laughed? Silence.

Why had she laughed?

Was the concept of me being interested in Alex so ridiculous that she found it funny? I shouldn't have said anything. Her eyes swept over me, and her brows raised. She had to be thinking about how delusional I was. Heat flared across my cheeks, and I tucked my chin to hide the creeping blush.

She gave a slow shrug and flicked her hair off her shoulder. "My brother is always a jerk," she said, rolling her eyes. "But I'll convince him."

Oh. Good. She wasn't laughing at me. Probably. She made a *"hmm"* sound. I followed her gaze across the lake, where Alex sat with one arm draped over the back of the lifeguard chair, his eyes hidden behind dark sunglasses.

A strange nervousness fluttered in my stomach. I didn't love the way she was watching him.

I huffed, more at myself than anything else, and heaved myself up from the lounge chair. "I'm getting in."

"Tell me if it's cold."

"It's always cold."

She was right, and I never could stand the slow creep of lowering myself in from the ladder. With a screech, I launched out over the shining surface of the lake. Legs tucked to my chest, arms wrapped around my shins, the biting cold of the water rushed over my head.

Down

Down

Down

I kicked my legs out beneath me, flipping and twirling on my way up through the dark. I broke the surface to find Sara staring down at me from the edge of the dock. Her blue eyes sparkled. Slowly, she removed one of the hair ties perpetually present on her left wrist and tied the masses of strawberry-blond hair up in a bun on top of her head. She watched me, and I watched her, and the small smile tucked between her lips never faltered.

Behind me, someone shrieked, and I spun around to see one kid drag another off the small floating dock at the edge of the roped-off section of the lake. They hit the water mid-giggle and came up sputtering and laughing.

"Mandy..." Sara sang my name: beautiful, taunting.

Not nearly enough warning before she crashed down on top of me.

Too fast. Too fast for a breath. Water rushed down my throat, filling my lungs instantly with cold fire. Couldn't breathe, couldn't see, couldn't stop myself from the cough that sucked in more of what would suffocate me.

Her arms around my shoulders. Hair tangling with mine. A leg wrapped around my hip, tight.

Can't breathe.

My hands searched, finding the bend of her elbow, the muscle of her thigh. I tapped, *let me go, let me go,* but she clung tighter and dragged us down.

Her face tucked into the bend of my neck. The tickle of bubbles, like she was laughing into my skin.

I screamed, and the screams turned instantly to racking coughs.

My body spasmed as my hands pushed against her shoulders, her chest, the softness of her stomach.

And then she released me and was gone.

Only panic remained, burning along my ribs and screaming through my head.

I scrambled for something, *anything* to get back to the surface, but there was nothing except the dark and the cold and *oh shit oh shit oh shit.*

There. Soft, fluffy mud beneath my fingers. I twisted, barely registering a stick as it scraped a line across my thigh. My toes squelched and I pushed off—up—but I was so dizzy, and God, I was shaking so bad.

Was it getting…darker?

Help me, someone.

A firm hand hooked beneath my armpit and yanked. The instant air hit the top of my head, I sucked in a breath of pure desperation. Too soon. My mouth wasn't fully clear of the sloshing water. My chest heaved. My shoulders shook.

Hair swirled around my torso, and two pale arms hooked around my chest.

A hard bump as I was yanked up the floating dock's ladder and onto the warm wooden boards. The force knocked another round of coughing from my lungs, and my stomach turned as spots flickered in my vision.

Sara's face swam into view, the silver heart charm around her neck flashing as it dangled inches from my nose. "Oh my God, Mandy, are you okay?"

I couldn't stop coughing long enough to answer.

"Mandy?" Another voice, deeper and less frantic than Sara's, but just as worry-laced.

Oh no. No no no—cough—no.

Alex. Coppery hair dripping wet over those deep, worried blue eyes. He knelt close, with one tan, muscled arm braced on his knee.

I rolled onto my side and vomited lake water all over the dock.

I was going to *kill* Sara for this.

4

NOW

SATURDAY AFTERNOON. ONE YEAR AFTER.

There's a betta fish on the dresser in the room my sister and I share, fringed tail waving iridescent blue, and somehow that's not the weirdest thing I find when I reach the cottage.

There are two sets of luggage here already.

I'm frozen just inside the doorway, staring. The smell of clean linen and wood polish is simultaneously comforting and cruel: a thousand beautiful memories and an agonizing few making a ruin of the rest. Kelsey dragging the covers off me in the morning. The sound of Mom humming from the sunroom while she drinks her first cup of coffee. Hot tears rolling down my temples, pooling salt in the corners of my mouth as I stare at the ceiling and silently sob.

I shudder. The quiet whir of the air conditioner is the only sound in the cottage besides my own breathing. Where is everyone?

And also: who is "everyone"?

The thought is sandpaper: all grit and fire as it scrapes its way through my head, leaving an uncomfortable rawness behind. Highmark is a *family* holiday. That's the rule. Or so I thought.

To the left, tucked against the far wall, the same yellow suitcase with the little white flowers that Kelsey has had for years is open at the foot of her bed, and a T-shirt is flung over the heavy dark-wood frame. But tossed against the floor-to-ceiling mirror doors of the closet between my bed and Kelsey's is a huge duffel bag. Clothes spew from the partially unzipped canvas, and a red backpack rests against what looks like...a camera bag?

I shrug out of my own backpack and drop it to the floor beside the dresser. *Thump*. The fish darts around the bowl in surprise.

"Sorry, buddy," I mutter, crossing the few steps to the mystery belongings.

Replaced. I've been replaced. I effed up and now she's replaced me.

The carpet is too thin to offer much cushioning, and my bare knees sting as they press into the floor. The front pocket of the backpack bulges outward and I yank the whole thing into my lap by the straps. What have we got in here?

And why am I digging through someone else's stuff? There's hand sanitizer. A whole mess of tangled charger cords. A notebook.

I flip open the notebook and scan the first page. It's a list of names, with additional notes scribbled next to some people, but not others.

Mandy (Kelsey's sister)

Well. That can't be good.

Mike and Rachel Jenkins (Kelsey's parents)
Charlotte and James Ellis (Sara's parents)
Finn (Sara's brother)
Alex (friend. Staff)
Mr. and Mrs. Miller (Owner. Second wife. 58. 31)
Leigh Miller (resort owner's daughter, age? 17)
Hannah (staff. Friend?)
Neighbors? Additional staff? Other guests?

Someone is gathering information. Why? And *why* are they staying *here*, in our cabin?

I fan the remaining pages quickly, and find it about half-filled.

"I'm not having this conversation again."

Mom.

I drop the notebook, air hissing through my teeth as I gasp.

The *thump-creak*, *thump-creak* of footsteps on the raised porch makes it hard to catch the words, but Mom doesn't like Dad's response.

I shove everything into the bag and scramble to the bedroom's open door.

Mom laughs, but in a "be careful what you say next" kind of way. "Sure Mike, you keep thinking that. But if she's struggling, then she's coming home, and I don't want to hear another word about your office. That's her room. Always will be, for as long as she needs it."

"Rachel, I didn't mean…"

I haven't heard either of their voices since Christmas, forcing our limited conversations into short texts. An ache swells in my chest. I miss them, but oh God, this is going to be painful. It's harder to pretend around people who really know you, and I'm already worn thin. What happens when they see the cracks? What happens when they apply pressure? I can't afford to fall apart.

I'm pressed so tight against the slim space between the doorway and the dresser that any second now I could melt into the paneled wood. Nothing but this wall, the sunroom, and a screen door on squeaky hinges separating me from my parents.

Smile, Mandy, and you better get used to it because they're going to be watching you close this entire trip. Smile. Wait, no. That feels wrong. I catch a glimpse of my face in the sliding door mirror across the room and wince. Definitely wrong.

I scrunch my nose and roll my shoulders back and try again. Better.

The screen door whines open, carrying a warm breeze and the sound of rustling branches. I step into the sunroom at the same time as my parents.

"Hi, Mom. Dad."

Mom yelps, which of course is a great reaction to have

when seeing your child. She freezes with one foot on the porch and one on the thin green carpet. My stomach twists, and I can't look at them like this, with their faces struggling to land on an appropriate expression.

The sunroom is all windows on the side overlooking the river and the woods beyond. I want to plant one boot on the plum-red sofa, crank the windowpane open, and launch myself straight through the mesh screen. A quick twelve-foot drop, and I'd be in the river, swimming away from confrontation. Or I'd break an ankle in the shallows.

Instead, I shove my hands into the pockets of my jean shorts, forcing the tiny space to make room for my fists.

"How are you, honey? How was the drive?" Mom asks. Her smile is overbright and doesn't quite mask the worry in her eyes, but it's better than the silent way Dad searches my face.

"Fine," I say. The same answer for both questions, but it's a lie for only one.

"That's an interesting color," Dad says.

Ah, so close. I thought he would say something about the new piercings. My mistake.

"It is." Mom's tone is different, but she doesn't manage to sound *pleased*. "Such a pale shade of blue. I like it." There's a second's pause. "Does it wash out?"

"No, it's dyed." I reach for the ends of my hair where it hangs just past my shoulders, but drop my hand quickly. Don't fidget, Mandy. Don't be nervous. "But I'll probably let it grow out. It was fun to try."

Already, I'm shrinking.

"I do love your blond hair," she says.

I resist asking her why she still calls my hair blond when it's been a light brown for years. "Whose stuff is in our room?"

"We should have told her," Dad says under his breath, but not so quiet that he didn't clearly intend for us to hear. He crosses to the small end table tucked against the wall between the two rooms and pours himself a tumbler of scotch.

I've stepped into the middle of an argument between my parents.

Mom wrings her hands together once, twice, and then thrusts her arms wide. "A hug for your mom first? Before we get to catching up?"

The second when her smile falters gives her fear away. She doesn't know if I'll accept. Before...*before*...I would've hugged her without question. Let her warm arms pull me close and squish my muscular body into her plump one. Mom loves hugging, and I loved to let her.

Now, my upper back is stiff, and not just from the long drive. I force my shoulders down and step into her arms, letting her give me a brief squeeze. It's not really the hug itself I want to avoid. It's the scent of chamomile that envelops me: the same Herbal Essences shampoo she's used for years. It's her beautifully graying hair that she never wanted to dye tickling my cheek.

It's how being here makes me want to cry, and what if a second of softness cracks me?

I indulge in one deep, floral inhale before I pull away.

The smell is safety and a love that feels more like a memory than anything else. How did this become our new normal?

It takes more effort than it should not to cross my arms over my chest as soon as she releases me.

~~Who else did you invite into this nightmare?~~ "Who else is here?" I have to know.

Mom clasps her hands together but drops them to her side almost instantly. "Your sister brought a friend this year. She needed, she, we thought she could use a friend after—"

She cuts herself off abruptly.

My gut clenches.

Suddenly everything is hot and tight, like we're trapped inside a greenhouse. Or insects beneath a magnifying glass. There's a beat of silence as neither of us knows how to restart. Dad crosses between us, patting my shoulder as he makes for the armchair.

Mom blinks and finds her voice again. "Yes, let's sit. Sit." She gestures to the sofa pushed up against the wall of windows. A swaying sea of mottled leaves and deep green pine needles are blurred through the glass and metal mesh screens.

I could be there again in an instant: dirt beneath my nails and the lake drinking my tears.

"Kelsey brought a friend from school," Mom says, and I snap out of the spiral. She sits and thumps the seat next to her, making plenty of space for me.

I have one leg off the ground, ready to shift my back against the armrest like I always do, when I freeze. "A... friend?"

"Yes. Natalie Carpenter. Her parents are in Italy visiting family, but Natalie is afraid of flying, so she's really excited to be here instead. She's a sweetheart but, hmm, well you'll see. Let's say she's got a lot of energy," Mom finally settles on.

"Do I know her?" I don't remember a Natalie in Kelsey's life.

"She's a new friend. From the soccer team. They've been hanging out a lot this year. Practically joined at the hip all summer."

I don't know if I like that, but I can't say why. ~~Jealousy, worry, confusion, Sara.~~ I'm being weird about nothing. So what if Kelsey brought someone else to hang out with?

The *why* clicks. Because she's got a frickin' list of people who were directly impacted by Sara's death. It's creepy. It's suspicious as hell.

It could be a *big problem*.

Dad glances at his watch. "Our dinner slot is at six-thirty, did you tell the girls that?"

Mom nods. "They know to be back in time to change." She inclines her head to me. "You brought dinner clothes, right?"

As if after six years of vacationing at Highmark, I would suddenly have forgotten that dinner is no place for jean shorts and scuffed-up boots. I open my mouth.

~~Nope. Nothing but what you see on my body right this second.~~

"Duh." Okay, was that really an improvement?

Mom's mouth thins and she gives me a Look. "Don't be

difficult," she says, but she reaches over to rub my knee, and her hand lingers for a gentle squeeze.

~~Love you too, Mom. Even if I can't stand being here.~~ "I'll go change."

A stampede of feet and a spill of laughter comes from the porch. My stomach drops. The urge to bolt swamps my limbs. I'm on my feet, rooted in place, when they burst into the cottage.

Kelsey is first through the door. Her round face is split in a grin, her dark blond hair pulled up in a haphazard bun, and she's half-turned toward the girl who I assume is Natalie. "Mom, we got the scavenger hunt list," Kelsey proclaims, a green flyer clutched in her hand. "We're going to be—"

She sees me, and her eyes widen, her expression bleeding all the laughter away until what's left is a look I've never seen from my sister before.

It's not hatred, which is a relief. But I didn't expect...

Fear.

5

NOW

SATURDAY NIGHT. ONE YEAR AFTER.

The guests at the resort are all the same. I don't know whether it's because I was wrapped up in Sara before, or because I'm one big bundle of annoyance now, but the energy is…suffocatingly bland. With everyone packed into the dining room, they run together like endless copies of each other.

It's strange, knowing not even a violent death could permanently disrupt Highmark life.

The sea of slacks and dinner jackets move in a slow dance with summer sundresses. Most of the people are middle-aged or older, and white, though not all, and everyone—*everyone*—makes sure to say hello to Mr. and Mrs. Miller on their way inside.

I can't see the entrance doors from my seat at our table, but every cheerful "Hello" and every rumbled "How are you?" makes my shoulders climb higher up my neck.

I keep expecting to hear her.

Mandy! Hey, Mandy, come sit with us!

Last year started out so…normal. Until it wasn't.

Help me, Mandy.

Stop. Sunflowers, Susans, no, wait, it's black-eyed Susans.

The chicken Parmesan sitting in my stomach sours. I push the remaining bite across my plate, flinching when the metal tines of my fork squeal against the porcelain. Over the top of his wineglass, Dad shoots me a look that says, *stop playing with your food*, and I pull the inside of my lip between my teeth. Highmark's long window-lined dining room is filled with the tinkling clatter of silverware and polite chatter, and I'm supposed to mind my manners.

Just like everyone else.

The pressure chafes worse without Sara. Sara never cared so much about what Highmark, or her parents, wanted from her. Sometimes she didn't care what *I* wanted either, but at least I got to tuck myself inside her little bubble. Better to belong with Sara than with no one.

I set the fork down and take a sip of coffee, chasing away the thought.

"You're going to be up all night," Mom says, reaching for the bottle of red.

"I'll sleep fine," I lie. I haven't slept fine in a year.

Two lines form between Mom's brows, and her lips pucker. "Are you eating right at school? Chips and coffee—"

"Aren't a meal," I finish for her. Some things never change. "I'm eating fine, I swear. I'm just tired from the drive. I don't want to crash by eight o'clock on our first night here."

This earns me a nod of approval from Mom at one end of the table and a small chuckle from Dad at the other. He probably suspects, correctly, that I'm lying to appease Mom.

Across from me, Natalie whispers something to Kelsey. They've been whispering since the cottage. I'm not a fan.

Natalie might've been overshadowed next to my sister, her thin frame bent toward Kelsey's round one, except that Natalie is nearly a head taller than Kelsey, who's only five foot two. They slouch into each other, and their hair smooshes together: Natalie's short brown curls mingling with Kelsey's straight hair.

Kelsey shakes her head, and Natalie nudges her shoulder. My sister huffs. Natalie grins. There's something about the intensity in their eyes. Shades of mirrored brown.

Who is this person who has so comfortably taken my place?

"Y'all play soccer together?" I ask.

Kelsey drops her hands into her lap. When she lifts her gaze, she doesn't look as openly afraid as she did in the cottage. A different sort of light has seeped in: determination. "Varsity."

A one-word answer. Great.

Natalie clears her throat. "Well, *you* play varsity. I show up and kick a ball around because my mom says I have to do at least one social activity that 'isn't just internet friends.'" Her voice contorts into a screechy, off-kilter imitation that I assume is supposed to be her mom.

The version of me from before Sara died could relate to

that. Tired of tennis and pressure. Off the court I'd been too awkward. Too…uncertain. Always on the edge but never let in. Except with Sara. Sara let me in and made it easy. I *belonged* ~~to someone~~ for those brief, perfect two weeks each year. Until they weren't perfect, and everything fell apart.

The new me just wonders what Natalie does that keeps her online so much. Maybe she's a gamer. Or super into DIY.

Or she's a creepy stalker…making lists about my family. About Sara.

"Internet friends?" I ask. I'm going to make an effort, for Kelsey's sake.

Natalie draws her narrow shoulders back, puffing out her chest and lifting her pointy chin so that she's all sharp angles and an even sharper smile. "Friends, *and* followers. CrimeChatWithNat. I talk about old true-crime cases, and sometimes newer ones, by request."

Well, that *can't* be good. "True—" I choke on my own spit. "True crime? Like…"

"Like missing persons. Bank robberies. Murder," Kelsey says. On the surface, her face is as sweet as ever. Round, with a slight flush to her cheeks and wide-open eyes, but there's challenge in her voice.

My pulse kicks against the side of my neck.

"Have you heard of her?" Kelsey continues. "She's pretty big on Instagram. And YouTube. People really like her channel because she's so good at putting the pieces together and working with families who want their stories told."

Mom says Kelsey's name in quiet warning, but stops

short of pointing out why it might be awkward to talk about death at this particular dinner table.

Putting the pieces together, putting the lies together, putting the truth about what I did to Sara together, and spewing it all over the internet. Now I know what that list was about.

We're her suspects.

The room is hot, loud, and oppressive, and there's a panicky sound caught at the back of my throat—alive and wriggling. My sister is obviously digging for a reaction, but she's come in with a backhoe when all she needed was a spoon.

I push back from the table, stumbling when the chair doesn't move enough. My knee smashes into the table leg, and there's a second where the bottle of red wine wobbles, and Dad's hand shoots out, but the neck slips through his fingers.

The bottle shatters against the wooden floor, spilling burgundy over the polished boards.

"Mandy," Dad snaps.

"Mike, it's fine. Here." Mom's eyes are extra wide as she tosses her napkin to me. "Girls? Girls, pass Mandy your napkins, quickly."

There's an entire bottle's worth of wine on the floor, and my family is chucking napkins, like little white ghosts, onto the puddle. It's chaos.

"Mandy?"

The buzz of the room floods my ears for half a second. I think it's Sara, but no. It's her *mother*. Charlotte Ellis sweeps across the dining hall from the entryway, with Mr. Ellis a step behind. Oh, *God*. What were they *doing* here, and why hadn't I thought to ask my parents if they were coming? The soft light of the dining hall momentarily grows even softer at the edges of my vision. Is there any chance this isn't real? That I don't have to face them? Can I run?

No. No, because where would I run to? There's no running from this trip.

They're only a few feet away, so I breathe as deep as I can manage and hold the breath tight in my chest. Sara's dad has put on weight and grown a beard—I've never seen him with facial hair before, much less a beard—and Charlotte has trimmed her once long hair to just below her ears, but mostly they're...the same as always.

She locks eyes with me, and I swear I see the desperation hiding behind her blue eyes. I just hope she doesn't corner me again. I don't think I could stand it.

Mr. Ellis nods to Mom and Dad. "Mike. Rachel."

He avoids looking at me directly, like he can't quite stand the reminder that his daughter should be standing next to me.

Mrs. Ellis wraps me in a careful hug, her arms barely brushing my shoulders even though the embrace lingers a beat too long, before she puts a healthy two-foot distance between us again.

"It's so good to see you," she says, but her voice hitches.

My cheeks heat. How can they stand being here at all, when they know their daughter's body was found at the lake's edge, face mangled and—

Stop. My eyes are watering, I have to stop. Hibiscus, hydrangeas, camellias, chrysanthemums, crocuses.

"Good to see you too," I choke out.

Mr. Ellis manages a lukewarm smile and the briefest of eye contact, and then goes around me to talk to Dad.

"What in the world happened?" Mrs. Ellis asks, indicating the broken glass and spilled wine, and even as I open my mouth to answer, a server bearing several dish towels swoops in to sop up the mess.

"We knocked over a whole bottle," Mom interjects. "Such a waste."

I appreciate the "we."

Sara's mom laughs, even though it's not actually funny. "Well, Mandy, I'm glad you're here. We almost didn't come this year, you know, with…with…what happened." She's can't say it. I don't blame her. "But we wanted one more goodbye. It'll mean so much to have you say a few words at the memorial." The look in her eyes is achingly fragile, and I hate myself for putting it there.

Wait. The what?

"The what?" Oops.

"Charlotte," Mom says warily. "We hadn't brought it up yet. Mandy only arrived a couple hours ago, and we've been getting settled."

Mrs. Ellis presses manicured fingers to her lips. "Sorry, Rachel. Well now that I've already brought it up, you'll speak at the memorial for Sara, won't you Mandy? If it's too difficult for you I understand, but you were her best friend here. I know Sara would've wanted it."

I know she and her husband have mixed feelings about

me. I'm alive and their daughter isn't. All of Mrs. Ellis's frantic questions about what happened and Mr. Ellis's chilling "so you left her out there alone" the next morning seem to have been set aside, but I know those feelings *must* still be in there, lurking beneath the surface.

I'm a link to Sara, and they can't afford to shun me. Not if they want to keep Sara alive through new stories—new pieces of the daughter they didn't pay enough attention to when she was alive.

I don't want to share our story.

"Sure," I say, wishing I could take the word back the instant it leaves my lips. There's a very real chance I'm going to pass out if this conversation goes on any longer.

Mrs. Ellis leans in, which means I must've whispered.

"Sure. I'll speak. Thank you." Why, for the love of caffeine and carbs, am I thanking her?

As the Ellises depart, I focus on not dropping my forehead to the tablecloth and burying my face in my arms. That was worse than I expected, and better than I deserved. I guess I should be grateful all the Ellises want from me is a few words at a memorial for their daughter, even if the thought makes me want to vomit.

"Mom, Natalie and I are going down to the lounge," Kelsey says, pausing only long enough for Mom to voice an objection, if she'd had one, before my sister and Natalie are gone.

Oh, right. I'd been fleeing too, before the wine and the horror of facing the Ellises. I frown. Not quite "the Ellises." Even without Sara, there's still one missing. Sara's older brother.

"Dad, is Finn here?" I ask, praying the answer is no. Last I heard he was at college in Georgia (and not doing great, according to Mom). Maybe he's staying down there over the summer. Please, anywhere but here. I can't face him.

"You know what, sweetheart, I'm not sure. Charlotte said Finn's coming for the memorial, but I don't know if that means he's getting here ahead of time, or if he's here already, or maybe not until the day of, which will be Wednesday, by the way. That way it'll be happening the day before all the Summer Bash events start on Thursday."

I nod, because that's the best I can manage. As painful as seeing Mr. and Mrs. Ellis was, seeing Finn would be...will be...worse. After the secrets and the arguments that got out of control last year, I'd rather he didn't show up at all.

Hell, if he hadn't showed up last June, everything might've been different. Everything might've been...okay.

Sara might be alive still.

6

NOW

SATURDAY NIGHT. ONE YEAR AFTER.

My armchair is oversized with fraying green fabric and dark clawed feet. It's always been my chair, but I can't get comfortable. Last year, Sara would've been perched beside me, leaning her shoulder against mine while she tried to convince her parents not to give her a curfew for the night. I shrink away from where Sara would've—*should've*—been, and pick at the beginnings of a loose thread.

Our not-so-little group is tucked into one corner of Highmark's bar and lounge. Outside, guests walk past, their ankles illuminated by the lighted pathway while the rest of them is cut off where the squat windows end. Being in this part of the lodge is like being underground, even if the sloping landscape means the far end of the lounge leads straight out onto a small patio, where a cool breeze rolls in through the glass double doors.

My eyelids droop, and it's only nine o'clock. That's

embarrassing. I need to wake up. I need caffeine, but the ceramic mug wedged between my thigh and the armrest contains only a sip of lukewarm coffee.

Unfortunately, the only way I'm getting a fresh cup is if I brave Kelsey and Natalie over at the bar. Their heads are *still* bent together, feet swinging from the barstools.

Across the coffee table, Mom and Mrs. Ellis are in the middle of needling Mrs. Miller under the guise of polite conversation. I'm pretty sure Mrs. Miller knows.

"And how's the candle business going?" Mom asks Mrs. Miller. "It must be so nice to get to make so many crafts."

Mrs. Ellis sips her wine. Mom doesn't give a crap about Mrs. Miller's "silly hobby," as she so bluntly put it last year, turning the pine-scented candle back and forth to read the label. Stay Awhile: Highmark Inn & Resort, with *by Alicia Miller* in small script at the bottom. They'd smelled nice to me, but Mom had been unimpressed. She and Mrs. Ellis would've been unimpressed with anything the Replacement did.

Mom had really liked Mr. Miller's first wife, but Alicia has been around for three years. Seems like time to let it go.

Mrs. Miller's smile cuts a perfect, perky curve across her face, but there's a second when her eyes are a little too wide. She *has* to know they don't like her the way they liked the first wife. There's a spark of pity flickering against my chest, because I know that look. The one that screams, *Let me in! I'm part of this too.*

Mrs. Miller isn't deterred. "I'm hoping to expand the

line and do a special edition for the Summer Bash next year. Really memorialize all the great times people have had here."

Mom darts a look at Mrs. Ellis, almost too quick to see. Neither of them responds for several bone-achingly awkward seconds, until Mrs. Ellis says slowly, "Yes…a lot of memories of the Summer Bash."

Mrs. Miller pales, and Mom's twisting her hands together so hard I half expect to see the skin split over her knuckles.

Mrs. Ellis recovers quickly, a cold smile forming. "And is your darling *step*daughter looking forward to the celebrations? How *are* you and Leigh getting along? Any better?"

Nope. Big nope. Mr. Miller's seventeen-year-old daughter hates her dad's new young wife, and everyone knows it. Then again, Leigh's not exactly friendly to anyone. That girl is stuck up, always has been. She wasn't around when Sara and I were younger—off at sleepaway camp somewhere—but when she started coming a couple years back, she mostly ignored us.

Mrs. Miller's neck flushes red, and I'd rather face Kelsey and Natalie than keep watching this disaster. I haul myself out of the chair and head for the bar, passing Dad, Mr. Ellis, and a handful of other guests. Cards spill out across the worn wood coffee table between them. They used to let Sara play with them some nights. I never joined. My poker face was shit. Ironic, since so much of my life is a lie now. My steps slow, my gaze lingering long enough to imagine Sara huddled around the table with them, but I grit my teeth and keep walking.

Kelsey's laugh rings out from the bar, and she wheezes as she tries to stop the laughing fit. Her Shirley Temple, which appears to be half maraschino cherries, sloshes as her shoulders shake. Natalie snorts, clutching a napkin to her nose.

A pang of jealousy grips my chest and yanks, momentarily stealing my breath.

That was Sara and me.

But not always.

Remembering the laughter hurts almost as badly as remembering the violence.

My gaze flicks to the far end of the bar, where the lounge's giant wooden mallard, Lucky, watches with shiny black eyes. No, not watching. Remembering. Green paint peels from around his chipped beak: more evidence of how volatile my friendship with Sara had been last summer. .

I'd told her no. She'd stepped in close. Fighting. Breaking apart.

Don't leave me—

Stop. Wisteria, waterlilies, calla lilies, carnations, clovers.

A quiver builds in my hands, and I slam my mug down way too hard on the counter. The cute bartender turns toward me, arching her dark brows and making me wonder if it would be more or less embarrassing to simply run away.

I clear my throat and will the heat building in my cheeks to *chill*. "Sorry. Uh, coffee please?" I am *so* eloquent.

She pours the coffee, strong and slightly acrid from too long on the burner, and passes me a paper carton of milk. I cradle the warm cup of liquid avoidance and tell myself a lie that's taken up a starring role in my rotation over the past year: that tonight, if I stay up long enough, when I do sleep, I will sleep so deeply that the nightmares won't be able to find me.

Five more hours will take me to two a.m., then three, then four, and by then maybe I'll be able to pull an all-nighter, but, no, I can't do that the whole trip so really what's the point and—

"What?" Kelsey stares at me, eyes wary, as she leans around Natalie.

From the look on her face, I'm pretty certain I've said some of that out loud. "Nothing."

She shares a look with Natalie, and it's not a particularly gracious one. I fold my arms. I don't want things to be like this. I want Kelsey to *want* to be around me again. I want things to be like they were before. I just don't know how to make that happen.

Kelsey rolls her eyes, puts a hand on her hip, and says, "You're being weird."

"Gee, thanks," I mumble, hugging myself tighter.

"I guess it's not surprising," she shoots back.

I blink at the acid in her voice. "What's that supposed to mean?"

Her eyebrows arch, disappearing beneath her long bangs. "Just means you've been *weird* eversince"—she stumbles on the words—"since last year. Why would I expect something else?"

I had ignored her for months, because it had been easier

to be selfish. Detached. Kelsey had always looked up to me, even when I didn't deserve it. What if, after Sara, Kelsey sensed the rottenness in me? If my little sister, who overlooked all my other flaws, couldn't get past this terrible thing I'd done, how was I supposed to keep myself together?

I'd dodged her texts and DMs, and I stayed in my own little bubble at the holidays. I knew she'd be mad, but I'd thought it was better than the alternative. It wasn't. I hurt her, and now she looks at me with a miserable cocktail of sadness and suspicion, waiting for me to keep failing her like I have all year.

If I want to reconnect with Kelsey—and I *do* want to—I have to make a real effort to meet her halfway. Be friendly. Be interested. Don't snap at her. I'm the one that broke this, so I'm the one that has to fix it. But the only person I have to lean on for support is…me. And I'm terrible support. The worst. Absolute trash.

It takes everything in me to pull my shoulders back and lower my hands to my sides. I'm sticking this out, even if I'm so uncomfortable my skin crawls.

I'm going to get my sister back.

"I didn't mean to ignore you," I say, though the words come out more uncertain than I'd hoped. They're a start, though. A genuine start. I'm trying, can't you see? Please see, Kelsey.

She frowns. She opens her mouth. She frowns again. "Yeah, well. You did."

Fail. I take a long sip of coffee and lick my lips. They're

both watching me. Judging me. Okay I don't *know* what they're thinking but it *feels* like they're judging me. "I was really busy with school, and...and..." I wasn't busy with shit. I was partying and having superficial conversations with people who were easy to keep at a distance so I wouldn't have to worry about anyone noticing how my insides had been eaten away by guilt. Nothing left to give.

There are several seconds of uncomfortable silence, before Natalie says, "It's weird having me here too, yeah? Sorry I'll be in your room this year." She shrugs. "But since Kelsey and I are sharing a bed, you still get your own, so it's not a big deal, right?"

Natalie's voice is overenthusiastic. The skin at the back of my neck prickles, and I glance at the sofa. Mom's eyes are fixed on us.

Normal. Stay normal.

If talking to Natalie is part of the requirement for spending time with Kelsey, then fine. Tonight is my first, well, *second* chance to show Kelsey I'm really interested in reconnecting after being a crappy sister. I can do better than the spilled wine incident at dinner, right?

"It's fine. Really." Not really. Not at all. At the very least, her being here could've been a nice buffer between Kelsey and me, but nooooo New Girl Natalie had to be a true-crime fanatic.

Natalie's grin wrinkles the bridge of her nose. "Kelsey's told me a lot about you and this place. About what happened..."

She doesn't need to finish the sentence. I'm already shaking my head, back and forth, back and forth.

Natalie pushes her dark curls back from her face with a quick ruffle. The gesture is casual, but the slight shift in her expression isn't. She props an elbow on the bar. "It must've been scary," she prompts, without specifying *what* must've been scary.

My eyes dart to Kelsey, half begging her to shush Natalie, but instead my sister drops her gaze to her lap.

"I don't want to talk about Sara." Firm, but not mean. I can manage that, right?

"But you got *questioned*." Natalie pushes onward. "By the *police*. Did they try to trick you? I bet they lied about the scene to try to get you to say you were there when she died. They like to do that, you know? Did they say anything about the firework?"

I'm blinking too fast, trying to keep up with the question dump. "Yes?"

"*Really?*" Her eyes shine.

"Wait, no. No, I don't think they mentioned the firework. Not to me."

"I bet you know some pieces that people would want to hear, though. Can I maybe interview you tomorrow? I'm trying to solve the mystery of what really happened to her, for my channel. You'd be a big help."

Natalie's light brown eyes are sharp, and hungry. She's way too passionate about this, and that terrifies me, because I know she's *right*, and every time I have to insist Sara's death was accidental steals a little piece of what's left of my sanity. It seems like there are so few pieces left, lately.

"Sara's death was an accident." Liar. You absolute dirty liar. Monster. Liar. Killer. "There is no case." My throat is collapsing in on itself. I can't breathe.

"Cops are wrong plenty. Or they lie. There's *no way* Sara lit that firework herself."

Is it hot in here? It seems hot. The off-white walls are crammed with so much outdoor-themed art it seems as if the aging resort photographs, landscape paintings, and cross-stitched ducks might actually be structurally important. Those overcrowded walls are closing in on me.

Especially the ducks.

Natalie keeps going. "If you'll sit with Kelsey and me and help fill in some of the gaps, I bet I can figure out what really happened. Get her justice. She deserves that. *Everyone* deserves that."

There won't be any justice for Sara. After she died, I kept thinking, *The truth will come out; it has to.* But the weeks passed and nothing happened. And then what else could I be sure of, if not my own guilt?

The role I played in my best friend's death is a wound I've picked and poked at for so long, folding it into the layers of myself, that now it's a hot, festering thing trapped beneath the surface. I hate Natalie for making me think about all this, but she's Kelsey's friend, and I have to be nice.

I swallow, and all that *niceness* burns on the way down.

"I said I don't want to talk about Sara. I'm going for a walk."

"But she was your friend," Kelsey says.

I freeze with my mug halfway to the bar. My sister sounds so sad.

Same.

"Of course she was."

"Then why won't you talk about her? Why don't you want anyone to know what really happened to her?" Kelsey asks.

Her challenge is almost too soft to hear over the noise of the bar, but it tethers me in place as surely as any rope.

How do you tell someone you love that you're a killer?

7

NOW

SATURDAY NIGHT. ONE YEAR AFTER.

Kelsey and Natalie stare at me, waiting. This is a nightmare.

No it's not. The nightmares are way, way worse.

But if the only way Kelsey will let me in at all is if we talk about Sara…

"I don't want to talk about how she died. I can't."

"That's okay," Natalie says, then launches in with a new strategy. "What was Sara like?"

Perfect. Frightening. Warm. Gorgeous. Petty. Brave.

Sweat prickles along my hairline and beneath my armpits. Come on, Mandy. Say something, *anything*, that won't invite more questions. But how do I explain Sara?

"People liked her." I offer. ~~Especially me. Except Finn. Even Alex. Except when…~~ "She was really popular."

Natalie cocks her head. "Was she?"

"What kind of question is that?" I blurt out.

"Sorry. It was just a question," Natalie says.

I don't think she's sorry at all. I bite my tongue. Don't cause a scene. Not here. Not in front of Mom and Dad... *Sara's* mom and dad...a lounge full of guests who would whisper about me and my "outburst" the minute I left the room. If they wait that long.

"It's fine." If I have to hear myself say, "It's fine," to one more person today I'm going to start screaming. "Yes. Everyone liked her."

Kelsey huffs, and it comes out ugly. Mean. It's a sound I'm not used to hearing come from my sweet little sister.

I focus on Natalie because it's easier than confronting Kelsey. "It's a really bad idea to go looking for a story on Sara. Please, Natalie, you should let this go."

Natalie's face lights up in a way that's entirely discouraging. She's not listening to me at all. "Why? Because it *wasn't* an accident?"

Shit. I've backed myself into a corner here. I bite my lip. "No. Because a girl died, and you're going to hurt her family. It's wrong."

A look passes over Natalie's face. I can't place the expression...guilt? Consideration? Fear? For a second I think maybe I have convinced her, but nope. No luck.

"I know what I'm doing. Sara's going to be my next story. I think there's more to her death, and people need to know." She tips her chin up. Stubborn. Determined. Annoying as hell, and possibly a *big* problem for me.

I change tactics.

"Kelsey, please. This is a really shitty thing to do. If I tell Mom and Dad they'll make you—"

Kelsey's face goes stormy. "If you tell Mom and Dad, I'm never speaking to you again. You can't just show up and boss me around."

I exhale, slowly. If I betray her to our parents I might as well kiss any hope of making up with my sister goodbye. And I can't do that.

"Okay. Fine. I won't say anything. But what you're doing isn't fun or funny or whatever the heck y'all think plastering Sara's story all over the internet—*again*—is going to be."

"At least *Natalie* cares about what happened to Sara."

The *unlike you* hangs unsaid, but heavy, between the three of us.

My jaw drops open. My tongue dries and there's a scratching at the back of my throat, and yet I can't seem to close my mouth. The pounding in my chest is mirrored behind my eyes. I can't believe she said that.

"What the fuck, Kelsey?" I don't mean to shout, but the quiet that settles throughout the lounge leaves only the sound of crickets trilling outside.

A startled, "Oh," comes from the couch, and Mrs. Ellis says something about "language." Mrs. Miller nods, eager to agree with Sara's mom's disapproval.

Kelsey's eyes shine. Hurried footsteps approach from behind, and Mom catches me by the arm. Her tone is harsher than her touch. "What is going on?" she hisses.

"I'm leaving," I reply, furious at the way my voice shakes. I have to get out of here or I'm going to scream.

"That's probably best, if you're going to yell at your sister like that." She keeps her own voice low. We are in public, after all, and I've already embarrassed us enough. "Absolutely unacceptable."

I jerk free a little too hard, and her nails make a slithering sound over the leather of my jacket.

I'm a few steps from the open doors, from freedom, when Dad stands and blocks my path as discreetly as anyone can detain another person. "You owe your sister an apology," he says quietly, but firmly.

I know I should just do what he says, but my throat is closed too tight and even though my skin crawls with shame, I can't turn to my sister and make the apology come out. I'm not wrong. I'm not the *only* one wrong. Everything about this is so screwed up, and Sara should be alive not the subject of some true-crime spectacle with me—guilty, guilty me—as the lens through which her story is told.

Mom wrings her hands together, but it's impossible to tell whether she's worried about Kelsey's feelings, or about how long this scene has already drawn out. I'm taking too long to wrap this up. How dare I?

"Sorry," I croak out, but I don't think I'm convincing anyone.

I dodge around Dad and head for the doors.

"I want you back at the cottage tonight by eleven," he calls after me. "We're having breakfast as a family in the morning!"

I have nothing to say, so I keep walking, until walking turns into running. At least the stars won't ask me what happened to Sara.

They already know.

8

THEN

Sara turned her face up to the slit of starry sky showing through the canopy of leaves. Her legs kicked out, scuffing the heels of her sneakers in the existing divot of dirt. This had been our spot for years—a secret little path carved out between two hiking trails. She was saying something, but I'd been having trouble concentrating, which I figured was fair. After all, I'd almost drowned a few hours ago. *She'd* almost drowned me a few hours ago, even though it was an accident. I picked at a piece of bark coming loose from the slanted tree limb that formed our makeshift bench.

A sharp, quick sting—pinch—on the fleshy part at the back of my arm, and I jerked away. "Ow! Too hard!"

I hated that she did that to get my attention, but I loved that she *wanted* my attention. It was our thing. Just like this was our spot. And the weeks at Highmark were our time, tucked away in the warm summer nights. But damn, sometimes she got a too-small chunk of skin between her fingers and it hurt like a bitch.

"Sorry," she said, and without missing a beat, "You weren't listening."

"I was too."

The lie is obvious, and she rolls her eyes. "Never mind."

We were surrounded on all sides by trees, with only the narrow path running between two parallel trails alongside the lake to lead to our secret spot. Just her bare knee tapping restlessly against mine.

I nudged her knee in return and said, "No, tell me. What were you saying?"

Her leg stilled, and the comfortable quiet shifted. Was she biting her lip?

"Sara?"

She sighed. "I, uh, I need to tell you something."

Shit. "What?"

"Please promise not to be mad, okay?"

I frowned, trying to catch her eyes, but she kept them fixed on the spindly trees and scraggly bushes in front of us. "Why? What happened?

She shook her head, and the smell of rose shampoo swirled around us. "Promise."

I inhaled deeply, both because I loved the scent of her shampoo and because it's better than saying what I'm thinking out loud. How can anyone promise not to be mad? Ridiculous. Also, I probably *would* be mad, and she knew it. "Just tell me."

She turned her face from me and in the moment before she smiled, I could've sworn she looked scared. But the illusion disappeared almost instantly. She drew her shoulders back and curled her fingers around the curve of the low-slung branch. "I made out with Alex."

I blinked. She...she *what*?

"I know you said you thought Alex was cute, and I did too, and we got to talking after I pulled you out of the lake." She fixed her wide blue eyes on me and dared me to say what I thought.

"What is wrong with you?" My stomach hurts, like she's punched me. How could she? She wasn't always like this—she can't have been, because how could I be friends with someone who would *immediately* swoop in on the boy I liked?

"I—" Her mouth hung open. "I'm *sorry*. I didn't mean for it to happen."

"You made out with him right after you almost drowned me," I said, half statement, half question.

"That was an accident! I already told you I didn't mean to land on top of you like that!"

I pressed my lips together, tight, to keep from snapping at her. I wanted to believe her, but I also wanted to stay angry. I'd earned it.

Her forehead wrinkled, her mouth turning down. "Come on." She scooted closer. "You don't really think I did it on purpose? I pulled you out as soon as I realized something was wrong. And you were *fine*. I wouldn't have let anything happen to you."

The line of her torso was warm beside me. The fact that even now I wanted to lean in was extremely annoying.

I unclenched my jaw and exhaled slowly. "I know you didn't mean to do it. But I threw up all over the dock." In front of Alex. Who you apparently proceeded to make out with. "It was gross. And so embarrassing."

She laughed. "It wasn't that bad. You mostly just threw up water anyway."

I made a face and ran my tongue over the roof of my mouth. "Still gross, Sara."

"I'll make it up to you. Even though it was an accident and I saved you." Crickets and the lapping of the lake filled the quiet for a few seconds before she continued. "We're going to have an amazing summer, I promise." She laughed, and there was a slight edge to it. "My friends back home will be so jealous."

"Okay." I was pretty sure I believed her. After all, she didn't do it on purpose. The drowning part. The Alex part... well... She had always thought he was cute too. And besides, what was I going to do, beg her to let me have him? That would be too pathetic, and also creepy and entitled. Alex was going to like whoever he liked. Hook up with whoever he wanted to hook up with.

But I sure wished it had been me, not Sara.

"If my parents really do let my jackass brother take the car, then I have a lot of missed fun to make up for while we're here," she pouted.

"Wait, Finn's getting the car? The one y'all share?"

She gave me an exasperated stare. "See? You weren't listening to me earlier."

I racked my brain. College. He was taking the car to school in the fall. "No, I just blanked. He's taking it to college." Nailed it. "That's so unfair."

"They don't care. It's so he can 'come home for the holidays' or some bullshit. I think they just don't want me to have a car. They've been so pissy since Finn told them I'd almost failed history." She frowned. "And French."

I did my best to keep my face neutral, but some judgment slipped in.

"What?" she asked, but didn't wait for an answer. "I didn't do some of the homework, and my teachers are super strict about assignments. Not everyone is bailing on their senior year like you."

"I didn't 'bail on my senior year,'" I stressed the air quotes. "I graduated early." I don't want to have this conversation again already.

Sara shrugged. "Same diff. I can't imagine missing out on being with all my friends senior year." Her voice dipped funny, but she cleared her throat and was back to normal. "*And* we were supposed to go to school together and be roommates, and now we're not. You're going to William and Mary. Bail.ing." She stressed the syllables in the same passive-aggressive way I had a second ago.

"You'll be fine," I muttered, but the doubt I'd been working hard to lock down pushed against its cage. I wasn't even dating Dan anymore. What if going to college a year early was a huge mistake? Already, I can hear the distance in Sara's voice that my decision is carving out between us, and I don't like it. Not one bit.

Sara waved her hand. "I know I'll be fine. *But* if Finn takes the car, I'm going to miss out on so much this year!"

"Can't you get rides from someone?"

She waved her hand away. "Duh. But that's not the point. The point is that they're giving Finn the car when he doesn't need it. He's been such a jerk lately, I swear he got me in trouble on purpose, which is really unfair. It's not like he's perfect, despite what my parents think. And now—"

She cut herself off abruptly, and her eyes darted away from my face, but not before I caught the sadness creeping in.

"Now, what?"

When she smiled, all traces of sadness were gone, replaced by determination. A bright, excited gleam making the blue of her irises shine in the sea of shadows falling across her face. "Help me get back at him."

I leaned away, putting a few extra inches between us. "How?" Finn could be a jerk. She wasn't wrong. If she wanted to mess with him, well, why not?

She had an answer all ready to go. "Let's steal something."

My mouth popped open and I was shaking my head before I realized what I was doing. "From who?" Wait, what? What was I saying? I waved a hand in front of my face. "Hold on. No. No we can't do that."

She nodded fast, up and down, up and down, her knee

bouncing as she tapped her toe against the dirt. "Yes, we can. Something from the resort. Not something too big, don't worry; I know you won't want to get in *trouble*."

I wasn't a fan of the way she said that last part, like it was an insult. Too boring. Too afraid. No fun. Not worth dating. Not worth being friends with. I gritted my teeth. "I'm not scared."

"Reeeeally?" She drew the word out.

I opened my mouth. Say you're not scared of getting caught. Caught *stealing*. "I—" Nope. I was definitely too afraid of getting in trouble.

She pinched my thigh, which hurt less through the jeans. "Hey. Mandy? Come on, are you going to help me? We could steal Lucky!"

I gaped at her as she giggled.

"We can't. People love that duck. He has his own plaque." Lucky might just be a wooden mallard presiding over the bar, but he's also a beloved unofficial mascot. He has his own little shrine, for God's sake, with golf tees and poker chips and napkins with doodles on them. The resort is *not* normal about him.

"If we get caught, we'll act like we were taking it for the scavenger hunt."

"The scavenger hunt is for things like interesting-shaped rocks and leaves. Pamphlets. Or things that get *returned* at the end. I assume you don't plan on immediately handing the duck back over to Highmark?"

She rolled her eyes. "No, Mandy, we wouldn't just give

him back. Kind of ruins the point of blaming Finn. Come on, it would be perfect."

My pulse counted the seconds as they dragged by. "No. I know your brother is annoying and an ass for telling your parents about your grades, but stealing stuff from the resort and blaming Finn is…" A massive overreaction? A little frightening? Or was I really just boring? Maybe her idea wasn't as ridiculous as it sounded.

She huffed and hopped up without warning, and the branch swayed beneath me. I shot my hands down to brace against the rough bark.

"Fine. I don't want your help if you're going to be such a bummer about it."

I watched her trudge down the leaf-plastered path, her shoulders straight and her hair swinging down her back. She was my friend, and I adored her, but…

But.

If Sara thought this was normal retaliation for her brother snitching on her, I wasn't sure I wanted to know what she'd do when faced with a *real* betrayal.

I hoped I'd never find out.

9

NOW

SATURDAY NIGHT. ONE YEAR AFTER.

The night prickles at the back of my neck, and even though it's only ten, most of the other guests have already returned to their rooms. The old wooden paneling of the main lodge is a lonely, sleeping giant against the dark sky. I shrink away from its looming presence.

I don't consciously decide to go to the woods. To *our* spot. My feet decide for me.

I'm passing our cottage before I realize I had no intention of stopping. I'm heading for the beckoning woods and a darkness that hides so much, so easily. But I do stop, a faltering stutter-step, when I catch movement out of the corner of my eye.

The hair along my arm raises, and I don't know why my heartbeat is acting like such a loud, thumping stereotype right now.

"Hello?" My voice rasps. "Kelsey?" Why in the world

did I call out for Kelsey? I know exactly where my sister is, and it isn't out here, in the dark.

A low, slow creak comes from our porch, and my breath sputters out.

I suppress a shiver. Well, I mostly suppress a shiver. On the balls of my feet, I pick my way over the uneven stones, keeping close to the bushes as I approach the porch. This is paranoid. I know it's paranoid. My family isn't spying on me, they're back at the lounge, probably discussing all the ways I've screwed up, and I'm going to find nothing but weathered boards and empty chairs overlooking the water when I round the corner. Still, my pulse is slick candy at the back of my throat.

I step into the middle of the path and get a clear view of the porch.

Empty.

No one. No door clicking closed. No Kelsey and Natalie plotting their next set of intrusive questions for content. Just one of the old rocking chairs shifting slightly—back and forth over the boards. The wind? I wait and watch as the chair stops. A rustling comes from beneath my feet, like a small animal skittering down one of the wooden supports.

This is ridiculous. No one is watching me.

Probably.

I hurry away from the creepy creaking and follow the path to the wooden footbridge that crosses over the narrow section of the river. The main property recedes behind me, and the damp night air draws closer. I imagine the swirl of dark sky wrapping around my shoulders as I slip unseen into the trees. This place swallows you. The lake, the trees, the sky... It's easy to avoid watchful eyes out here.

Sara knew that all too well.

We both did.

The planks creak with each step, and I shiver. The slow gurgle of water moves beneath me, adding its soft glug-glug-glug to the rustle of leaves. As soon as I step off the bridge, the cover of trees grows too dense for sufficient starlight to reach me, but I trudge along, not wanting to turn on my phone flashlight yet.

I'm in no mood to be seen.

I widen my eyes and try not to twitch at the shadows shifting in the trees and tucked under protruding roots. They're nothing but the result of eyes ill-suited to darkness, and yet... Does that one look a hell of a lot like a person? Did that one make a sound? No, a twig snapped beneath my shoe, and I'm a big baby.

I take the trail running along the edge of the lake and, as the forest closes in around me, hiding me from view, I smash my fingers against the flashlight icon. The burst of light illuminates the winding path. A line of trees and shrubs and crawling vines separates me from the lake, but flashes of water shining with the reflection of the stars peek through every few paces. To my right, the earth slopes upward more aggressively, leaving the trail slightly slanted so that I have to watch my footing.

Where the heck is the entry? I must have gone too far.

Everything feels different in the dark, and the opening to the trail that cuts between this one and the one running parallel a little way up the mountain is hard to find, even in the daytime. I swallow and double back, quickening my pace.

Sara always walked in front of me when we came here. She always went first.

The only time I came here alone…

Drunk. Reeling. Senses in shambles.

Dirt beneath my nails and mud-stained jeans.

I chew my lip.

There. There's the opening. It's almost impossible to see when coming from the resort, because the one-person-wide walkway cuts backward from that direction. I push aside a hanging branch and move slowly. My pulse roars in my ears. Keep breathing. Keep moving. The fallen leaves on the initial incline are slick with decay. The smell of rot and dirt envelops me, growing stronger with each step.

When the branch I know so well, growing horizontally on one side of the path, comes into view, my breathing catches and sweat slicks my palms. I sink down onto the branch, gingerly, half-expecting the wood to give way beneath me— dry and rotten.

I shouldn't have come here. Not *here* of all places. Not where I buried—

My thoughts collapse in on themselves, messy and heartbroken and afraid, oh God, so afraid because my fingers itch to bury themselves in the dirt and hold ~~her my~~ that cold piece of guilt in my hand one more time.

My gaze slides to the washed-out hues of green and brown opposite the narrow, trodden patch of dirt. Fused tree limbs and somewhere beneath the scrubby foliage, a rock.

Shit.

I'm not going to sink to my knees. I'm not going to dig it up. I'm not.

10

THEN

WEDNESDAY NIGHT. MINUTES AFTER.

I staggered to her as the world tilted around me. Was I going to be sick? No. No, I couldn't get sick right now. That would be like...evidence, right? *More* evidence.

The sky flashed, and I yelped, dropping to a crouch. Another firework? No that was lightning. I pitched sideways and a stick jabbed at my already raw hands. Shit. No balance. A crack of thunder rattled the trees. The ground shook.

A whine slipped out of my mouth—one that ended in a gag. The entire clearing was littered with "evidence." The rock I smashed her face with. The plastic bag full of empty airplane bottles. Footprints and blood and hair, probably.

Sara's dead body.

My stomach rolled, and bile climbed up my throat. Breathe. I had to check on her. I had to know for certain. A warm drop splattered on my cheek—the first drop of rain loosed from the churning sky. I wished I could dissolve into the night. Be swallowed by the lake. Be buried by the dirt.

Sara was crumpled in a heap several feet from the lake's edge, near the center of the clearing. Up close, there was nothing to check. There was no way Sara was alive. The left side of her face was a bloody mess atop a mangled neck.

I sagged beside her as the first tears slipped out like a silent apology. No apology could ever be enough.

I was sorry. I didn't mean for any of this to happen. But that didn't really matter, in the end, did it? I grazed the side of her face that wasn't a red ruin with trembling fingers.

"I—" I choked. The words wouldn't come.

My head swam. Between having ditched my contacts and the swelling shock, the night was fuzzy in more ways than one. Rain pelted the surface of the lake and battered the leaf canopy, loud enough to make it seem as if Sara and I were the only people in a weeping world. I exhaled and my lips formed her name, "Sara," and nothing else.

As rain soaked my head and shoulders and made the blood run watery down the curves of Sara's face, my thoughts slowed to a dull, empty crawl. What was I supposed to do? Think. Call an ambulance? Call the cops? No. Couldn't do that. God, I was going to throw up. No, couldn't do that either. Wouldn't. I hiccuped and tasted sour bile and liquor.

Maybe I'd wake up. That wasn't going to happen, why would I even think that? Or I could stay here and let the earth swallow me. Yes. That was the solution.

I lay down beside Sara on the soggy ground. I took her

limp, warm hand in mine and squeezed, wishing I could pump life back into her through force of will alone.

"Don't be dead, Sara." I whispered, my voice hoarse. "You're not supposed to be dead."

No answer.

"You can't be dead."

But she was.

The silver heart charm I'd yanked off her neck earlier pressed tight between our palms, the chain threaded through my fingers. Sara's necklace. My necklace. This was all I had left, but I couldn't keep it.

Could I?

I could.

No, I couldn't, right? Was that incriminating? I couldn't get my alcohol-soaked thoughts to line up straight.

I needed to bury it.

11

NOW

SATURDAY NIGHT. ONE YEAR AFTER.

The last piece of Sara that I held in my hand wasn't her wrists, or her hair, although those pieces are the loudest haunts; it was her necklace, which was also my necklace

I have to find it. Hold it. Just one more time, and then I'll put it right back where I buried it. That'll still give me enough time to return before Dad's curfew. It doesn't matter that I'm eighteen and have been away at school for a year. Dad said eleven and he's still my dad. I don't want to disappoint him more than I already have tonight.

Or that other night, when I heard Mom and Dad talking about what might've been, if only I hadn't gone off with Alex and left my drunk friend alone in the woods. How they couldn't believe I'd done something so irresponsible, and thoughtless.

My throat closes in a tight knot.

If they knew the truth, they'd never look at me the same again.

I swing the flashlight to the ground, searching for the rock with three distinct circular pools worn into the surface, but all I find are thin, twisting branches and a layer of leaves both dead and alive.

I keep the phone aimed with one hand and use the other to remove branches and overgrown vines. I tell myself to stop, sit down, leave, run, but my fingers continue to curl around one gnarled twig after the next.

Where the hell is it? The rock should be here. Right here. Shouldn't it? I've imagined this place so many times—been *haunted* by this place so many times—and it should be *right* here. In front of the fused trees. I was drunk that night but not *that* drunk. Okay, maybe that drunk, but it should be here.

Could someone have moved it? It was an interesting rock. Someone could have taken it. Crap. How am I supposed to find a random patch of dirt?

Leave it buried. Leave it lost.

A shiver rolls up my spine and into the base of my skull. Alone. I'm so alone, and yet I can *feel* Sara at my side. In my head. Around my throat.

I can't let ~~her~~ it go. I keep clearing.

The toe of my shoe thunks against something hard. I squat, keeping clear of the damp dirt, and lift the rock with the three deep craters that look vaguely like empty eye sockets.

Jackpot.

I pitch forward onto my hands and knees and dig. Every other thought empties except for—

Dirt beneath my fingernails, water soaking my jeans.

My hands plunge into the soft earth like they're on auto-pilot. Branches. Leaves. Grit settles on my skin, my tongue, my hair, as dirt flings from my fingertips. Rocks and bits of twigs scrape over my palms.

Deeper. I have to go deeper. Is that six inches down? How deep did I bury this thing? Surely not more than a foot?

My nail beds ache, and my elbows are sunk deep into the hole when a small broken stick thrusts up beneath what remains of a fingernail. I curse as my eyes water. I've got my finger halfway to my mouth to suck the blood when I remember dirt clings like a rough second skin.

Every noise from the surrounding trees makes me flinch, and my heart beats fast. Faster. So fast the grayed bushes surrounding me swim at the edges of my vision. It has to be here. This is *definitely* where I buried it.

Where is it?

I expand the hole's circumference far wider than the side of the rock, and still there's nothing.

"Shit. *Shit.*" My throat closes so tightly around the curses that they barely squeeze out. I clench my fists in the piles of debris heaped beside me and glare into the hole. The light from my phone is so bright and so out of place that it creates a blind spot in my left eye where it points skyward.

"Where are you?" I ask the silence. And who took you? I can't even bring myself to say the second part out loud.

A sound in the distance, too far away for me to place, interrupts my furious stare-down with the empty hole.

Footsteps? A jumbled voice? I purse my lips and listen, but there's no follow-up sound: no rustle through underbrush, no crunching leaves.

Time to hurry. I don't want to be discovered out here—by a person, or a bobcat for that matter. I stare at the mounds of dirt. Maybe I missed it. The chain could've broken and slipped through my fingers. The heart-shaped charm could've been so tarnished I couldn't see the flash of silver. Her necklace has been buried out here for a whole year, exposed to dirt and rain. I run my hands through each pile of displaced earth. *Please be here. Please be here. Please be here.*

But there's nothing.

Gone.

She's gone.

Tears prickle the corners of my eyes.

The noise that isn't my own frantic breathing comes again. This time, the crunch of footsteps over twigs and leaves is distinct. Whispers and a low, urgent voice come from the higher of the two paths.

What am I doing?

Oh my God. Out digging up a necklace, taken from a girl on the night she died. Possible evidence, that I concealed. My stomach lurches. I have to get out of here.

Shit, shit, shit. I replace the dirt as best I can, and with a shaking hand place the stone over the disturbed ground. I hastily kick the surrounding leaves, and sprint toward the lake.

I'm less careful this time, and my foot slides out from

under me just as the cut-through opens onto the main trail. My phone slips from my hand, bouncing and throwing light in chaotic bursts through the dark.

"Did you see that?" a voice asks as I scramble to kill the flashlight.

I clutch the phone to my chest and take small fast breaths. Dizziness swamps me as my pulse hammers at my temples.

"No. What'd you see?" A girl's voice. One I recognize. Maybe.

"I thought I saw a light. Wait, listen."

I hold very still.

"Chill, Leigh, there's no one else out here. Pass me the bowl."

I slam my hand against my mouth to stifle the anxious laugh that bubbles up. My palm smells like dirt. Christ, Mandy, get it together. Scared half to death by Leigh Miller, out to smoke weed away from her dad and the stepmom she can't stand. Even though she'd been off at camp a lot of those early years and never seemed to like us all that much when she finally did start spending part of each summer here, it's not like I have any reason to be *afraid* of Leigh.

~~Unless~~.

No, no, no. Wisteria, waterlily, willow, that's a tree, close enough—

Out in the quiet, the crackle of their lighter carries, and a moment later the telltale skunky smell reaches me and one of them starts hacking, which is my cue to get the hell out of there.

Can't linger and risk them seeing me. Leigh might complain openly about having to spend a month each year at her dad's resort, with all its fake niceness and side-eyes over the rims of iced-tea glasses, but I don't want *anyone* asking questions about what I'm doing skulking around the woods by myself.

Especially now. The necklace isn't here.

But I was alone that night ~~by the time I buried that little piece of Sara~~.

So who knew about the necklace?

And what else do they know?

12

NOW

SATURDAY NIGHT. ONE YEAR AFTER.

At ten minutes past eleven, I tiptoe over the porch boards, trying and failing to dodge the ones that creak. Every year the humidity brings new sounds to the aging wood.

A yellow glow of light spills through the slits in the sunroom blinds. Someone's still awake.

Zap. A moth flies into the porch lantern.

I stop. Who's in there waiting for me? Kelsey and Natalie? Mom? Dad? I rub my hands up and down my arms, scrubbing at the dirt stubbornly clinging to my skin. My nails are cut too short for much dirt to hide there.

Dirt beneath my nails, water soaking my jeans.

I shiver, even though the night is warm.

Zap.

I remove my glasses and carefully wipe away a smudge. This is as good as it gets.

The screen door whines softly, and I slip inside. Mom

looks up from her paperback mystery. Shadows collect in the corners of the room, washed out in the light of the single lamp. I don't touch the switch on the wall; the less light the better.

"Hey," I say, barely above a whisper.

The doors to both bedrooms are closed, leaving us alone in the strange quiet of an otherwise sleeping house.

Mom stares at me for a long time. Long enough I wonder if I'd be wrong to simply cross the carpeted floor without another word exchanged.

Finally, she shakes her head. "Why are you covered in dirt?"

I look down at my arms and hands. They're clean, mostly.

She stands and comes close enough to gently push a lock of blue hair away from my temple.

Oh. Right. My face.

When she lowers her hand, she has a twig pinched between her fingers. Her brows raise.

"I was walking by the lake."

"And what did you do? Fall in?"

She isn't being serious. I'm not wet. But I don't know what answer she's looking for.

"No."

"You stormed out of the lounge in such a huff. You really upset your sister. And in front of Alicia. And the Ellises. It was inappropriate and frankly, Mandy, just plain rude."

"You don't even like Mrs. Miller," I grumble, on the defensive.

"I don't dislike her," Mom insists. "And that's not the

point. She's Eric's wife, and they own the resort. We don't exactly need to be causing them any more problems. Not to mention Charlotte, sitting right there, watching my two sweet girls fight with each other when her own daughter's gone." She chokes up at the end. "Just terrible."

My chest aches as the air runs out of me. Trembling. Crushing. "That's not fair."

But it *is* fair. Sara is gone. We can't fight anymore, no matter how much I wish I could change that. I would give *anything* for a do-over.

A cry pushes at my chest, eating up the space inside me. I had my chances for do-overs.

I wasted every single one of them.

Mom sighs, long and disappointed, and I know it's not my twig-tangled hair or the dirt on my cheeks she's disappointed in. It's me. All of me. I hate this place and the person it made me. Maybe Mom does too. How could she not?

Killer. Liar.

I bite the inside of my lip.

Don't cry, don't cry, don't cry.

"I really think you should consider taking a year off from school and coming home," she says. The gentleness of it only makes it worse.

"Mom—" My voice is strangled. I can't get the rest of the protest out.

"We've been worried about you. We *are* worried about you."

I have to swallow twice to loosen my throat enough to

speak. "I'm fine, Mom. Really. Coming home isn't"—I lick my lip—"I don't want to take a year off."

"I'm not saying you have to." The *not yet* is loud in between the words. So, so loud. "Just think about it. Please, honey."

I clench my jaw as if that will somehow help keep the tears in too. Nod. Quickly. Just agree with her to make this end. My head rattles up and down and a tiny dead leaf falls onto the carpet. Perfect.

Mom raises up on tiptoe and I know what she wants. A kiss good night like when I lived at home. A kiss good night and a daughter who isn't being slowly devoured by the endless, crushing guilt.

I tuck my chin because I want that too. She brushes her lips against my forehead.

"Good night, honey."

"Night, Mom."

My skin is over-tight, my shoulders cramping, as I lock the bathroom door behind me. Careful. Have to be quiet. On the other side of the wall, Kelsey and Natalie are indistinguishable lumps beneath the covers of their bed. My pajamas sit on the toilet lid, but I can't put them on when I'm covered in so much dirt.

A mirror hangs above the small pedestal sink, and I start with the remaining debris tangled in the ends of my hair. There. Marginally better.

As I run my hands under the faucet, the present slips away like water down the drain, and I sink into memory.

Dirt beneath my nails, water soaking my jeans.

Blood swirls in the sink—wait, no, it would've been mostly dirt then too—down, down the drain. A few tiny cuts between my fingers and crisscrossing my palms sting. Breathe, Mandy. I have to breathe because I have to think. Think. Before the cops get called. What else do I need to get rid of? I hiccup and liquor burns up my throat along with the bile. Swallow. Oh, God, she's *dead*. She's dead dead dead dead dead dead—

—Stop—

Dead dead dead dead. It feels like my brain is melting down. Dead dead—

In the mirror, a sea of small blue flowers decorating the shower curtain fill my view. I wonder what they are. Cornflowers? Hydrangea? She's dead, and I'm thinking about flowers. I wince. A shower. Start with a shower, and where the hell is Kelsey? Never mind, just hurry.

But...no...no that's not right. I struggle up through the flashback. Kelsey isn't missing. She's a few feet away. Asleep in bed with her friend who's determined to drag Sara's death back into the spotlight.

I gasp, like coming up for air, pushing away the last grasping fingers of the worst night of my life. With my pulse pounding in my head, I frantically lather enough soap to cover every inch of skin, all the way to my elbows.

When all the dirt is gone, even the bits that clung to my neck like glitter on glue, I stall. My feet won't move, and I stare at the wild-eyed girl in the mirror.

The flowers on the shower curtain are in fact hydrangea.

If I stay in the stark, bright bathroom, I can put off seeing Sara's eyes—so hurt, so angry—in my dreams.

But there's no *escaping* her.

She's everywhere. Everything.

Inevitable.

13

THEN

SUNDAY AFTERNOON. THREE DAYS BEFORE.

"Help me!" Sara's voice was shrill.

"Shhh," I hissed, eyes darting around the temporarily empty lounge. "And put that down."

She frowned, but she didn't let go of Lucky—the bar's unofficial mascot and unlucky target of Sara's revenge scheme against her brother. "Just come here. If you open your bag, we can shove him in real quick and get the hell out of here."

My teeth ground together. I'd told her no out in the woods. I was not going to help her steal from the resort, just to get back at Finn. "I said *no*."

She stepped in close, clutching the wooden duck under its rounded belly, as if it were alive. There was an empty space surrounded by a ring of tributes to Lucky on the corner of the bar.

"Sara, stop. They're going to notice him missing immediately. I don't want to do this. We'll get in trouble."

"No we won't, that's the point. Finn will. And I bet he'll barely be in trouble anyway. It's just a duck. Even if everyone is super weird about…" She gestured at the poker chips and miscellaneous offerings. "…all that."

I shook my head. She was right, maybe? But what if she wasn't? I couldn't think. I needed more time to…to think about it…to decide. Sara wanted to steal the duck, and I wanted to be like Sara, but…

But.

"I can't." I took a step back, too slowly.

Sara's hand shot out to grasp at my bag, slung over my shoulder. Her fingers hooked around the canvas strap, but I jerked my shoulder away and she stumbled forward.

Lucky fell.

Smack, beak-first into the thin carpet floor.

Shit.

"Shit," Sara said.

He looked okay. His neck wasn't snapped. That was a good sign, but I couldn't make myself kneel to look closer.

Sara scooped up the wooden duck and turned him for an inspection.

"Oh my God," I said. "We chipped his beak."

Sara lifted her eyes to mine, seething. "If you'd let me put him in your freakin' bag, this wouldn't have happened, but no, you couldn't just go with it. You know you worry way too much, right? Getting in trouble with your parents is not literally going to kill you."

Heat crept up my face. So, Sara thought I worried too much. Great. Guess I'd worry about *that*, now. I scowled right back at her. "I know."

I said the words with as much of my own anger and force as I could, but I didn't quite believe them. I was scared—all the time—and Sara wasn't. Why did that make me feel so... ashamed?

"Whatever. I'll handle Finn on my own." She set Lucky on the bar, where he reclaimed his post just as before, minus a small chip of beak. She turned for the door, ignoring me.

She was mad. I was mad. But...but I...

Don't leave me. I'll fix it, I swear. I can do better. I can be more fun. I'll figure it out.

I shivered. I couldn't watch *another* person walk away. Like my ex-best friend, Brianna, who upgraded her friend circle in middle school. Like Dan, who liked me, but not enough to actually stay with me in college. Like Mom, almost, but...no. No, that didn't bother me. That wasn't about me, that was about Dad. I shook the train of thought out of my head. So what if she almost left him—left us? She didn't. Everything was fine.

"Wait," I called, hustling after her. "I'm—sorry." I barely tripped over the apology.

"M'kay." Passive-aggressive and squeezed through pursed lips.

I squashed the little flicker of answering anger. I didn't want to be mad at Sara. I wanted the perfect summer she'd envisioned for us. I'd put distance between us with my decision to go off to college a year early, to a school I *knew* she probably wouldn't be able to get into. And now she seemed hell-bent on picking fights with, well, everyone, but I could smooth things over. "Let's work on the scavenger hunt list instead. We've only got three days to get it done. If we want to win..."

I let the end dangle. I knew Sara wanted to win, which meant she'd have to forgive me and work together.

She slowed and her face brightened. I loved the smile that lit her face. She flicked her hair over her shoulder and nodded. "You're right. We need to get started."

Good. Easy. That worked.

"Let's split up to search. We'll get the list done faster that way," she finished, and my heart sank a fraction.

She was right. This would be faster. But it was hard not to follow as I watched her pick her way down the steps toward the lake.

Over by the storage shed, which was almost certainly called something fancier than that, I knelt and pushed clumps of uncut grass out of the way. The "something bouncy" item on the list was practically begging people to scrounge up forgotten golf balls. Come on, where are you, you little suckers?

I did an awkward kneeling shuffle along the sides of the shed, rummaging through the grass as I went. There. A flash of scuffed-up white. I snatched the ball out of the cool dirt and slipped it into my bag.

Behind me, on a faraway hole, a golfer yelled, "Fore," and across the curved stretch of lawn, the patter of Ping-Pong came from the lodge's porch.

What else could I check off the list? How was Sara doing with her half?

There was a dark line of shadow to my right. The shed door was ajar. It was off-limits, for sure, and I couldn't take anything *real* from the resort, but I was annoyed with Sara, and myself, and feeling reckless.

Interesting. I dug the list out of my pocket and scanned the items we hadn't crossed off yet.

SOMETHING WITH "HIGHMARK" ON IT
SOMETHING BLUE AND GREEN
SOMETHING PLASTIC
SOMETHING WITH A FLOWER ON IT
SOMETHING SHINY
SOMETHING SMALLER THAN A DIME
SOMETHING THAT SMELLS GOOD

Hmm.

I glanced around. No one was watching, so I eased the creaky door open and ducked inside. Maybe there'd be an old Highmark flyer, or a garden tag with a picture of a flower that I could use. The air was humid, pressed in tight, and tasting faintly of pine and dust. Light poured in through high plain windows.

Boxes of fireworks were stacked in piles against the far wall. Sparklers and rockets and Roman candles, all for Wednesday's Summer Bash.

Those would be...exciting. "Best Summer Ever" material. And they'd show Sara I wasn't totally boring.

Aren't you worried about stealing, *Mandy? You'll get in trouble, Mandy. Wouldn't want to accidentally be too much fun, would you, Mandy?*

Sara's voice echoed inside my head, her earlier disappointment like a poison seeping through me.

I clenched and unclenched my jaw. Crushed my fingers together.

I could do this. I could make myself into someone exciting enough to keep around. I messed up earlier, but this would show her I could be better.

My pulse pounded as I shoved as many fireworks as I could fit into my bag. The weight was terrifying. Thrilling. With breath trapped in my chest and my arm tucked tight against the canvas bag, I hurried out of the shed and into the blazing sunshine.

In the distance, beneath a crop of giant old oak trees, a woman with gray hair lowered her binoculars and stared at me.

Crap. Was the door open while I stuffed the fireworks into my bag? Could she see the tips protruding under my arm? The bulge against the canvas?

She was still staring, and blood rushed up my face in a flush of heat, but I couldn't go back inside now. It was too late.

I ducked my head, hunched my shoulders, and hurried away.

It was fine. This was fine. Nothing bad was going to happen, I was being weird for no reason.

By the time I reached the side of the resort facing the lake, where Sara was supposed to be working on her half of the list, the weight of my bag had knotted my shoulders. Or maybe the stress had tightened my muscles. What was I thinking? Fireworks? What was I going to do with fireworks?

Nothing, that was what. Which meant… I couldn't show them to Sara, could I? She would *obviously* want to set them off. Duh. This was such a bad idea. I could show her the Roman candles. Or maybe only the sparklers. I—

"I don't care." It was Sara's voice, harsh and dripping scorn. "Tell them you don't want the car, or I'll tell them about—"

"Damnit, Sara!"

Finn. That was Finn, and if Sara's voice was harsh, his was absolutely furious. I crunched my way farther down the pebble walk, until Sara and her brother came into view, over near the gazebo built into the trees separating the lawn from the river.

Finn jumped, whirling around to look at me. His hands stayed locked tight around Sara's upper arms, like he'd stopped in the middle of shaking her. Even from a distance I could see the indent of his fingers in her flesh. But she didn't look afraid or worried. She looked pleased.

After several frozen seconds, Finn released her and stormed off, leaving Sara and I staring at each other.

"What was that about?" I asked.

She looked me up and down, quirked her lips into a strange smile, and said, "Nothing."

Which was obviously a lie.

Why was Sara lying to me?

14

NOW

SATURDAY NIGHT. ONE YEAR AFTER.

There's a pinching at my thigh, soft at first, then more insistent. No. *Please*, no. Move your arm, Mandy. Make her stop. You could make her stop; all you have to do is take her hand in yours.

Again, a pinch at the fleshy curve of my hip. Sharper.

I roll my head to the side, slowly, like time's gone syrupy. I want to see, have to see, and yet if I could stop my head from turning, I would.

The coolness of the pillow cradles my cheek. Sara is waiting. Her head rests on the pillow beside me, her skin pale and smooth and whole. The curve of her cheekbone glints in the moonlight.

My pulse is tissue paper fluttering in the wind. She traces a fingernail from the base of my chin to the hollow of my throat.

"Do you hate me, Mandy?"

Pinch. Right over my collarbone.

"No." Maybe.

Her lips curl, and at the corner of her mouth, the skin splits, just a little. A spiderweb of red crackles across her cheek.

I've stopped breathing. I always stop breathing.

"Then why, Mandy?"

Her jaw blackens, the flesh peeling back from her gums to reveal long exposed teeth—down to the roots. Her neck is a bloodied hollow.

"I didn't mean to," I croak, knowing the excuse isn't enough. It's not enough for either of us.

Skin crackles, blisters, peels. Bone gleams white, and her jaw sags, leaving her mouth lopsided. The smell of gunpowder and mud crawls up my nose and lodges deep in my throat. When crispy orange wisps of hair float into her eyes, she blinks, but doesn't wipe them away.

I flinch.

"Do you love me, Mandy?"

Tears glide from the corner of my eyes, over the socket and the bridge of my nose. Warm wetness pools into my pillow.

"Yes."

I wake with my cheeks wet and the stench of sulfur still clinging to the edges of my consciousness. My head pounds in time with the panicked hum of my heartbeat. *Sara.* I squeeze my eyes shut, blocking out the wooden boards of the ceiling. Sara is gone, and that was quite enough remembering for one night. I should have never gone to our spot. That was a mistake.

A wet, crackly sound comes from beside my bed. My stomach clenches. I'm still dreaming, but this is new. Sara has never *crackled* before.

It's horrible.

I don't want to look. Don't want to see her ruined neck and face again. Not yet.

The sound shifts, becoming more like a moan. Ugh. Look, Mandy. Look or this will never end.

I turn to find the whites of eyes, and they aren't Sara's. I recoil. A scream gets caught in my throat and for several seconds I can't hear over my roaring pulse.

Kelsey crouches on the floor, inches from my face. Wh—

She leans forward and her hands touch the edge of my bed. The mattress shifts.

Oh God. Oh God, this isn't a dream. I can't seem to get any words out. Kelsey, what's happening? Kelsey, Jesus Christ, what are you doing? Kelsey, *why*?!

Her cheeks shine—tear-streaked and soft in the light of the window.

I raise up on my elbow and my chest constricts. There's something so…lost about her expression. A blank look in her eyes, filled only by faint ripples of sadness and fear.

Kelsey follows my movement, but she doesn't seem to be looking directly at me, nor does she stand from her position beside the bed.

The air in my lungs is dust. Dirt. Withered and dead.

"Kelsey? What's wrong?" I manage, but I get no response. She continues to stare at me, but her gaze is fixed more on my cheek than my eyes. "Kelsey?" I hate the way the words break apart in my mouth.

She's sleepwalking. She must be. But very real emotion presses up against the waking world, seeping in salty tracks down her face.

Natalie sleeps in blissful ignorance. Kelsey never sleep-walked growing up. Is this new? The urge to wrap her in my arms and make the tears stop hits so strongly that I have to reach out. I have to let her know I'm here, even if she can't see me through the grip of nightmares.

Her eyes drift to my outstretched hand, and her lips pull back as if she means to scream.

Or bite me.

I yank my hand back. "Kelsey," I say her name louder this time, half hoping to rouse Natalie as well. "Wake up. What are you doing?"

A fresh tear slips down, into the crease of her mouth, but she doesn't answer. She doesn't react at all.

There's a crawling sensation at the back of my neck, and I'm suddenly way too aware of the window directly behind me. I move slowly and carefully to press my spine against the headboard, so I can keep my sleepwalking sister *and* the window *and* the door in view.

Watching. Always watching. Always waiting.

The beat of my heart keeps a tally of the silence.

Finally, Kelsey rises from the floor and walks steadily back to her own bed, like she's moving on an invisible track.

That was...

Fucking awful.

I stare at Kelsey as she lays her head down on her pillow and goes back to sleep. I hope. The alternative is that she's staring sightlessly at the ceiling, which is incredibly unnerving.

"Oh my God," I mouth the words, balling my hands so tight in the sheets the bones ache. Poor Kelsey. When did that start? It has to have been in the past year, right? I would have known, otherwise.

I might have known anyway, if I'd been a more attentive older sister.

Pinch—along the curve of my neck.

I gulp down a ragged scream and nearly throw myself out of the bed. My pulse is a hammer, smashing against my skin. I search the dark, but I'm alone. No one pinched me. The pang was a muscle spasm.

I force myself to draw one breath after another until they're steady and I've pulled my focus back to Kelsey and *only* Kelsey.

An uncomfortable twisting in my stomach mirrors the tension in my shoulders as I inch down under the covers. Something is bothering Kelsey. Haunting her. And I certainly know about restless nights and tear-soaked sheets. Maybe she'll want to talk, or maybe she won't, but I can at least offer. I can try to help.

At least then, I'll be able to help *someone*.

Because I definitely didn't help Sara.

15

NOW

SUNDAY MORNING. ONE YEAR AFTER.

I step off our porch and into a nightmare.

MURDERER.

It's spray-painted in sloppy, red letters along the slate walkway in front of our cottage.

MURDERER. Someone is angry. Someone *knows*. But that's impossible. They can't be angry at me because they *can't* know...right?

But the necklace is missing too.

The world tips away into one big swirling, dizzy mess. The hand I cast out to steady myself against the railing might as well belong to someone else entirely. I'm floating. I'm not here. Not really. I'm gone. Just like Sara.

I crash back into my body with such sudden, terrible clarity that my stomach lurches and my knees buckle, and it's all I can do to swallow the bile coating my tongue with the sour, slimy thickness of guilt. And fear.

MURDERER. There are speckles of red paint dusting the grass where the wind carried the accusation off the path.

"Mandy, honey, are you—oh my God." Mom's voice filters dimly through the roaring in my ears. Her fingers, tight, too tight, digging into my shoulders. Her sharp intake of breath, hissing through her teeth. Her urgency as she whispers, "Come on, get up," in my ear.

We aren't alone.

Maybe we never were. Maybe the small crowd gathering in the grass and on the walkway had already stopped to stare before I discovered the message. I have no idea.

As soon as MURDERER hooked its fuzzy red claws into me and splattered my heart against my rib cage, I'd lost track of everything beyond the defaced walkway.

But now their panicked voices rise around me like a wave ready to batter me against the shore.

Mom hauls me to my feet, and numbly, I move with her, back to the safety (safety? ha!) of the cottage. Kelsey and Natalie shove open the screen door, and Natalie barely pauses on her way into the fray, cell phone out. Kelsey hesitates. Her eyes land on mine, filled with that same fear that I saw a flicker of yesterday, and then she hurries after Natalie.

A firm voice cuts through the chatter of the crowd. "Everyone, please, clear away. We've got staff on the way to clean this up. Please. Go, enjoy your day. Leave this to us."

Mr. Miller, I think. I don't really care.

The fear and guilt twists, morphing into anger. This is bullshit. Who would do this? *Maybe the only other person*

~~there that night, that's who. No, they don't know about me. They can't. DON'T THINK ABOUT THAT.~~ This is horrifying.

What am I supposed to do? A whole resort full of people, devouring the fresh gossip. MURDERER laid out like fuel on a fire and I don't want to be the tinder but I don't know how to stop it. I could run. Flee back to school, but could I really? Mom and Dad would be pissed. They might even be mad, or worried, enough to insist I come home to "get better." And Kelsey and Natalie are dragging secrets to the surface. With this message, the name on everyone's lips will be mine. I'd hoped to keep my head down and avoid drawing attention— *risk*—to myself, but that's out the window. I'll have to be careful. Distract Kelsey and Natalie from looking into Sara's death. Figure out who spray-painted this mortifying message. And for the love of God, make sure I can still count Alex as a friend, despite our awkwardness yesterday. I need *someone* to be on my side, and there are too many people here who could be...dangerous.

I grit my teeth against the thought of ~~who else~~ what else lurks behind Highmark's polite, charming facade.

~~I can't do this~~.

I can do this.

16

THEN

THURSDAY MORNING. HOURS AFTER.

Everyone had to have been thinking it: murder. Sara had been murdered. How could they be thinking anything else, in between the tears?

Finn hugged his mom tight to keep her head turned away from Sara. Mr. Ellis knelt in the dirt where I'd done the same only a few hours ago. Although…not *quite* the same spot? Was it? She'd been farther from the lake's edge, hadn't she? No. No…I must've been misremembering. Everything felt a little fuzzy, like the lines of individual memories were already warping and bleeding into each other.

Mr. and Mrs. Miller stood off to the side, Mr. Miller on his phone while his wife hovered at his side. Dad was a wide-eyed, grim-faced statue beside Mr. Ellis.

I couldn't feel my hands. Or my face, for that matter. My body was one buzzing mass of terror and shame. Bark scraped my thighs where I sat next to Alex on a fallen log. I'd been unable to bear putting jeans on this morning. I couldn't stop remembering how they'd felt, soaking wet in the mud beneath the dock.

My eyes cut to the left. *That* dock. Right there. I slid my hands under my knees to hide the shaking.

Thank God Mom had stayed at the cottage with Kelsey when Mr. Ellis stopped by to ask for help looking for Sara.

Alex leaned his shoulder into mine. He'd shown up not long after the search party converged on the clearing. "You okay?" he asked, and his voice trembled.

I shrugged. "No." And I needed to tell him about the lie I told my mom. A lie I needed him to back up.

He took my hand and squeezed. I didn't let go.

Hannah stood on the opposite side of Alex with her eyes fixed firmly on the ground at her feet. Her staff polo was as wrinkled as the pinched lines crinkling her forehead. I couldn't tell if she was scared, or confused, or both.

"Come on, Hannah, sit with us," Alex said. "The wood's only a little damp."

No. The thought was sharp and sudden. I winced. I had to be normal. Be calm.

"I'm fine," she said, but she wouldn't look at us.

He patted the small open spot to his left. It had rained all through the early hours of this morning, and puddles dotted the soggy ground.

"I said no!"

A few heads turned toward us, and she lowered her voice, but the acid remained.

"Your girlfriend is over there dead and you're sitting there all cozy with Mandy? Not a good look, Alex." Finally, she did look at us. Or, more accurately, at our hands.

Sara wasn't his girlfriend. I winced. That wasn't important now.

"Well screw you too, Hannah," Alex snapped, but he gently withdrew his hand from mine.

Hannah glared, and Alex sighed.

"Sorry. I'm just...freaked. This is messed up," he said.

"Super messed up. How'd *you* even know to come out here? I didn't see you this morning when Mr. Miller was asking people to help look. I thought you were still asleep before your shift."

Alex recoiled, which pressed him more firmly against my side. He craned his neck to meet the accusation in her eyes. "Jesus, Hannah. I know this is stressful, but are you actually accusing me of having something to do with this? I'm *here* because Finn texted me that something was wrong and that Sara was missing. We were all out here last night. I figured this was the best place to check. Just like the rest of you."

She looked Alex up and down and shook her head. "Dunno, man. The other night you seemed pretty pissed at Sara for using you to make her brother mad."

Alex stilled. "I was mad. But you know I wouldn't *hurt* her. That's ridiculous! Horrible!"

I took several shallow breaths. Why couldn't I get enough air?

Because Sara was dead. Right over there. Right where I abandoned her.

I pressed the back of my hand to my lips and swallowed bile.

Hannah shook her head and glanced toward where the Highmark staff nurse was kneeling beside Mrs. Ellis. The nurse made slow, gentle motions as she talked. A single wet line traced down her cheek.

We settled into silence, but Alex broke it again.

"I didn't... I would never have done...whatever the hell happened to her," he said.

She exhaled, and her voice shook.

"I know. I'm sorry. But seriously, the cops are definitely going to ask you about her. What are you going to tell them?"

The cops and paramedics would be here any minute. They'd been called almost half an hour ago, but we were remote, and there was a lot of property to cross even after they arrived.

I shifted, my ankles grinding against the dirt. This was my chance. Once the cops showed up, they'd investigate and take statements, and surely everything would start to come together.

They'd learn—

Someone would—

She—

The knot in my throat pinches painfully. I needed to have my side of the story—my lie—locked in place before then.

"Alex couldn't have had anything to do with this, Hannah. We left together last night. And hung out after."

Alex's intake of breath was barely audible, and he stiffened beside me, but a second later he nodded.

"Well...that's good, then, I guess." Her nails dug hard into her forearms where she continued to hug herself tight. "Gosh, her poor parents. Poor Finn." She spoke his name softly, and seemed to forget we were still sitting there.

Alex faced me and held my gaze, a question burning in his eyes. He mouthed, *Are you sure about this?* breathing just enough life into the words for me to make out what he was saying.

I nodded. He didn't need to know that this wasn't some selfless act on my part. I'd already committed us to this lie, and myself to so many others without conscious thought.

~~I stayed back with Sara.~~ No. Alex and I left together.

~~I wanted Sara dead.~~ No. We had a little fight.

~~I knew she was sprawled in the dirt by the old crumbling dock.~~ No. I didn't know where her parents could find her.

~~I knew she was murdered.~~ I had no idea what happened to her.

~~I'd seen someone else last night.~~ They must not have seen me.

~~What really happened?~~ It didn't matter.

~~I was going to scream.~~ I would be fine.

17

NOW

SUNDAY AFTERNOON. ONE YEAR AFTER.

God it's hot. Mountain nights may be cool enough for sweaters and jeans, but the days are another story. My brain melts into a mushy puddle. Good. Maybe the sun will scorch the last coherent thought from my head, and I'll slip into oblivion. Dramatic? Sure. A genuine wish? Also yes.

MURDERER. The accusation is painted onto the backs of my closed eyelids. It slithers through me like an unwelcome whisper.

The lake is busy with kids and parents alike, out on the beach and grabbing an easy lunch at the Snack Shack, but Kelsey, Natalie, and I are mostly alone on the smaller dock.

Could Kelsey and Natalie have been the ones to leave the message? They wouldn't…would they? Who else would've left such a ~~truthful accurate~~ confrontational message outside our cottage?

Not Alex. Well, probably not Alex. Not unless he wants

things to get real ugly real fast, since he lied to the cops too. Hannah? She hadn't seemed very happy to see me. I hate that the most likely candidates *are* my sister and Natalie.

The uncertainty hurts, like a fist closed tight around my heart. I want to believe Kelsey wouldn't do something so cruel but...

Would she? Do I really know my sister?

The memory of her lost eyes and quiet tears fills me.

I shiver. Is she looking at me now? Staring at her sister the murderer? Mom would probably be here hovering too, if Kelsey and Natalie hadn't jumped at the chance to "keep me company" by the lake. Ninety-nine percent sure Mom asked them to babysit me. I can't even say I blame her. My body still doesn't feel quite like it belongs to me. Drifting. Rattled.

Guilty, guilty, guilty.

My skin prickles, like I'm being watched. Duh I'm being watched. By my sister, by Natalie, by the other guests and the staff, all thinking the same thing. MURDERER. *Murder? Who got murdered? Oh that poor young girl last year? Yes. A firework accident, the cops said. Weren't they friends? We all thought so, but you know how teens are. Could she have done it? I wonder...*

Stop. Gladiolas, gardenias, geraniums, chrysanthemums, mums, marigolds.

"I am getting so much interaction on the 'murderer' teaser," Natalie says to Kelsey as she scrolls down her phone. "You think we can get some shots of the spot where Sara died tonight? I want to have something else big ready. Showing them what Sara would've seen is pretty good, right?"

I shudder at the passion in Natalie's voice. This is going to end terribly—for them, and for me. It's not safe. I need a way to stop them.

"We can go tonight after dinner," Kelsey says. She sounds almost as eager as Natalie. "It won't be totally dark yet, but dusk should be good too, right? And then we can hang around until you get what you need."

Nope. Don't like that one bit. I take a sip from my thermos of iced coffee. I swallow wrong and gag as the painful lump travels down my throat, like a golf ball sinking into my chest. I press my fingers to my breastbone and wince.

"You good?" Kelsey asks.

I nod. "I'm good." No, I'm not. I need to stop this. "Actually, no. I know we got in a fight last night, but I meant what I said. Y'all shouldn't make a story out of Sara's death."

Natalie spins in her lounger to plant her feet on the deck and lean toward me, with Kelsey alert in the chair between us. They're in coordinating red swimsuits: a united front.

"We're not," Natalie says. "Whoever killed Sara made it into a story. We're just telling it for her. Someone knows more than they've said. Maybe talking about her death will get them to come forward. Besides, someone here also clearly thinks you murdered her—shouldn't you want to help?"

I'm pretty sure my cheek twitches. Was it you, Natalie? Did you and my sister leave that message to push me into helping you? I swallow the accusations. I don't know if I could stand if the answer was yes.

"I don't care what some spray-painting weirdo thinks," I say, flatly, in total contrast to the laughter, wild and furious, ringing in my head. Liar. You are *such* a liar. This is a disaster, and I do care. I care *so goddamn much*. I have to care, because it's not over. It might never be over.

With the incident bleeding through the resort's gossip circles, if I can't get Kelsey and Natalie to drop the story, I'll have to muddy the waters. Keep them distracted with Sara's life instead of her death. Maybe in some roundabout way, I can lead them to the conclusion that her death really *was* accidental.

I hide the way my mouth pulls down behind my thermos.

"It's not just one person who thinks you could have killed her," Natalie says, as if she's telling me water is wet.

I tense, but I keep my voice sarcastic and hope it hides the fear. "Yeah, because people on the internet *always* know what they're talking about." I swallow a scoff. They look for a place to point the finger. They oversimplify. With Sara, nothing had ever been simple, especially not her death.

But I don't want to turn this into a fight. I want to win Kelsey and Natalie over.

I want to protect them, ~~if it comes to that~~.

Natalie looks like she wants to argue with my take on internet critics, but she glances at Kelsey instead, like she's asking silently for my sister's support. Or permission.

Kelsey frowns. "We're not talking about online. We've asked around the resort."

Right. That creepy list they've been making of people involved.

"Who?" Suspicion washes over me, and my voice holds a harder edge than I intended. My sister can't find out. She can't know what I did. I'll die. I will curl up and die right here I swear to God.

Kelsey shrinks.

Natalie takes over without missing a beat. "The girl who brought us extra towels yesterday."

"What girl?"

"Hannah. I asked her about what Sara was like last summer, and whether anyone was acting weird. And she said that the weirdest thing was that you would've left Sara out there, because you and Sara were always together. She said we should talk to *you* more." Natalie raised her brows.

I scowl. Interesting that Hannah would point the finger at me. If I were braver, I'd go confront her, but I'm not. At least Kelsey isn't on the list of people who ~~know~~ think I'm responsible for Sara's death.

"Well, she's wrong." I sit up straighter, facing them like we're coconspirators. I'll give them a harmless detail. "Look. Here's something other people don't know about Sara. She'd just broken up with her boyfriend, and she was obsessed with 'the perfect summer.'"

"You're sure she broke up with her boyfriend?" Natalie asks.

"What do you mean?" Isn't that what I just said? "Like were they actually still together? No, they definitely broke up." Unless Sara lied. But why would she lie about something like that?

Natalie shakes her head. "No. Did *she* break up with *him*. Or did he dump her? Maybe he came up here and murdered her."

Wow, she really went to a true-crime place with *that* one, didn't she? I've made a mistake. Natalie is going to plaster ridiculous speculation about Sara's love life all over her channel and I've enabled her. I resist the urge to drop my face into my hands and scream.

All I meant to do was imply that maybe Sara really *had* been reckless and had an accident during her summer of fun. "She broke up with him." I leave it simple.

"Why?" Kelsey asks.

Even if I wanted to answer her, I can't. Why *did* she break up with him? Did she not tell me, or was I just being a bad friend and not paying attention?

"I don't know," I say, more to myself than to them.

"She didn't tell you? Nothing? What about anyone else she might've been fighting with?"

I shake my head and Kelsey gives an exasperated sigh. Sara could be really hot and cold. Sometimes she was the easiest person in the world to get along with, and other times it seemed like she pissed off everyone she spoke to. Me, Hannah, Leigh, Finn, Kelsey… Hell, Sara even occasionally rubbed my parents the wrong way.

"Finn, I guess," I blurt out. Shit, though, that's too close to the truth.

Natalie darts a confused look that I don't understand at Kelsey.

"But just sibling stuff," I add quickly. I know Finn didn't kill Sara. Not directly, anyway.

"That's all you remember?" Kelsey asks.

"Yes."

"I don't believe you," she says.

I wince. Smart of her, honestly. Sara shouldn't have trusted me either.

"Kelsey, I'm…" She's not going to talk to me about a damn thing if I can't even tell her I'm sorry. "I shouldn't have ignored you so much this past year, but I'm trying now. Really."

Her mouth twitches down, and for a brief, horrifying second, I think she's going to cry. But the moment passes.

"I needed to talk to you, and you weren't there." There's a hard lump of resentment in her voice, and something else I can't quite place.

My head hangs, and I chew my lip. I should ask her about last night. About coming to me, tears trailing her cheeks. About why she was so sad. ~~The answer might be me.~~

"When did you start sleepwalking?"

Her forehead wrinkles, deepening the appearance of the purple tint beneath her eyes. "I don't sleepwalk."

"You were sleepwalking?" Natalie says at the same time.

I hesitate, not wanting this to sound like an accusation when it's not.

"Are you sure?" I ask.

She nods and readjusts the bikini tie around her neck. "Pretty sure."

"It seemed like you were sleepwalking last night. And… crying."

I let the statement hang.

Her face, already a little pink from the sun, flushes. "Really? Did I say anything?"

Is she embarrassed, or worried, or both?

"No, I don't think so." Why? Did she have something to hide? Oh God, absolutely not. I can't be suspicious of my sister. Not like…

Stop. Hibiscuses, hydrangeas, azaleas—

A wave of dizziness hits me, and vaguely I consider that I hardly ate breakfast and I've had more coffee than water all morning. Deep breaths. But deep breaths are hard and it's so hot out here and it feels vaguely like I'm tipping off my lounger. I keep the calm smile plastered to my face through sheer desperation. Can't let the panic show. The dizziness relents, slowly.

"That's pretty weird," she says. The relief is thick in her voice.

Hmm.

"It was super weird, Kelsey. And I… You seemed… scared. And sad."

An unreadable look passes over her face. Her lips part. Her teeth scrape her bottom lip, gently. "Sorry. I don't know what it was about. I was asleep, like you said."

And with that the moment is gone, but her face as she crouched there in the dark, is not.

Watching silently.

Dirt beneath my fingernails, water soaking my jeans.

MURDERER, spray-painted in bold and bleeding red.

Seriously. Who the *hell* wrote that? And could they have seen me that night, as everything fell apart?

18

THEN

MONDAY AFTERNOON. TWO DAYS BEFORE.

Sara wiggled down the couch until she could poke me with her foot.

"Are you *sure* you don't want to go down to the lake?" she asked.

It was a perfect afternoon for swimming, but Alex would be there—either on the stand or in the Shack. I didn't really want to go watch them flirt.

Her toes caught an exposed bit of skin where my shirt rode up.

I swatted at her, and she laughed and yanked her foot away.

"That *hurts*, Sara."

"Fiiiine." Her tone was dismissive, but she curled tighter into herself on her end of the couch. "I was *going* to say that I have dirt on Finn. Real dirt, and it's *big*."

I arched a brow. Somehow, I didn't believe she hadn't manufactured this "dirt" herself.

Her expression hardened, almost too slightly to notice, but I knew she wasn't happy about my hesitation.

"What is it? Did perfect Finn dent the car?"

"No," she said, forcing the eye roll into her voice. "It's something major. *Perfect* blackmail. But I can't tell you if you're not totally on board. You have to promise to help me and keep it secret."

Ugh! Sure, I was curious, but I was also sick of her insisting on promises and trying to get me to back her up on terrible ideas. She definitely didn't used to be this...controlling... did she? All these ultimatums were weird.

"Why are you so obsessed with this? Just tell me. I don't want to promise I'm going to help and then find out it's something awful."

"You don't trust me?"

The unexpected question staggered me. No, I guess I didn't trust her. Not this year. She'd had a one-track mind lately and everything was...out of balance. All I wanted was for things to be *normal* between us.

"Sara, you've got to stop trying to get me to help you screw over your brother. I don't want to get involved." I was way too loud by the end, and Sara jumped off the couch.

"Shh!" she hissed, waving her hands at me. "My parents are downstairs."

A beat of quiet passed, and my breathing evened out.

Sara straightened and smiled, but it was oddly brittle. "Fine. But don't expect me to keep trying to include you in things if you're going to be so insufferably boring all the time."

I felt my mouth fall open. "Is that a threat?"

"What?"

"If I won't torture your brother with you, you'll—" I hated that I choked a little before I could continue. "Stop being my friend?"

She recoiled. "*No—*"

"I hate you!"

Sara and I both jumped, ready to fight before realizing the insult hadn't come from either of us.

We looked to the screen door, where beyond the Ellis porch, the shouting continued.

The Millers were fighting.

I jumped off the couch and followed Sara out onto the porch. She snatched my hand in hers, her fingers lacing through mine and squeezing tight, and pulled me down beside her.

With her face a few inches from mine, she raised a finger to her lips. Her face glowed with excitement. I couldn't resist the grin tugging at the corners of my lips. God, she loved drama, and sometimes, she carried me away with her. The knot in my throat eased. Maybe I was being difficult. Things with Sara were always simpler when I let her lead.

We crawled to the edge of the porch, keeping low and searching for the source of the shouting.

There was no one outside the Miller cottage, but a window on the side facing Sara's cottage was open.

"Eric," a voice said, insistent and angry.

"Dad, I'm not going to sit at a table and make conversation *by myself* with your girlfriend."

"Leigh!" Mr. Miller shouted. "She's not my girlfriend. She is my wife."

"Well she's not my mom."

There was a pause, and Sara turned wide, perfect sky-blue eyes to me. *Oh my God*, she mouthed. I snorted, and she shifted enough to nudge my foot with hers. I nudged back.

"She's not actually sad, Dad. She's literally just crying so you'll side with her."

Someone—had to be Mrs. Miller—gave a frustrated scream. A door slammed, and a second later, Mrs. Miller stormed down the walkway from their cottage, wiping her eyes with the back of her hand.

A metallic whine came from behind us. Sara gasped. We whirled around clumsily, bumping our shoulders and knees together.

"What are you doing?" Finn asked, one eyebrow raised. He wore only jogging shorts and sneakers, and he ruffled his golden hair while he waited for an answer.

When neither of us said anything, he shook his head.

"Y'all are ridiculous," he said, but he laughed as he said it.

Sara scrambled to her feet, holding a hand down to me. She pulled, and I brushed random bits of leaf and twigs from my butt.

"Are you still going to build a fire with Alex tonight?" she asked her brother.

"Yes," Finn said slowly.

"Can we come?"

He made a face. He was going to say no. Why would he want his sister and her friend hanging out with him?

"You would show up anyway, so yeah, sure." He shrugged. "Now move out of the way you weirdos. I'm going on a run."

Sara watched her brother jog down the stairs and turned to me.

"Help me pick out what to wear tonight?"

She didn't wait for a response before pulling me along with her.

Things weren't perfect between us this summer, but if I could find a way to hold on to more of the moments like this, and fewer of the ones that felt like a battle, maybe we'd be fine. We *had* to be fine, because I couldn't stand the thought of losing Sara too.

I let out a breath and kept her hand firmly in mine.

19

NOW

SUNDAY AFTERNOON. ONE YEAR AFTER.

If Kelsey and Natalie are running around asking Highmark staff and guests about Sara, I owe Alex a warning.

He sits perched in the wooden lifeguard chair, one tanned ankle crossed over the opposite knee. My feet slow despite how badly I want to be near him. Our first conversation hadn't gone well. Alex had seemed less than pleased to see me.

I couldn't blame him.

His head swivels and he waves me over. I think he's smiling, but without my glasses I can't be sure. I leave the gravel path behind, cutting across a strip of scraggly grass and through the sandy patch that little kids and their parents use as a beach. The coarse sand is surprisingly cool as it squishes between my toes, and I tap my flip-flops rhythmically against the side of my thigh as I approach the short set of stairs.

The Snack Shack looms, in perpetual need of a fresh coat

of paint and staffed by a bored-looking girl at the counter's window, behind the lifeguard roost.

My stomach growls, and I drain the last of the coffee as I cross the raised platform to Alex's side.

"Hey, Mandy," he says.

I've always loved hearing him say my name. I squint up at him, and now I can see that he's definitely grinning.

The sun glints off the whistle around his neck, and there's a sheen to the sweat slicking his chest that glows nearly gold. Up close, the definition in his chest is, uh, distracting.

"Hey." I shuffle from one foot to the other. It's incredibly tempting not to bring up Sara or the…complications my sister and Natalie are creating.

It doesn't matter. Alex does it for me.

"Who's your sister's new friend?" he asks, lifting his chin toward the opposite dock.

Diving right in. "Natalie. Her parents are in Italy or something and my mom and dad didn't want Kelsey's only option to be *me*, I guess."

"That's nice for her. It's not like you and—like we ever wanted her around much anyway." Alex's face is frozen for a brief, flickering instant.

I know he'd been about to say, *You and Sara,* and he'd have been right. Kelsey was always the younger sister and therefore the annoyance. We'd ditched her as often as possible. I knew it wasn't right, but we did it anyway.

"Yeah well, I came to warn you that they might track you down and grill you about Sara, so I'd wait before you go thinking that it's 'nice' for Kelsey to have a friend here. They're being super persistent. And annoying." *Annoying* is a wild understatement.

"Oof. Hannah mentioned they'd cornered her when she was dropping off towels. Thanks for the extra warning. And I'm sorry," he says.

"About...what?"

"About yesterday. If I was weird." He rolls his eyes skyward. "Of course it was weird. But I'm glad you're back. Really. My parents didn't want me working here again this summer. They wanted me to hang out around home and do... well...nothing, before going back to school." He shakes his head. "All through high school my mom was all over me about 'Get a job, you have to have a job, you can't just sit there doing nothing.' Super mixed messages."

I scrape my nail over the skin at my thumb and shift my weight. "Why did you want to work here this year, though? If I could've spent this summer somewhere else without pissing off my entire family and ending up yanked out of school, I absolutely would have. But my parents insisted I come. Like a test." I laugh. "I think I'm failing."

I *know* I'm failing. But I can fix it.

Alex studies me, and his tone is careful when he says, "I definitely didn't expect to see you here." After a pause where I don't offer any response, he continues. "But I always liked working here. Even after...everything."

My brow scrunches. "I'm surprised they wanted you back."

A startled laugh bursts from his lips. "Yeah, well, they called and I accepted. Maybe a face-your-fears kind of thing, I don't know. But I didn't say no."

"I guess I did the same when my parents told me I had to come. I could've argued harder. I could've come up with a valid excuse." Saying it out loud...why didn't I? Was I trying to face the same fears as Alex?

No. Impossible, because whatever guilt Alex holds, it can't compare to mine.

"Why don't you come out to the staff cabins tonight? A bunch of us are having a party. It'll be fun."

A strange joy sizzles in my chest. I ignore it and say, "Really?"

"Really what?"

"I—sure." I cut myself off, but I'm surprised to warrant an invite now that Finn isn't around and Sara is rotting in a grave—*nope*. "Which cabin are you in this year?"

"Same as last year. Number two."

"Cool."

"You'll come then? Most of us should be hanging out by nine, so any time after that."

Most of us.

"How—how many people?" What if they ask me about Sara? What if they *don't* ask me about Sara, but they're clearly *whispering* about Sara? What if they're wondering whether there's really something to the 'MURDERER' spray-painted in front of our cottage?

Or worse, what if whoever else I saw that night is there?

I grit my teeth and tell myself it wouldn't matter. That the time for accusations and revelations is long past, regardless of Kelsey and Natalie's schemes.

His face softens. "You're worried."

I drop my gaze as a frown tugs at my mouth. "Kelsey and Natalie are already bugging me nonstop about Sara." Her name comes out rough.

He sighs and hops down from the lifeguard tower. "People have asked me about her too."

"Really?"

"Yeah. But they dropped it quick." He reaches for me, and when I don't pull away, he gives my shoulder a squeeze. "Please come. I really am happy to see you."

"I'll be there."

He smiles broadly and my heart flutters. How clichéd.

The history we share is decidedly less clichéd.

But despite everything, I'm happy to see him too.

Really happy.

20

THEN

MONDAY NIGHT. TWO DAYS BEFORE.

Sara was tipsy, but that only made it easier to hover at the edge of her warmth—a twin fire to the flames crackling in the middle of the circle—and imagine a life where I knew how to shine that bright. Hannah groans at something Sara said but I couldn't hear.

An imperceptible shift in the wind brought curls of smoke to where I hunched forward on one of the benches. My eyes watered, and I waved a hand to clear space for a clean breath.

In a blink, my marshmallow caught fire.

I yanked the blazing marshmallow out of danger and blew until I was left with a bubbly, blackened hunk of sugar. Pinched between my thumb and forefinger, the crispy outer layer crackled and white oozed over my skin.

"Here, I'll take that one," Sara said.

"What?"

"You don't like them burned. I'll eat it."

I opened my mouth, and she plucked the marshmallow from my outstretched hand and squashed it between two slabs of chocolate—no graham cracker.

"Okay."

"What? You always say you like your S'mores golden brown." She paused. "Do you want it back?" she offered, her eyes dancing as she waved her abomination of a S'more between us.

"No. You eat that one." My fingers were sticky with the remnants of melted sugar and blackened flakes. I scraped my teeth over my thumb as I licked away what was left.

"I can get us more S'mores stuff," Hannah volunteered, and leapt up from the bench, nearly skipping over to the plastic bags full of chocolate, marshmallows, and graham crackers on the ground beside Finn's chair.

"Hey Mandy?" Sara's tongue flicked out to catch a stray bit of chocolate. She washed it down with her drink: vodka bought with one of the staff members' fake IDs and orange juice.

"Hmm?" Raspy from smoke. I cleared my throat.

"Are you having fun?"

"Of course I am."

"You don't look like you're having fun."

How would she know? She hadn't been looking at me, which I knew, because *I'd* been looking at *her*. She'd been stealing glances across the fire to where Alex and Finn were bent over Finn's phone, their faces lit by dual lights.

Finn smirked, and Alex laughed, but when his eyes cut to Sara's brother, he frowned.

Even his frown was lovely. An ache pinged in my chest. "Well I am."

Sara pouted. "Then why are you mad?"

"I'm—"

She pinched my arm, but not hard. "Don't deny it. You're mad about something. Or sad. Which is it and how can I help?"

Her eyes swam with sincerity and alcohol, and I really thought she meant it. She wanted me to be happy, but...

But nothing. Sara was my friend, of course she wanted me to be happy, just like I wanted the same for her.

I smiled brightly, the fire warming the left side of my face and leaving the right cool. Sara's face was cast in mirrored light and shadow. "I'm good, I swear. I'm out of drink though. Going to get a refill."

"Me too, *pleeaasse*," Sara said, and drained the remains of her cup. When she finished, her eyes landed on Finn, Alex, and Hannah, and she frowned.

Hannah knelt by the marshmallows and graham crackers, but she was busy talking to the boys. Touching Finn's hand.

"Doesn't she have a boyfriend? Who she's supposedly in love with?" Sara asked.

The disapproval dripping from her voice surprised me.

"That's what she said. But I'm sure that's nothing," I said, jerking my head in their direction. And sure enough Finn stretched, removing his hand from where it had touched Hannah's. She went back to gathering up S'more supplies as if nothing had happened.

Sara huffed. "Everyone cheats these days and it's gross."

"O...kay?" It came out a question. I was standing there holding two empty plastic cups, and I really wanted to just keep walking but, "Sara...did something—"

She flashed a bright, firelit smile, and cut me off. "Go on. Go get us new drinks." She waved me off, and as I walked away she called, "Alexxx?"

I rolled my eyes and trudged to cabin two, where Alex's room was. I made the refills weaker. I was pretty sure more alcohol was a bad idea tonight. I was halfway to the front door, clutching cups full of more orange juice than Sara would be happy about, when shouting started.

Great.

Just *great*.

We couldn't all sit around and stuff our faces with chocolate and marshmallows for one night?

I shouldered my way outside and marched over to where Sara and Finn were arguing. Sara had stood up from the bench, and Finn faced her, hands clenched at his sides. Alex and Hannah both hovered nearby.

Sara and Finn were *terrible*. They hadn't always been this bad, had they? No, definitely not. Sure, they'd fought, but this year Sara couldn't seem to let anything go.

And Finn was rising to the challenge.

I frowned and met Alex's eyes across the fire. They were wide and guilty. Hannah stood beside him, mouth set in a scowl.

I crunched my way across the wood chips and lumpy dirt

to stand beside Alex. The smell of smoke and some woodsy soap clung to his skin, and I resisted the urge to lean closer.

"Hey, man, we didn't mean—" Alex starts, but Finn cuts him off with a glare.

"Didn't mean what? You didn't mean to hook up with my little sister?"

Ohhhh.

Uh-oh.

"Suddenly you want us to be in each other's business," Sara shot back, giving her brother's shoulder a jab with her pointer finger.

Finn made a garbled, frustrated noise and threw his hands up.

"No! But you don't even like Alex." He stared his friend down, brows raised as if Alex were missing something very, very obvious. "Seriously, dude. She's just using you. She's bored and mad at me and she knows hooking up with you would piss me off."

Alex scoffed, but his eyes slid to Sara.

She was too busy glaring at her brother to notice.

"Shit," Alex muttered.

"I can't believe you, Alex," Finn said. "Ew. I don't want to talk about it anymore."

Finn stormed off toward the path back to the main grounds of the resort. He walked fast enough that the darkness swallowed him quickly.

Alex started after him, but Sara grabbed his arm.

He whirled on her. "What do you want, Sara?"

"Stay here. He doesn't want to talk anyway."

"Are you serious with this? Why the hell would I stay with *you* after that? Did you really just get with me to annoy your brother?"

I hated that he sounded like he actually cared. I'd always thought there was something between us—that he liked me—but apparently, the thing between us was Sara.

She glanced at me for some inexplicable reason. This was so not my fight. I wasn't going to back her up on *any* of this.

She must've expected him to side with her, because surprise, and uncertainty, bled into her voice. "I—no. No, that wasn't totally why."

"You're kind of a bitch, you know that?" Alex said.

It took a lot to make Alex angry. Part of me was glad to hear him turn on Sara, but did it mean he liked her enough to care that she'd been using him? I felt a pang of guilt too, unsteady and sour, about rooting for my friend's downfall.

But she'd started it.

Sara crossed her arms. "It took two of us to get in this situation, you know. You're not perfect."

Hannah muttered "slut" under her breath, and I whispered "shut up" right back.

"What did you say?" Sara snapped at Hannah, who rolled her eyes. Sara pressed forward. "Why are you even here? Didn't you say you had to call your boyfriend tonight?"

"I do, *later*. And *you* can go back to your cottage if you don't like the company here. In case you hadn't noticed, these are the staff cabins, and I don't have to justify myself to you," Hannah snapped.

She shoulder-checked me as she stomped away. Rude.

Alex sighed.

"Do whatever y'all want, I'm leaving," Alex said, and took off after Finn.

Sara turned, her brow furrowed, her lips parted, like she couldn't quite understand what had happened. Where it had all gone wrong.

I felt bad for her, I did, but when her eyes found mine I had no comfort to offer.

She was playing games with us all, and I was tapping out.

NOW

SUNDAY NIGHT. ONE YEAR AFTER.

They're whispering.

They're making an effort to hide it, but not a *strong* effort.

Coming here was a mistake. What's taking Alex so long? I twist, forcing my eyes to go straight to the doorway that leads to a simple shared kitchen. Can't let any of the other staff catch me staring at them. I don't want to invite their questions. Everyone's either seen, or heard about, the "MURDERER" spray-painted in front of the cottage where I'm staying. Half these people were here last year when Sara died. They're probably trying to remember what they'd heard when the police questioned me at the time.

It's not ideal, and I'm convinced my skin is crawling off my bones.

Alex strides through the doorway and into the common room, and the knot in my chest loosens by a fraction. He throws himself down onto the couch beside me, handing over a plastic cup that crackles with the fizz and pop of Coke and—*sniff sniff*—a lot of rum.

"Yeah," Alex says, taking in my expression. "It's cheap stuff, but it's what we could get."

"No worries." I know how it works. Kids with fake IDs and kids who swipe their parents' alcohol. Kids convincing older kids to buy us vodka in a plastic bottle. Can't be too choosy.

I take a sip and fight a grimace, but I'm not going to pass on the drink. Not while I'm surrounded by people who all definitely know about Sara. Did one of them have to try, and fail, to scrape the spray paint from the sidewalk outside my cottage? Did they take pictures? I can't blame them. I would have.

A chilling thought settles like a misty cloud around my shoulders.

Did one of them do it? MURDERER.

~~Did one of them do worse than that?~~

No, don't go there. Not now.

Hannah sits on the other couch, talking to a guy with glasses. She'd said a frosty hello when Alex welcomed me inside and introduced me to the group, but otherwise, she's ignored me.

"We're going to play two truths and a lie," Hannah announces. "Whoever's turn it is will tell the rest of us two truths and one lie, and as a group, we'll guess which is the lie. If the group guesses wrong, they all drink. If the group guesses correctly, the bad liar drinks." Her eyes, curious and vaguely hostile, settle on me a second too long as she sweeps the room.

I stiffen. Beside me, Alex does too. He relaxes almost immediately and scoots closer to me, making room for two more people to join us on the couch.

"Everybody got it?" Hannah asks the group of seven.

Oh, I got it, but I wish I didn't. Lies. I'm lying all the time but the truth isn't much better, is it? I should be good at this game. I play it every day.

A brunette with their hair trimmed short and violet lipstick goes first. "I collect soaps. I sleep with my baby blanket. And I'm allergic to strawberries."

While the group debates, Alex's knee settles against mine, and he doesn't move away. Maybe he hasn't realized. That's ridiculous, of course he's realized. But maybe he hasn't, somehow, because wouldn't he have moved?

I drink, because I'm being absurd.

His leg is warm.

Alex goes next, which means my turn is coming soon. I twist to watch his face, and have to incline my head because he's so close to me. The line of his jaw is perfect. Gorgeous. I want to trace my fingers along his cheek, and end at those soft lips. Pay attention, Mandy. Jeez. Was I always so attracted to him? I liked him, but before there was always Sara. Sara and Alex, Sara and me. Sara.

"I've read twenty books so far this year. I've never been north of Virginia. I have a girlfriend."

I look away from Alex just in time to see Hannah's mouth twitch. I don't have the courage to chime in with the one I *hope* is a lie. Please don't have a girlfriend. Please don't have a girlfriend.

The group correctly guesses that Alex doesn't have a girlfriend. He drinks. I drink too, mostly to stop myself from staring at him. Alex with his tanned, muscled forearms. Alex in that black T-shirt that fits perfectly across his broad chest. Is my mouth dry?

He leans his shoulder into mine. "Your turn."

Yeah. My turn.

The rum makes me bold, and I hold his gaze when I say, "I have a boyfriend."

That earns me a smile, but I need two truths.

~~I killed a girl.~~ "I can't whistle."

~~I'm afraid my sister hates me.~~ "I'm afraid of moths."

"You don't have a boyfriend," Alex says smoothly, and raises his cup to his lips, peering at me over the rim while he waits.

"Hey!" Hannah shouts, but Alex is right.

I take a long drink, giving him his answer.

"You didn't know that was a lie," I say.

"No, but I hoped."

I forget to breathe. His hand, which rests on the back of his leg, slides over enough that his fingers brush against my thigh. Holy shit, holy shit, holy shit.

"Want more?" he asks, and for a brief, skin-flushing moment, I think he's asking if I want him to touch me more, but he nods to my now-empty cup.

I nod. "Please."

Hannah's voice cuts in. Her turn.

"I've never broken a bone. I sometimes steal stuff from guest rooms." A heavy pause. "And I've never killed anyone."

The room swoops around me. She's not looking at me, but one by one other heads turn. One person blushes. Several grimace. The corner of Hannah's mouth lifts.

Alex? Alex, come back. I'm screaming it inside my head but no sounds are coming out. My armpits sweat and it's hot. So hot. My pulse pounds.

A girl on the other couch with a pitying expression gives a weak laugh and points out, "You were literally bragging yesterday about a pen you took. You definitely steal stuff. And you haven't killed anyone. So the lie is that you've never broken a bone."

The words are muffled through the roaring in my ears.

"What the hell, Hannah?" Alex's voice comes from behind me.

She gives innocent eyes. "What? I *haven't* killed anyone."

"You're not being funny," he says, scowling.

She shifts, but quickly squares her shoulders. "I didn't say *anyone* here was a killer. If you're making assumptions, that's on you. Though I can see why you'd jump to conclusions, with all that spray paint…"

My eyes burn with shame. Don't cry. Not in front of her. I bite my lip.

Roses—uh. Uh. Violets.

Shit.

"That's not fair and you know it," Alex says.

"Yeah, yeah. You and Mandy were together that night. Even though you'd been hooking up with Sara all week." She gives a not-super-innocent shrug.

"It wasn't like that," Alex mutters.

"You three were messy, and now her own sister is out there stirring up *more* mess. I'm not the problem. That's all I'm saying."

If I hold myself any tighter I'm going to crack a rib.

"Come on, Mandy," Alex says, and the sound of him saying my name, tight with anger but not at me, pulls me around to face him instead of the vultures in the room.

He ushers me, drinks in hand, through the door and onto the porch, before kicking the door closed. Wood slams against wood hard enough that I jump.

Alex's mouth is set in a hard line, but he presses his eyes shut and after a few seconds his face smooths. "Sorry," he says. "Let's sit?" He makes it a question.

I want to leave. But also I don't want to leave, because if I leave, Alex will stay and what if he doesn't extend another offer to hang out?

I lower myself onto the edge of the porch and swing my legs. My heels scuff the dirt.

Alex sits on my left, keeping a sliver of space between us.

I don't like the remaining distance, but I stay put.

There's no roof out here, only a stretch of boards and two stairs down into the dirt path. Above, stars glitter around a half-full moon. The night smells clean, like pine and earth.

Folding chairs have been set up off to one side, near the fire-pit. I look away, not wanting to remember the last time I sat around that fire.

"It's nice out," he offers.

It's a weak attempt at normalcy, but I'll take it. "Yeah."

There are crickets somewhere, or more like everywhere, and even though there's hardly any wind, the faint sound of shifting branches and rustling leaves creates a raspy murmur around us. I sip my newly filled drink, quickly, and hope the anxious thrumming inside me quiets soon.

Soon the world is softer-edged. No need to worry about the people inside, because you're out here with Alex and that's what you wanted all along. To be with Alex, right? My skin is warm despite the cool mountain air, and even though I know I probably shouldn't, I finish off the last sips of my drink instead of saying the words that are forming on my tongue.

I like you. And also your face and your arms and your chest are nice. And kissing you would be great, thanks.

I giggle, and then frown at the fact I've just giggled for no apparent reason.

Alex cocks an eyebrow. "Something funny?"

I lean forward, staring at my feet as I knock the toes of my boots together. *Tap, tap, tap.* "Not really."

He's silent for seconds that seem to drag on for an eternity beneath the blanket of midnight sky. The moment hums, electric between us.

"I really like your hair like this," he says. "The blue is great. Really fits you."

My breath catches. Alex likes the new me. Or at least, part of the new me.

He reaches out, hand hesitating a fraction from where my hair grazes my shoulder.

I smile, hoping he'll brush the side of my neck as he runs his fingers through my hair. But I don't know how to *tell* him that's what I want. He grins and drops his hand to his thigh.

Shoot. I blew it.

Again my eyes stray to the firepit. I can almost see Sara there, at the center of her own self-made storm.

"Do you know when Finn's supposed to arrive?" I ask. *Why* did I ask that? That's not at all what I want to talk about. In fact, talking has nothing to do with what I want right now.

A flicker of guilt passes quickly over Alex's face, and he takes a drink before responding. "Actually, no. I've texted him, but he didn't respond. He and I haven't talked much recently, but still. Dick move not to text back."

Cringe. I'd ignored soooo many texts from Kelsey, and she was my own sister. Definitely a dick move. "My mom said he was coming before the memorial, but that's all she knew."

Alex groans. "I've been trying not to think about that."

"*You've* been trying not to think about it? I'm supposed to speak. How...?" My shoulders hunch. "How am I supposed to do that?"

He sighs. "I don't know, but I don't envy you. It's been really hard for me too." He reaches over, his fingers hovering above mine before giving my hand a firm squeeze. "I'm sorry I never texted you. I wanted to, but you know you never actually gave me your number, and I was… I don't know. I guess I was scared. Especially since we…"

He trails off and I whisper the words I know he planned to say. "Since we lied to the cops?"

Saying it out loud makes the alcohol in my stomach slosh. Oof. This is not a good conversation. Not now, not ever, but we're in it and he keeps touching my hand, which is nice.

His lips press together, and I swear to God kissing him is seeming like a better and better option: both to stop myself from talking, and because I'm convinced he'd be good at it. His fingers move up to my wrist, trail along my forearm. His brows are drawn together though, like he's having to think really, really hard about what he's saying. "Do you think we did the right thing? You know, looking back, was it even worth lying about? It shouldn't have been a big deal, right?"

His touch and his words are pulling me so hard in opposite directions—excitement and panic, thrill and horror—that I'm dizzy. Or I'm drunk. Probably (definitely) both.

I lick my lips and they taste sweet, like Coke and rum. "I don't know if we needed to lie or not. It seemed like a good idea at the time."

And I was scared.

Help me.

Dirt beneath my nails, pine in my lungs, water soaking my jeans.

Only the warmth of Alex's shoulder pressed against

mine keeps me from bolting. Warm. Safe. He's a friend and friends don't hurt each other ~~yes they do they hurt each other all the time~~. I gulp to keep down the bile rising in my throat.

"I guess I spent so much time stressing over their questions, over what they'd find. Whether it was an accident or—" He stops and swallows, pulling his hand back into his own lap. *Don't leave me.* He shakes his head. "I, uh—I need to tell you something."

The anticipation and anxiety are impossible to untangle in my chest right now.

"Hm?"

"I may have...sort of...accidentally told Finn that you and I didn't leave together that night. We talked briefly, a few months ago, and I mentioned feeling bad for having left y'all out there." He speeds through the rest as the last of the desire swirling through my limbs evaporates.

"But I explained everything and it's okay, I mean, I think it's okay. I told him you'd only lied because I'd panicked."

My throat collapses and it aches, forcing the words out. "Was he...mad?"

He sighs. "I don't think so. Not...more than he was already."

I wonder if Alex can see how hard my heart is beating. If he can see the fear clawing at my chest. Belatedly, I realize I'm shaking.

His hand comes up to cup my chin, gently turning my face toward him. "I didn't mean to tell him. It's my fault if he's a jerk to you when he gets here and I'm so, so sorry. I'll try to fix it."

But there's no fixing this, because nothing changes the fact that Sara's still dead. I lurch up from the porch, but I'm drunk, and I plant my right foot on an uneven mound of dirt. I trip forward.

It's a slow-motion fall. My left knee thuds against the ground, and my palms sting as dirt and small rocks bite into them.

"Jesus!" There's a shuffling as Alex stands and jumps down from the deck.

The memories of the last time we were all here together wash over me.

The expression on Sara's face after Finn and Alex left. The rift between us growing wider, and neither of us doing anything to stop it.

We made it worse.

I curl my fingers into the dirt. My chest is tight and throbbing, ready to burst all over the walkway.

Help me. But I didn't.

I push myself up, teeth gritted and flashes of that night strobing across my vision.

Sara looking down at me, her legs pinning me on either side. A hand pinning my hair and a challenge in her eyes. Always a challenge and I was so fucking tired of fighting.

How could she have known how it would end? I didn't know myself.

Anger burning through my veins, searching for a way

out. The cool surface of the rock when I clutched it in my palm.

I didn't mean to hit her that hard.

Or maybe I did.

I force a deep breath and smile, even as tears glass my eyes.

"Oh, Mandy," Alex says softly. "I swear I haven't slipped up and told anyone else. And her death was an accident, anyway. It's going to be all right. I'll talk to Finn when he gets here. Want me to walk you home?"

I shake my head. "No. I'm okay. It's just really hard, talking about her." And not completely melting down as I realize you've messed up my alibi. I'm already dealing with Kelsey and Natalie and whoever spray-painted the walkway. I don't need Finn getting suspicious too. "I'm gonna go."

I turn to flee down the winding path to the main property, just like Finn had a year ago.

Alex hurries to my side. "Are you sure you don't want me to walk with you?"

I shake my head, but stop quickly. The ground spins too much when I do. "It's fine. I'll text you when I get back."

"You don't have my number though, remember?"

Right. We just talked about that. Sara had his number though, and an old annoyance bristles. I pull out my phone and have to concentrate extra hard on punching in the numbers he provides.

What a disaster.

As I walk away, letting the shaded path swallow me, I steal one last look at Alex. He hasn't moved, watching me go.

He smiles, but the guilt ruins the effect.

22

NOW

SUNDAY NIGHT. ONE YEAR AFTER.

My stomach heaves, and I empty its contents into the toilet bowl. *Ughhhhhh.*

Sticky heat crawls along my neck and the room spins faster. I gag again as my stomach seems to shove its way into my throat. This is garbage. Trash. The absolute worst.

I take a few breaths and focus on the floral pattern on the shower curtain, but that only makes things worse when the little blue hydrangeas start to move. I pray Kelsey and Natalie are still asleep outside the bathroom door, but I'm almost too miserable to care.

When it's over, I rock back on my heels, breathing heavily. The tile is cold and hard against my knees, and I push my damp, sweaty hair away from my eyes.

"Oof," I say to no one. I wash my hands, enjoying the cool water on my skin, but the room still has a slightly wobbly quality. I cup palmful after palmful of water, sucking down as many gulps as I can.

The sink is cold, my fingers gripping the porcelain edges. What are you doing, Mandy? I sigh, and it seems to last forever. The one and only perk of the alcohol is that maybe, just maybe, I won't dream.

It's a big perk.

After brushing my teeth and washing my face, I flick the lights off and venture to bed. The room is fuzzy with the faint light filtering through the curtains. Barely light enough to see as I wiggle out of my jeans, only toppling over once, and toss my sweater to the floor. Pajama pants and a T-shirt are a welcome comfort.

Sweet, sweet bed. I am *so* ready to sleep this awful night away, and ideally forget about Alex telling *Finn,* of all people, that we lied. I yank the sheets back, and my eyes shift longingly to the pillows.

But there's something on the pillow closest to me. Dirt?

No. Dirt isn't shiny.

Am I dreaming? My feet are frozen in place. Arms locked at my sides.

A silver heart in a tangle of chain.

I can feel my pulse on my tongue, and for several seconds the room disappears. My hands are buried in dirt, and twigs scratch at my arms. Where is it? Where! This is where I buried it, but it's *not here.*

Not in the dirt where I *know* I left it, and now Sara's necklace is on my pillow.

I didn't put it there.

Someone dug it up.

Someone knows I buried it.

Who? Who would have known? And—oh God—whoever dug the necklace up was in my room. My pulse jumps and I turn, like moving through mud, to Kelsey and Natalie. Were they there, asleep, when someone was creeping through the dark?

I shudder.

I'm going to be sick again. This is too much. It's all too much.

Silent tears spill down my cheeks, and I press knuckles to my mouth to keep the cries silent. I want to scream. I want to pick up the necklace and throw it to the floor. Smash it beneath my bare feet even though I know I'll only hurt myself on its edges instead.

I want Sara not to be *fucking dead*.

I push my palms over my eyes until I see explosions of red and tears paint my temples. I have to get myself under control before Kelsey or Natalie wakes up.

Okay.

The necklace is on my pillow.

The necklace is on my pillow.

My skin is cold.

Breathe.

I reach out and lift the charm, letting the chain slide between the cracks of my fingers. Silver glints dully in the dark, but the metal is pristine. Perfect. Unmarked.

My brows wrinkle. This...

This isn't the same necklace. It can't be. It's too clean. My knees go weak beneath me, and I dip toward the ground before catching myself.

There's no way this necklace has been buried in the dirt for an entire year. There's next to no tarnish to the silver, no dirt in the delicate etchings across the surface in the heart or caked into the links. I run my fingers along the chain. There aren't even any kinks.

How?

I lick my lip and try not to let nausea make me sick again.

Someone is messing with me.

I turn slowly. The shadows pressed up against the walls on either side of Kelsey and Natalie are almost thick enough to swallow the sleeping pair, but not quite. Suspicion crackles hot and angry in my chest.

Liars. *Liars*. All of us.

I take a step forward, but what am I going to do? Shake Kelsey awake and demand she tell me what the hell is going on? Why in the world she's torturing me like this? How she knew exactly what would cut me the deepest?

For fuck's sake, they had to have gone out and bought the necklace before coming to Highmark. Sick. This is sick.

But what if it wasn't them? What if it was someone else?

A visual of red spray-paint splashes across my mind.

MURDERER.

How long did I take to walk back here? Could Alex have run ahead? He wouldn't. Would he? No, no, he wouldn't. But

Natalie? For her channel? Almost certainly. God, what if she brings too much attention to the case and the cops reopen it? Is that a thing? I'm going to pass out.

I squeeze the necklace tight in my fist. Whoever left this meant to scare me, confuse me, tell me they're watching.

~~Like I watched them that night, a year ago?~~

I turn slowly, unsteady on my feet, and scan the windowsills, the corners, the dresser for any light that would give away a hidden camera. There's nothing. Where could Natalie have hidden a camera with a clear shot of the bed?

Ha! The space behind the bedside lamp. I tiptoe over and peek behind the ceramic base, but again, I find nothing.

Damn it. Am I being ridiculous?

No. This is bad. Really bad.

Frustrated, I haul myself into bed but don't lie down. My head buzzes and the thumping against my chest won't calm. My eyes keep darting to the door in front of me. To the windows to my left. To Kelsey and Natalie sleeping to my right.

I'm surrounded, and unless I start getting some answers, ~~we're all~~ I'm in dangerous waters.

23

THEN

SEVEN YEARS AGO.

"This is Sara," Mom said, pushing me toward a girl with long blond hair. Not blond the way mine was, which was still dark at the start of summer, but like there was red in hers that made it shiny instead of dull. I reached for a strand of my own hair, hanging limp from the car ride.

Why was Mom making me talk to some random girl? I wanted to complain, but also…no. What if I made Mom mad like Dad did? What if she left again? I tried not to shiver at the memory. She had come back after one night, and they'd gone to therapy, which I wasn't supposed to know about either, but I did. Had it really worked? How soon was too soon to know for sure? I swallowed the lump rising in my throat and focused on Sara instead of Mom. That was safer.

"Hi," I said. She didn't say anything, so maybe I'd been too quiet. "I'm Mandy."

Her eyes moved over me and eventually she smiled. I

liked her smile. It made the freckles over her nose and cheeks squish together. "Cool shirt. Did you make it? I'm so bad at tie-dyeing."

I fiddled with the hem of the tank top. It was one of my favorites. I was glad I'd picked it for today.

"Yeah, I made it last summer."

Sara nodded like she was impressed.

"My mom said we could do the scavenger hunt together. She said you're the same age as me. Do you want to be my partner?"

I looked to Mom. "Scavenger hunt?"

"It's new this year, honey. They're adding it to the Summer Bash. We have a list in our cottage."

Oh. "Oh." A tiny flutter beat inside my chest. New girl. New girl with eyes that crinkled when she smiled and who didn't seem nervous at all when she asked if I wanted to be her partner for the scavenger hunt. Weird. Cool. "Yeah, I want to."

"Yay! I have to go unpack my stuff first or my brother will steal all the space, but do you want to come with me? We can go down to the lake after?"

I blinked. Did I want to go sit in her family's cottage while she unpacked?

Yes. Yes I did.

"Okay."

"Have fun, girls," Mom said, and left Sara and me standing in front of the lodge.

Sara flipped her hair over her shoulder and tipped her

head to the side. I fought the urge to squirm. What was I supposed to say now? Was I supposed to say anything at all? Probably?

Sara stepped over the slate and took my hand, giving it a shake that jiggled all the way up my arm to my shoulder.

"Your face looks scared. What are you scared of? Come on, let's go," she said, laughing.

She pulled me along with her, beneath the shade of trees and between the fresh cut grass.

"Do you have any siblings?" she asked.

I nodded, but she wasn't looking at me. "A little sister."

"Is she here?"

"I think she's in our cottage with my dad."

"Do you like her?"

I laughed. The question was so unexpected.

"What?" Sara asked.

"People don't usually ask if I like my little sister."

"Well, I'm curious. I have a brother, Finn, that's his name, and I love him, but he's also the worst. So we don't really hang out. But maybe you like your sister."

Kelsey and I fought sometimes. I once put a worm down her shirt and she once cut off half my hair while I was sleeping. But I loved her. I was even pretty sure I liked her, just not all the time.

Something about Sara made me lie. "Nah, my sister's the worst too. Super annoying. I try to ditch her whenever I can."

Sara beamed, and a warm, soft feeling spread across my

skin. I ignored the pang of guilt in my stomach. Kelsey didn't need to know what I'd said.

"Good. So it can be just you and me this week."

A whole week with this girl who wanted to spend her vacation with me. Only me. I'd never met someone who made me instantly feel like I belonged in their circle. If she wanted to hang out with me, I wouldn't do anything to change her mind. Excitement thrummed up my arms, especially where her hand still clutched mine, swinging back and forth as she walked.

She glanced my way, and in that half turn I swore she was the prettiest girl I'd ever seen. I was so jealous of her perfect hair, her perfect grin.

"By the way, I *love* your necklace," she said.

I'd forgotten I was wearing the small silver heart charm around my neck.

"Do you want it?" I blurted out.

"Oh my God, *yes*! Really? That's so nice." She dropped my hand and stopped.

Had I really thought she would say yes? No, because I hadn't thought at all. But she liked something of *mine*. She wanted something of *mine*. And I wanted to be her friend, so I undid the clasp and let the heart and chain pool in my hand.

Sara plucked the necklace from my palm and fastened it around her own neck, nudging the charm with her finger to center it on her chest.

"How does it look?" She beamed.

It made me happy, how excited she was.

"Looks good," I said, and it did.

My own chest felt bare, but that was okay, because Sara smiled and pulled me alongside her, talking about all the things we'd do this summer.

Just me and her.

24

NOW

MONDAY MORNING. ONE YEAR AFTER.

I frown so hard that the hangover headache behind my eyes throbs. Fresh mountain air and woodsy pine swirls around me, and the forest sings with birds calling and squirrels racing through the trees. I hate all of it. These freakin' woods and this horrible resort and that goddamn empty hole in the ground where Sara's necklace was *supposed* to be safely buried.

I don't know what I'd expected to find, coming out here. Footprints? Well, sure, but that wasn't helpful. A scrap of fabric? What was this, a cop drama? Nope, if there was anything useful to find, I wasn't finding it.

The ground is… Well, it's messy. Disturbed. Because I disturbed it two nights ago and went running off when Leigh and her friend showed up to get high. So, yeah, someone's been digging, but that someone was me, and was probably *only* me.

I force my fingers to unclench from around the silver imposter necklace crushed against my palm and stare at the sinister little piece of jewelry. It sure *looked* like Sara's necklace, *my* necklace, before I gave it away, but it couldn't be It had to be a fake.

I swallow. There's nothing here, and I shouldn't be here either. There's a sinking feeling in my gut that I don't want to acknowledge, but—but—but—

It has to have been Kelsey and Natalie, right?

I sigh and stand. This was a dead end, so what do I do next? I can't confront Kelsey and Natalie straight out. I have a sneaking suspicion it's what they *want* me to do. Leave the necklace, make me mad, lure me right back into their obsession with dragging Sara's story back into the spotlight. No thanks, I'll pass.

I snatch my thermos up from the leaf-covered ground and shove off the branch. My stomach is still upset from last night, but the coffee provides enough of a kick that I'm able to function. I definitely need to eat some actual food before the hike at noon. My stomach makes a gurgling sound. Maybe sooner rather than later.

The ground is soft and slick with leaves as I make my way down the slope toward the lakeside path. The water is visible only in shining bursts between the row of trees that rings the lake. I pause to watch the sun flash off the glassy surface.

I want to leave Highmark, I want to leave *so badly*, but I can't. One, Mom and Dad—mostly Mom—will be so worried about me that they'll make me come home from college for sure. My teeth grind together and my skull pounds. Two...what if the person who sprayed the accusation on the walkway is the same person who—

Nope. Nope, nope, nope. Can't think about that. I grip the thermos tight between both hands to keep them from shaking, and press my eyes shut tight. Orchids, oleanders, poppies, daisies.

I'm fine. I'm fine, I just have to slow down this runaway train before it runs us all over. I take a step, and my stomach swoops. Oh, shit. Heat crawls up my neck. The shakiness in my hands isn't from stress or exhaustion or dehydration, or...not *just* those things... It's because I'm about to pass out.

Slowly, I sit down on the side of the path, setting my thermos beside me and drawing my knees up. Calm down. I don't have anything to eat with me, but sometimes it passes if I can just *calm down*. I take slow, steadying breaths and rest my forehead on the back of my folded arms. My skin isn't clammy yet, which is a good sign.

While I try to slow my heartbeat and keep the panic down, the crunch of footsteps and a soft whistling comes from the path in the direction of the bridge.

"Hello?" A rough but kind voice asks. "Are you all right?"

I lift my head enough to prop my chin on my arms and peek at the owner of that voice.

A woman in her seventies hikes down the path toward me. Her short gray hair is the color of an overcast winter sky, and the lines in her olive skin are deep around the eyes. She stops a few feet from me, her hiking boots caked with dirt. She looks…familiar.

"Are you okay?" she asks again.

It's a smoker's voice: all gravel and grit. I reassess how old she might be. Maybe midsixties. I've definitely seen her around, but it's more than that. My pulse jumps as I try to sort through my sluggish thoughts. I flick my tongue across overdry lips before responding. "I'm a little dizzy."

I don't elaborate because it seems like too much effort.

"Are you diabetic?"

I shake my head no. I'm not. I was tested as a kid. But I also pass out occasionally. *More* than occasionally, this past year. Stress, blood pressure, blood sugar—something inside me is routinely displeased with the way I'm running the operation.

My cheeks flame. "Do you happen to have anything to eat? I…" I hate to ask, but I'm not sure I'll make it back to the cottage otherwise.

"You know, I do have a packet of trail mix in my pouch."

And by pouch, she means the bright pink fanny pack situated on her hip. She unzips the bag and hands down a tube full of nuts and chocolate.

I accept with shaky fingers and it takes me two, three, goddamnit four, tries to get the package open. My mouth is almost too dry to swallow, and I wash down every weakly chewed-up bite with the remaining sips of lukewarm coffee.

I feel like lukewarm garbage.

"I'd join you down there, but these knees would fight me

on the way up," the woman says. She grunts to herself and sits in the dirt next to me anyway. "You'll help me up, won't you? Course you will." She studies me, eyes flicking from my face to the trail mix clutched in my hands and back. "You're white as a ghost."

I wheeze, hoping she knows I intend it to be a laugh. I've eaten half the packet, and the dizzy feeling has subsided as swiftly as it came, but I eat one more mouthful before offering the rest back to my gallant gray-haired rescuer. "Thanks," I say.

I really should've eaten breakfast before heading off into the woods. I knew I should've when I left, but I didn't. Why?

It's not important.

I don't think about it.

She waves away the nut mix. "You keep it. I wasn't planning on a long walk anyway. And I'd feel better if I knew you had the rest. Just to be safe."

In the wake of the near-fainting attack, my shoulders slump, and there's a quiet but persistent urge to scream building at the back of my throat. My head hums. I nod and twist the top of the plastic wrapper between my fingers.

I'm too uncomfortable to look at the woman beside me, but I can feel her staring at me. Why do I remember her? Just another guest, or am I forgetting having met her before?

"That's Sara's necklace, right?" she asks, and I stop breathing.

The necklace in question dangles, half-forgotten, from my fingers. The heart rests against my shin.

"Wh—what?"

Her eyes are intense, and finally, I notice the small dark binoculars hanging low against her stomach.

It's *her*. The woman who saw me coming out of the storage shed, the fireworks bulging out of my bag. And now she's seen me with a dead girl's necklace. I'm dizzy again. The edges of my vision of fuzzy. I'm going to pass out—

Gasp.

Oh. I wasn't breathing. Okay now I have to say something. Or run. I could run. No, I quite literally cannot run at the moment.

"I said, that's Sara's necklace, isn't it?"

I shake my head. "No. It's…" How am I supposed to explain this? "It's a look-alike."

"Ah," she says softly.

"How did you know Sara had a necklace like this?"

"I've been cottage-neighbors with the Ellises for nearly a decade." Her tone dips so markedly into gentle, like you'd soothe a wounded animal. "And she had that thing in her mouth more often than not."

I don't know what to say to that. I'm too busy fighting tears and a panic attack. Does she remember me from the shed? Does she believe me about the necklace? Am I totally screwed? Every nerve wails, and I'm so close to shattering.

Oh my God, did *she* write MURDERER on my walkway?

I swallow a laugh, and it hurts all the way down. No. This old lady wasn't running around in the dark with a can of spray paint.

Probably.

"You miss her, don't you?"

There's no judgment in her voice, just pity, and I burst into tears. I don't deserve pity. I don't deserve to be sitting here trying to cover my tracks and avoid blame. I swipe at my face, trying to eliminate signs of the outburst even though she's clearly seen, but the tears *will—not—stop—coming*.

"Shit," I whisper angrily, and then bite my tongue because oh no I shouldn't be cursing in front of nice older ladies who may or may not have seen me stealing future murder weapons from the resort.

"You know what? It is shit."

I nearly choke on a laugh, though the tears only come faster.

She continues. "It's absolute shit, and that's okay. There's nothing wrong with missing people when they're gone. It's normal to be sad."

My shoulders tense and my jaw locks. *She means well*, my brain hisses. She means to help, but…

IT'S NOT OKAY IT'S NOT OKAY IT'S NOT OKAY. Furious alarm bells blare through my head. Nothing about what happened to Sara is ever going to be "okay," and why is she being so nice? Is she trying to trick me? I'm so confused.

With effort, I unclench my jaw and mutter, "I guess."

She blows a small puff of air through her nose. "You don't believe me, I know. I don't mind. The morning is beautiful and I saw a woodpecker on the way over here." She taps the binoculars hanging around her neck. Ah. She's a bird-watcher. But what else has she seen in her years at Highmark? I fight the urge to squirm.

She continues. "And most importantly I had a snack to share. I'd say the morning is shaping up pretty nicely. Who's to say a quick cry here and there can't be part of a good morning? Someday thinking about her won't make you so sad. Trust me." She grins. "And help me up."

She's wrong. Thinking about Sara and what I did will always be a rotten, miserable nightmare. There's no escape. But—I wipe the last of the tear tracks from my face—if I can figure out who's leaving grim notes in spray paint outside my cottage and stop Kelsey and Natalie from making everything a million times worse, I might actually make it through the rest of this trip with my sanity.

I heave myself to my feet and extend a hand to my lake trail companion.

"I'm Virginia," she says, gripping my hand in hers. "And it was nice to officially meet you, Mandy. I hope the rest of your day is filled with fewer tears and more smiles."

I give her one of the desired smiles and hope it doesn't look as fake as it feels.

25

NOW

MONDAY MORNING. ONE YEAR AFTER.

The family hike is at eleven, which gives me twenty minutes to curl up on a bench seat by one of the windows in the lobby of the main lodge. Time to stalk Kelsey and Natalie's social media accounts. I start with Instagram. As I open the app, I absent-mindedly munch on a mini blueberry muffin from the tray next to the coffee station. Moist and sugary and probably not what I should be eating, but it's delicious and easy.

No notifications on my own account, but there's a message waiting in my inbox. It's from Em, but I'll have to read my roommate's message later, because I need to see what I can find on Kelsey and Natalie's pages before the hike.

I scroll through Kelsey's posts first, but there's nothing to give any clue into her interest in Sara or her work with Natalie. All I get is an overwhelming sense of how absent I've been from her life this past year. Natalie is in so many of these pictures, and before Saturday I didn't even know Natalie existed. She's posing with girls from the soccer team. There's an artsy close-up of the betta fish, which is currently swishing its long frilly tail around the bowl in our cottage. A long gap with no posts from July through September of last year.

I exhale through my nose. I don't have time to feel guilty right now. I need to figure out how much damage they've already done, and where they might be headed with Sara's story.

I scroll back up to a photo of Kelsey and Natalie posing together in front of a colorfully painted brick wall. They each have an arm around the other's waists and wear big smiles on their faces. Their free hands hold ice cream cones topped with rainbow sprinkles. **This chick is coming on vacation with me next month—had to celebrate!**

Natalie is tagged.

I click. The screen freezes for a moment, slow to toggle between pages with the weak internet, and I grind my teeth together. I don't have long before I have to head back to the cottage for the hike. *Hurry up hurry up hurry up.*

Natalie's profile loads. I hunch over the perfectly trendy aesthetic.

Shades of red and gray everywhere. Crisp shots of Natalie speaking into a mic. Creative "on location" style images. The whole account is geared toward her true-crime brand.

But it's the small rectangle near the top that pulls my brows together and sets the base of my skull tingling. **Follow Back.** Which means Natalie already follows me. My account is set to private, but I hadn't changed it until a few weeks after

Sara died, when the idea of anyone keeping tabs on me made my skin crawl. She could have followed me before I switched the setting. Who else might've followed me, before I thought to protect myself?

~~Could she…~~

Snapdragaon, sunflower, sage, salvia, sea holly. I crush that fear before it can bloom.

I haven't posted anything about Sara since she died, but the idea of Natalie poking around for clues about who Sara was and what we meant to each other before…before… makes me uneasy. I scrape my nail over the skin around my thumb. What had I shared in the past? I never went back through old posts about us. I hadn't wanted to see.

And I still don't.

Still can't.

I remain on Natalie's page and click an image of her face, taken from a slightly downward angle that keeps the Highmark lake and mountains framed in the background. She must have taken this yesterday at the dock. A tingle runs from my shoulders down my arms.

I tap to read more of what she's written. I can't resist, even though a rush of dizziness swamps me as I do.

First full video in the Sara Ellis series goes live TONIGHT! In the meantime, head on over to my YouTube channel CrimeChatWithNat and be sure to subscribe! Link is in my bio!

Tonight? Tonight?! That's not good. What's she going to do for the first video? Does she have enough to be a problem?

I scan the comments—holy shit, so many comments—below the posts. Sara's name jumps off the screen. And someone has named Highmark. The wave of interest already forming is horrifying. My eyes flit through the remaining comments, and—

I'll be watching.

Technically, it's an innocuous statement, but something about it is weird. Almost threatening. I click the username, "Sara_0078," and find an account set to private with zero followers and only fourteen people they're following.

Who the hell is "Sara_0078?" Could it be the person who wrote "MURDERER" on the walkway?

I am *so* not loving all these cryptic messages.

I bookmark the post so I can come back to that comment later, and I tap the link to Natalie's YouTube channel. I wait. The load bar grinds to a halt with an infuriating fraction remaining, and then the white space fills with video thumbnails. At the top of the screen, a black-and-white logo reads "CrimeChatWithNat" and is artfully splattered with blood. Maybe it's a little over the top, but her passion is obvious.

No matter how impressed I am, that doesn't change the fact that Natalie intends to make Sara, by way of insider details from *me*, the topic of her next series. And she plans to launch this terrible idea *tonight*. I chew my lip. How do I stop this? I could steal her phone. Her laptop. *I could steal her laptop*. That's a great idea. Except she'll know it was me, and then Mom and Dad will think I've totally snapped, stealing from a girl they welcomed on vacation with us, and that'll be another check mark on their list of reasons to pull me out of school.

I put the "steal the laptop" idea on the back burner. She probably already has the video edited and uploaded and ready to go if she's making it live tonight. Shit.

It's almost eleven, but I have to see her YouTube channel. One quick peek.

The banner and font match her Instagram, and her face with titles referencing cases I don't recognize fill the page. Each little square has a photo paired with it. A victim photo. Probably. There's a featured video at the top of the page. **MY story, YOUR story.**

Definitely watching *that*.

Too late I realize I haven't brought my headphones with me, and an overly perky ad for some pyramid scheme yells at me, and at the other Highmark guests. I smash the volume button until the audio is barely above a whisper and raise the phone too close to my face.

Natalie's eyes stare straight into mine, and I shift in my seat. *"Hi friends, Natalie here. This is CrimeChatWithNat, where I share new true-crime stories every week. So don't forget to like and subscribe! When I was little, Jessica, my babysitter, was like a big sister to me. She took me to the park, made us grilled cheese with extra cheese for dinners, and one night, she never showed up."*

I lean closer to the phone without thinking. She doesn't mean...

"I waited with my nose pressed to the window while my mom called Jessica. But I never saw her again. She'd been murdered. My parents didn't tell me what had happened, because I was eight, but they told me she was dead. I cried for hours. I was so confused. How could she be dead?" Her eyes are shiny, and she flicks a finger beneath her lower lids.

Okay, maybe I feel a teensy bit bad for Natalie. Doesn't mean I can let her drag me back into the middle of Sara's murder. It won't end well. Not for any of us.

"Later they told me the truth, and I had to learn more. I won't tell you the details. Her family said they don't want me to talk about it. But her murder was *solved with tips that came in after her story went viral. So now I talk about old crime stories, and newer mysteries and crimes by special request."* She emphasizes *special request. "If you have a family member who's missing or murdered, and you want me to talk about them on this channel, you can DM me. Or email me at the address in the description. Thank you all for being here for CrimeChatWithNat."*

I frown. Natalie only does current stories by request. Which means Kelsey had to have brought Sara's murder to her, right? Kelsey wasn't Sara's family, but I guess for a friend, Natalie made an exception.

She shouldn't have.

26

NOW

MONDAY AFTERNOON. ONE YEAR AFTER.

The flat expanse of rock that makes up the overlook rolls out from the pines and drops off sharply, tumbling down the mountainside in a cascade of green and brown. Mom and I sit side by side a respectful distance from the edge, watching plush clouds drift across the sky. The smell of pine and warm stone and dirt is thick up here, and the breeze keeps the blended aroma swirling around us in constant motion.

If I didn't know Kelsey and Natalie were lurking nearby, scheming, I might be able to relax.

I slide my hand between my hair and the back of my neck and lift, letting the sweat dewing on my skin cool. The hike up was a lot harder than I remember, and I hadn't been a fan of hiking to start with, much less hungover hiking.

Uh-oh. Mom's asking me a question, and I haven't heard a word.

"What was that?" I ask, shaking my head. "Sorry, I zoned out."

Mom sighs, but not entirely unhappily. "It's easy to get distracted up here."

"Yeah. Almost makes the hike worthwhile."

Mom shakes her head and smiles. "Thank you for coming. I know you didn't want to."

I stiffen. Is she implying I didn't want to spend time with the family, or is she acknowledging my dislike of hiking? I lick my lips. I choose to believe she's not trying to guilt me over having avoided them all for months.

"I'm glad you made me come. It's beautiful. And I'm even more glad the second half is downhill."

"You and me both." She rolls her right ankle from side to side. She has her brace on—support for an old injury— but I'm sure that the constant uneven footing of a rocky, root-threaded trail hasn't been comfortable. "You're having a good time, though, honey? In general?"

The worry in her voice hurts as much as it frustrates. She seems to genuinely want me to be happy, but why in the world would I be "having a good time" at the place where Sara died? How can she not understand?

I suppress a sigh and say, "Sure. I can't believe I didn't make it home before this, but yeah, I'm having a good time."

"Good. Good. And your speech? For Sara's memorial? Charlotte asked how it was coming, but I want you to know if you need help with what you want to say, I'm here. I know all this has to be hard for you. I'm really, really proud of you for making the effort."

There's a lightheadedness coming over me, and my throat chokes up at the mention of having to discuss Sara and her memorial with Mom. I can't. I won't. But I also can't completely ignore her offer. She'll worry, and I don't want her to worry.

"I'm good. I'm almost done." Lie. Big huge lie.

I haven't written a single word. No notes. No ideas. Between the spray-painted message and Natalie's crime channel and a messy night with Alex, suffering through speechwriting hasn't been high on my to-do list. I'll be putting that nightmare off as long as possible. The prospect of having to stand in a sea of respectful mourners as friends and family of Sara's give heartfelt speeches about who she was and what she meant to them is stomach-turning.

God. Natalie will eat the memorial up. I hope she doesn't film it. She's definitely going to film it. Is that even allowed?

"Good, honey. That's good. It's going to mean a lot to Charlotte and James. And Finn." She adds Sara's brother as an afterthought, and I tense.

"Did they say when Finn is getting here?" Do I sound casual? Doesn't matter.

She pauses and her lips purse. "Actually, I think Charlotte convinced Finn to get in later today. To give them a day together before Wednesday's memorial."

Finn could be at Highmark *tonight*, and now thanks to Alex, he knows I alone was the last person to see Sara alive.

"I have to pee," I say, and Mom raises her brows at my abrupt announcement. I have to move. Seeing Finn again will be miserable, especially if Kelsey and Natalie harass him too. Natalie's video implies she takes the wishes of victim family members into consideration, but she's clearly ignored that standard for Sara. I can't trust her not to poke Finn.

Just like Sara used to.

What if Finn tells Natalie what Alex told him, about our alibi?

Sweat coats the nape of my neck, and my hair clings, hot and itchy.

I push to my feet. The rocky surface is lumpy through the bottom of my sneakers, and I have to watch my step as I beeline for a large boulder surrounded by a less dense area of trees where I can slip away and hide. For a minute. That's all I need. Maybe I'll actually pee.

In the cool green shade of intertwined branches and fanned leaves, I lean against the roughness of the boulder. The back of my arms rest on a scruffy patch of yellow-brown lichen. I could stay here. Just me and the rock and the lichen. No family, no memorial service, no true-crime content. Just forest and vibes.

This is an unreasonable plan, but I indulge for a few minutes, hoping the silly fantasy will calm me down. It's not as effective as I'd hoped. My skin is still too warm, and I'm too keyed up to sort my breathing out. Also, I do have to pee.

I shimmy my shorts down and squat, annoyed at the fact I didn't slip a few sheets of toilet paper into the pocket of my shorts before leaving the cottage.

A twig snaps.

And then another, as someone enters the edge of the brush on the other side of the boulder.

I make a sound between a gasp and a screech and lurch to my feet, yanking my shorts up. One of my feet slips on a damp patch of decayed leaves. I pitch forward with one hand still on my shorts and the other flung out in a desperate attempt to prevent my face from being ripped apart by a thicket of scraggly foliage.

A sharp sting tears into my knees as they collide with the dirt, and I catch myself with the heel of one hand. I'm spewing a string of curses as I scramble to right my shorts when Natalie says, "Oh."

That's it. I'm going to run into the woods and never return. At least the bobcats and the deer won't play mind games with me. They might maul me, but that's not sounding so bad right now.

"What do you want?" I grumble, making more eye contact than strictly necessary. I have to compensate somehow for the fact I definitely didn't get my shorts pulled all the way on before she rounded the corner.

Natalie holds up her hands, and in the left, is her phone.

I see red—or is that gray—I don't know but that's how the saying goes and god*damn* I'm pissed. "Were you filming?"

Her eyebrows fly up and her mouth pops open. "No! Well, I was before, but I wasn't filming right then. When you were. When. Um." She huffs. "When you fell over with your pants down. My channel does true crime. I'm not interested in where you pee. Or…" She gestures at me. "Whatever you were doing."

I huff right back at her. "Yeah. You and your channel." I chew my lip. "Natalie, what can I do to get you not to publish the first video about Sara tonight?"

She smiles. "You saw my post?"

I nod. "I saw, and I need you not to post it. Please. How can you do this right now? You saw what someone wrote on our walkway. You *posted* about it." Then again, maybe you wrote it too. "This will make things so much worse."

"Sorry, but it has to happen."

My hands ache with how hard I'm clenching them. "Can you at least wait? Until after the memorial? Be respectful of her family."

Her eyes flick away from my face for a second, but I can't quite read her expression. There one second and gone the next. Not guilt, but…she's hiding something. She meets my gaze again, and the look is gone.

"I'm not waiting. Sorry." She doesn't sound like she means it. "I don't have as much material as I hoped, but it'll be a hit anyway. If you would've let me interview you…oh well. There's still time for a future video." She perks up and my shoulders tighten. "You and Kelsey together would make a *great* interview."

My mouth curls downward. I have to fight not to yell at her. "Are you and Kelsey even really friends, or are you using her? Is she just content to you, like me?"

She lifts her chin, a flinty hardness spilling into her eyes.

She takes a step forward, and I take a step back, nearly losing my footing for a second time when a sturdy vine snags across my ankle. My heart beats too fast, and I'm sweating, but I don't regret asking.

Sometimes people use people.

Sometimes friends aren't really your friends.

"Kelsey is my friend. I don't have to explain myself to *you*." She flings the words at me. "Your sister wanted me to do Sara's story, and she wanted me to talk to you. She doesn't believe it was an accident either." She wiggles her phone back and forth. "So, will you do an interview or not?"

My breaths come in short, shallow bursts, and I pluck at my T-shirt, fanning myself with the fabric. I'm not giving her any new information to pick apart. "No, I won't, and you better be careful," I snap.

Natalie makes a small sound and calls, "What does that mean?" as I pick my way out of the woods.

On the rocky flats, Kelsey and Dad are with Mom, looking at something overhead. A hawk rides the wind, dipping and swaying, and I'm hit with a touch of dizziness as I follow its path through the sky.

I give myself a little shake and wander to the edge of the overlook several feet away from my family. I don't want to be around them right now. I cross my arms. I didn't get a chance to pee, I'm hungry, and I should probably sit down, but my knees are locked and my spine is tight, and I can't seem to make myself do anything other than gaze down at the lake. Across the water, Highmark looms up out of the trees. There's the stretch of cottages lining the river. There's the swimming area and the Snack Shack. Is Alex perched in the speck that is the lifeguard stand? Has he been able to reach Finn?

The sun shimmers in waves over the surface. Mesmerizing. Swirling. Shifting.

Distantly, as if underwater myself, I hear footsteps and a voice. Mom, maybe. Nausea curls in my stomach and too late I realize that it wasn't annoyance making me so hot or toying with my vision, it was the slow creep of another crash. My head slides sideways. No, my vision slides sideways as great chunks are gobbled up by gray.

The ground goes out from under me.

27

THEN

What a disaster.

I gripped the racket in my hand so tight my skin tingled. I should have bailed; after last night, I was in no mood to play tennis with Sara. I was in no mood to *see* Sara.

I served the ball, imagining that green fuzz smacking her right in the face.

Sara flew across the court, shoes squealing and ponytail flying behind her. Her racket thwacked hard against the ball, sending a volley low over the net.

Pivot.

Sprint.

My arm reached, reached, reached, and triumph burst through my chest as the taut strings connected with the tennis ball for the return.

Back onto my toes.

Thwack.

Cut.

Sprint.

This one was easier, not as far to the opposite corner, and with a smooth, strong follow-through, I sent a volley whizzing past Sara to the very edge of the court.

"Game," I called, breathing heavily. My arms ached, and the socks I'd brought were all wrong for tennis. A sting at my heel said I'd have a nice blister by this afternoon. When I could catch another full breath, I said, "That's five-four."

Sara scowled and tapped her racket against the side of her leg. Once, twice, *thwack, thwack*. She wiped her arm across her forehead, where a thick layer of sweat glistened. The rings beneath her eyes were faint shadows from across the court.

She tried to smile, but it looked more like a grimace, and went to retrieve the balls on her side of the net.

I jogged to fetch mine, tucking them into the pocket of my shorts.

It was Sara's game to serve. She toed the white line, paused, and swept some of the clay dust away with the sole of her shoe. The ball twisted back and forth in her hand, the racket held down at her side.

Energy hummed along the muscles in my legs and forearms. Don't grip the racket too hard. Your palms are sweating. Ease up, it's just a game.

A game you don't want to play.

But I wanted to win.

I wanted to win at *something* with Sara.

Sara hit the first serve into the net.

"Fault," I called out of habit.

She shot me a venomous look and pulled the second ball from her spandex shorts. Seemed I wasn't the only person pissed off this morning. Her chest rose and fell, fast and deep. Ball up, the racket arced, *thwack*.

Sara grunted and I pushed off the balls of my feet, lurching forward. The ball made a soft thump as it bounced off the white vinyl headband of the net and dropped to her side of the court.

"Double fault," I muttered, straightening and relaxing my grip on the racket. A smile crept across my face. Easy point.

Sara yowled, an honest-to-God *yowl*, and threw her racket, sending it skittering across the scuffed clay.

I froze, afraid to draw her attention and wanting to rub it in at the same time. She wanted to play. She asked for this. She knew I was better, so what the hell right did she have to be angry?

I'm not supposed *to be better*.

The realization slammed into me.

It didn't matter that Sara was a swimmer, not a tennis player. She couldn't stand losing to *me*.

She snatched the racket up and turned to retrieve the nearest ball and lined up to serve.

"No," I said, shaking my head.

She hesitated. "What?"

"I don't want to play anymore."

"But we didn't finish."

The anger was hot beneath my skin. "Well I'm finished," I shouted.

"Why?" Her annoyance seeped into that one word. She stared at me, waiting.

I stalked toward the net, and she mirrored me on the opposite side. When we were face-to-face, I said, "Because I'm mad at you. Why did you have to have Alex, if it was only to piss off Finn anyway?"

"I *said* that wasn't why. I don't need Alex to get back at my brother." She leaned forward, getting in my face. Her shoulders shifted over the net, and my—no, her—silver necklace hung between us. My fingers itched to snatch it right off her neck.

Sara's free hand curled over the top of the net and clenched tight.

I was really getting under her skin. Good. It felt good.

"Yeah, right. Because of your big secret about Finn?" I roll my eyes. "You and Finn are always fighting about *something*, and then you move on, until you start up all over again. It's annoying, and I'm tired of being stuck between you two."

Her nose scrunched, smooshing all those freckles together. "You're my friend, not his. You're not supposed to be stuck between us; you're supposed to be on my side."

Guilt stirred, but I shoved it down. "And are you on *my* side?"

"What's that supposed to mean?"

"You got mad when I said I didn't want to blackmail your brother over a stupid car. And you hooked up with Alex after I said I was interested." *You also almost drowned me.*

"That's not the same."

"How?"

"I—it's just not."

I pressed my lips together. How was I supposed to respond to that?

Her throat bobbed. She didn't blink, and her eyes were shiny when she said, "So you're upset and now you're going to side with my brother over me."

You know what, screw it. "You tried to drown me!"

Turned out I hadn't quite let it go, yet.

Sara gasped, jerking away from the net, and from me.

"You really think I tried to *kill* you?" she whispered, her voice breaking.

I tried to hold her gaze, but it was too hard. I looked at my shoes and muttered, "I don't know. No. Maybe."

She fled, and her footsteps filled the sudden silence of the court. I didn't know how to feel about that. Triumphant? Oddly, yes. Guilty? A little.

Mostly, I was just confused.

28

NOW

MONDAY AFTERNOON. ONE YEAR AFTER.

The sky fades into view in blurry patches, partially obscured by a heart-shaped face and dark chestnut hair. Kelsey.

There's something lumpy and firm digging into my back, at the base of my rib cage. A leg. I blink, but Kelsey's face refuses to come properly into focus, and my stomach churns like an angry sea. A sudden flash of heat washes over me, bathing my forehead and armpits with sweat, and I roll off Kelsey's leg in time to weakly spit up bile onto the rock.

"Mandy, are you okay?" Mom's voice comes from above, and is laced with panic. "What in the world were you doing so close to the edge?"

"Are you hurt?" Dad asks, voice tight with worry.

Kelsey scoots away and comes up on her knees, but it's a few additional seconds before she lets go of my hand. Her eyes are wide. "You almost—" The words are barely above a whisper.

"Mom?" I force out, carefully pushing myself into a seated but slumped position. "Do you have anything to eat?"

"Oh, Mandy." The disappointment keeps my eyes trained on the ground. "Yes, hold on."

She slings the small backpack around and hands me a chewy peanut bar. The perfect combo of sugar, protein, and salt. I chew and swallow and chew some more. My mouth is cottony, and each bite works its way painfully down my throat.

Natalie sits down next to Kelsey and bumps her shoulder against my sister's, while Mom says something to Dad that I can't hear over the sound of chewing and the blood rushing in my ears. It feels like I've sprinted a mile when all I did was faint in one spot. An absolute champion.

An absolute failure.

"Are you going to be okay making it down the mountain?" Dad asks. "Do you need me to carry you?"

My heart swells. Dad can't carry me down the mountain. The path is too steep and there are several rock scrambles to navigate. I'm also a fully grown eighteen-year-old and Dad has the fitness of your average middle-aged office worker. It would end terribly for us both.

But he offered.

I twist my lips in the approximation of a smile and shake my head. "I'll be fine. Now that I've eaten. Thank you, Dad." I hope he can hear how cute I think it is that he offered.

Mom hands me an apple. It's that unappetizing shade of dull red where you know there's a ninety-five percent chance the flesh is going to be mealy and devoid of flavor. I'm pretty sure it came from the basket in our cottage that Hannah refills every morning.

I wonder if Hannah spit on it.

"Eat that too," Mom insists.

I don't argue. I do grimace at the first mediocre (and possibly spit-on) bite.

"When was the last time you had a fainting episode?" Mom asks.

I lie. "Before Christmas? But I didn't actually faint; it was fine. I'm being careful, I swear."

She frowns. "Obviously you're not, or you wouldn't have almost fallen off a cliff. You could've been seriously hurt. Or killed. This is a big deal. What if your sister hadn't been coming to get you for a picture? What—"

"Mom, stop," I plead, before catching myself and fixing my tone. "Please. I ate something right before the hike; it's not like I completely forgot. I don't know what happened." I leave out the part where what I ate was a sugar-filled, over-processed muffin, or that the vast majority of the liquids I've consumed recently have been caffeine in various forms.

She's unconvinced. Go figure. "This is serious, Mandy. Don't think I haven't noticed you eating all junk. When was the last time you ate a vegetable? Or drank a full glass of water, for that matter? It's just not smart. You know better."

If I crush my jaw together any tighter, I'm going to chip a tooth. "We're on vacation," I start, but Mom holds up a hand.

"We're on vacation, but that doesn't mean you should be eating like an unsupervised toddler. You say you're responsible, capable of taking care of yourself, but this isn't cutting it."

I can't give a real response without my voice wobbling, so I say, "Okay," and keep saying, "Okay," over and over until Mom reluctantly drops the issue.

But I can feel eyes on me all the way back to the cottage, and every time I glance around, Kelsey turns her head away quickly. I pretend not to notice.

29

NOW

MONDAY NIGHT. ONE YEAR AFTER.

It's quiet out on the porch, by myself in the dark. The water rolling past the raised boards shines black beneath the starry sky. I miss the joy that used to fill me up so easily here, like I was part of something magical and simple. Warm, pine-scented breezes and trilling crickets were a playlist to my favorite time of the year, but now the dark is claustrophobic. Crushing. The skin at the back of my neck prickles as I stare at the woods across the water and try not to picture Sara's body, bloody on the banks.

I press my eyes shut, hard enough to blot out the image. The memory sinks away.

I exhale. It's time. I have to see what fresh horrors Natalie shared on her channel. The video loads, I pop my headphones in, and Natalie's voice drowns out the crickets.

"Hi, friends, and welcome to CrimeChatWithNat, where I share new true-crime stories every week. As promised, our

next story is about Sara Ellis. Now, for those of you who don't know, Sara Ellis was a seventeen-year-old girl who was found dead on June twenty-third at Highmark Inn and Resort."

An image of Highmark's main lodge flashes on screen.

"The cops ruled her death an accident, but...let's get into it!"

I'd rather not.

"At ten fourteen a.m. on June twenty-third, 911 got a call from the resort owner, Eric Miller. Sara's parents had woken up earlier that morning and found Sara wasn't in her room. They tried her phone, but she didn't answer. They thought Sara might have stayed at her friend Mandy's, so they walked over to the Jenkinses' cottage to see if Sara was with her."

I tense, and my breath runs out in a huff.

"But Sara wasn't there. Mandy said she hadn't seen Sara since the night before, and Sara's parents, Charlotte and James, got the Highmark staff and the Jenkinses to start searching the resort for their daughter. Because Mandy told them she'd last seen Sara at the dock the night before, searchers started at the two main docks by the swimming area. But Mandy meant the old dock, which was much farther away. When Mandy told them which dock she really meant, the search moved there, at around ten a.m. In interviews, Mr. Ellis said that he was worried, but that he totally expected to find Sara alive. Instead, they found Sara's body. A staff member, Hannah Kennedy, was sent to wait at the resort entrance and bring police to the scene. When they arrived,

the investigation started. But I'm talking about Sara's story now, because I say the investigation should never have stopped when it did."

I'm cold. Like damp seeping into my bones, wrapping clammy fingers around the deepest parts of me, and choking out all warmth or happiness.

"I'm going to pause here because it gets a little graphic if anyone wants to skip ahead. I'll have this video time-stamped so you can jump past this part."

I hover over the bar and scan forward past Sara's death, and the autopsy. I don't need to relive those. But I do stop at the section labeled, Her story continues.

"And that's the backstory. I hope it's got y'all interested in Sara and who she was. Now, here's where I bring you new information about the case that isn't a case, according to the cops, and remind you that I'll be uploading part two on Friday."

I click the volume up, even though I can hear perfectly fine.

"After talking to a source at the resort, I learned something interesting about Sara and Mandy in the days leading up to Sara's death."

Well that can't be good. Who has Natalie talked to?

"Leigh Miller, the resort owner's daughter, told me that Mandy and Sara had been fighting before the night Sara died. In fact, not only were they fighting, but Leigh said that Mandy had to be dragged out of the lake several days before, and that Sara...might've tried to drown her."

Oh hell. I'd assumed since Leigh usually acted like she was too good to hang out with us, that she wasn't paying any attention to what we did.

"*So what do we think? Was Mandy more involved than she seems? Are there other guests who may have seen something? Help me decide who to talk to next by heading to my Instagram and voting in my story poll. And until our next chat, stay safe out there!*"

Ughhhh.

Reluctantly, I switch to Instagram, but when I search her account, no users show up, and I *know* she didn't deactivate. What the eff?

Natalie blocked me.

I search #CrimeChatWithNat for confirmation, and find the hashtag alive and thriving. *Really* thriving. Jesus. So is #SaraWasMurdered and the equally concerning #HighmarkMurderer. People are clearly excited about Natalie's content.

I breathe deep, sifting through hypotheticals, each one worse than the one before.

This is bullshit.

I switch into my messages and pull up the thread with my roommate, Em.

Hey. Can you look up CrimeChatWithNat on here? It's my sister's friend's account, and she's blocked me. I'm worried she posted something really bad.

Should I elaborate? Warn them? I only told Em the basics of what happened with Sara. They know Sara was my friend, and that she died, and that I'm back at Highmark this summer. The rest we never got into. College was supposed to be a clean break from my past.

I hit send. I need screenshots and I need them fast. Em's always on their phone. Come on, don't fail me now.

I wait and bite my lip, willing them to start typing.

Ah, yes! **One sec**, pops up on the screen, and it feels like forever, but my patience—or total lack thereof—is rewarded with a flood of screenshots, interspersed with, **Holy schnapps** and **what the frack is going on, Mandy?** If ever there were a time for my former roomie to break their commitment to creative alternatives to cursing, this would be it, but they stay constant.

There's a screenshot of a story showing the overlook, with **You better be careful**, typed over the image. It's what I said— part of what I said—to Natalie up on the mountain. Jesus Christ. I'd known better, but I'd been angry and tired and on the verge of passing out. The next screenshot is of a story poll.

Help me decide who to talk to next about Sara Ellis.
"No wrong answer," the poll proclaims.

A. Mandy (the friend)
B. Finn (the brother)
C. The inn's owner (what did he tell the cops?)
D. Hannah (the staff member)

Em has clicked *C* to get the poll to show them the results. I'm neck and neck with Finn, and that is one name on the list that I *cannot* let them interrogate, for so many reasons. But how do I keep Kelsey and Natalie away from Finn, if I'm not willing to give them the story they want instead?

I could offer to talk to Finn. Would that satisfy my sister?

I shake my head, as if there's anyone but me out here to see. Shit. I have to handle this. But I don't *want* to handle this. What I want is to keep my head in the sand and wallow in my own guilt like I've been doing all year. It hurts, but it's easier than confronting what happened that night.

I fire off a quick thank-you to Em, swear up and down I'll fill them in as soon as I can, and slip inside the cottage.

Kelsey and Natalie look up, wide-eyed, as soon as I walk into our room. They're sitting cross-legged on their bed, huddled around phones and Natalie's laptop.

"You saw it?" Kelsey asks.

I nod. Be calm. I have to be calm and make them believe I want to be helpful. If they start asking Finn questions, and he tells them Alex's and my alibi was a lie all along, everything will unravel.

"I did. Thanks for *blocking* me," I say.

"And?" Natalie asks, leaning forward with her elbows propped on her knees.

"I saw your poll."

"And you want to volunteer to talk to me?"

"I want to volunteer, but not for that. I'll talk to Finn for you."

Natalie's eyes narrow, and Kelsey glances at her friend.

"You…want to talk to Finn?" Natalie asks.

"Yes. We used to hang out. I can get him to talk to me."

Kelsey's face pales. What is wrong with her? I open my mouth but can't quite form the right question, and she says, "Mandy—"

But Natalie shushes her, giving her a sharp look.

"You know what, that would actually be super helpful. We were going to talk to Finn tonight, if you wanted to go find him…"

I grit my teeth. Natalie is such a little shit. There's no way they originally planned to talk to Finn tonight, but now that I've volunteered, she's pushing me.

And I can't push back.

"Great. I'll go do that now. *If* I can find him."

She smiles and says, "Great. And get video!"

Kelsey doesn't match Natalie's enthusiasm. In fact, my sister looks sick, but whatever's bothering her, she keeps her secrets to herself.

I guess it runs in the family.

30

THEN

WEDNESDAY AFTERNOON. THE DAY OF.

Mom had caught me sulking, trying to decide between meeting Sara for the kayak race and ditching her, and kicked me out of the sunroom. I stomped over the porch boards and each step trembled beneath my feet.

Was Sara still mad? Well, if she wasn't mad before, she was definitely going to be mad when I showed up barely in time for the kayak race. Oh crap, what if she'd found someone else to partner with? Could she do that, if we'd done the scavenger portion together? I walked a little faster.

I'd been too mean yesterday on the court. Sara might've been pissing me off lately, but it wasn't her fault I liked Alex too. And so what if she fought with Finn? He wasn't *my* brother, and he could handle himself. Let them fight.

In the moment, I'd felt justified in yelling at her, but now...I wasn't so sure. I definitely shouldn't have accused her of really intending to drown me. She would never. We were friends.

A squeal pierced my ears. Ugh. The kids chasing each other around the lawn that separated the lodge from the river were loud, and my guilt was making me cranky, go figure. I should walk faster. The longer Sara waited, the more likely we were to end up fighting again. I watched my step and hustled.

Smack.

A shoulder clipped me, hard, and I staggered around. My arm throbbed and a familiar scent—something citrusy and floral, like perfume—floated around me. "Hey, what the—"

Finn's broad shoulders and sandy-blond hair were already several steps away, and he extended a hand dismissively. Like *I* was the nuisance. Like *I* rammed into him. The gravel crunched loudly beneath his heavy footsteps.

What was his problem?

In the direction Finn came from, Hannah, Alex, and another staff member nodded along to whatever Mrs. Miller was saying. Hannah glanced over and her brow furrowed.

I filed it away to ask Sara later. Maybe. If she forgave me for the tennis match. For now, Finn's mood couldn't be my problem.

31

NOW

The Ellises have always stayed several cottages down the riverbank from us, closer to the docks and the lake than to the trail entry, but suddenly I wish they were farther. The walk is too brief.

Their cottage is two stories instead of the standard one-story, complete with the best view of the lake on the whole resort. Mr. and Mrs. Ellis take the first-floor master bedroom with the walkout porch, and Finn and Sara share the second floor.

Shared. They *shared* the second floor. Past tense.

My face crumples, and I press a hand over my mouth. Above, yellow light shines out of the second-story windows. The first floor is dark. Mrs. and Mr. Ellis are probably in the lounge with my parents, like every other night. Good. I'd hate for them to hear us.

Although eating glass sounds about as appealing as

talking to Finn, I have to bring something back to Kelsey and Natalie. I can't have them interrogating Finn themselves. Who knows what he'll say to them? Who knows what he'll say to *me*?

"Finn, can we talk?"

He'll scowl. Maybe he'll even say "no."

"Please, I have to tell you something and I feel terrible—"

"You should. You left her. You left her and you lied."

I'll blink back tears, unable to stop the furious blush rampaging across my cheeks.

Maybe he even asks what else I'm lying about, and it all comes spilling out and—

I shake the train of thought loose. Obsessing over it is only going to make the moment itself worse. I can do this. Move, feet. *Move.* I grip the wooden railing, and the first stair groans under my weight. I freeze, breath catching. Just keep going.

Footsteps come from above. I gasp. The door opens, squeaky on its hinges, and I hurl myself off the stairs and down the incline sloping toward the riverbank. The darkness beneath the stairs hides me, I hope, as leather flip-flops and ankles appear through the slats.

Hands in the dirt, and once again I'm frozen, watching through this narrow field of vision, waiting for danger to pass. Like a coward. I bite down hard on my tongue.

Finn's voice, low and harsh, rumbles through the quiet.

"I know about the walkway." He doesn't sound happy. "That doesn't mean she did it. But, well, Alex said something. Maybe…"

His tall, muscular frame is only visible in little pieces as he steps onto the walkway and strides away from the cottage.

"Fine. I'm on my way, but just to talk."

Is he...is he talking to...?

No.

He wouldn't be.

Would he?

32

THEN

WEDNESDAY AFTERNOON. THE DAY OF.

"You're paddling too hard on the right," Sara said from the front of the kayak. Her arms rose and fell with each stroke of the paddle, and the days in the sun had brought out a thicker layer of freckles dusting across her shoulders and down her arm.

"No. I'm not." I watched the spot right in the center of her back, where her ponytail swished back and forth.

"Well, we're pulling to the left and *I'm* not paddling harder on one side than the other."

Yeah. Sara was definitely still mad at me, but with each passing minute, my guilt was slowly fading into the background to make way for annoyance. Why was *I* always the problem?

I eased up on the right, even though I hadn't been the one messing us up in the first place.

The nose of the kayak straightened, putting us back on

track to glide along the far side of the river, opposite the lodge and closer to the woods. All we had to do was get to the archway set up on the distant golf green, grab our flag, and kayak back to the launch behind the Snack Shack first, and we'd win the year's scavenger hunt.

There was only one boat ahead of us, and we were getting closer.

"I'm sorry," Sara said, so suddenly I thought I had obviously misheard her.

"What?" I stopped paddling for a second and we slowed.

She twisted in her seat. "Hey, don't stop!"

"My bad."

Several strokes passed, and we settled back into the rhythm before she said, "I'm sorry me fighting with Finn is messing up the vacation. And I'm sorry I hooked up with Alex if you were seriously interested in him."

I bit my tongue not to correct her on the "if." There was no "if," and she'd known that, hadn't she? If she could apologize, I could too.

"I'm sorry I was such a bitch about it." My arms burned with how fast we were paddling. Sweat rolled down my neck and chest.

"You really were."

Gee, thanks. "I, uh, I ran into Finn on my way here. Literally. Ran right into him. And he stomped off without saying anything at all to me."

"Yeah, well I told you Finn was being an exceptional ass lately."

"He seemed really upset."

The soft splashing and the laughter of the other contestants as we all drew near the collection of flags dragged on with no response from Sara.

"Hello? Sara?"

"Don't worry about it."

I frowned. "Why? Don't worry about what?"

"Look, I don't want to talk about Finn. You didn't want to help me. And if you remember, last time Finn came up, it ended with you accusing me of trying to *kill* you. Honestly, maybe I don't trust you now. I'm handling it on my own."

I blink at her back. Had she gone ahead with blackmailing Finn without me? Was she going to do everything else without me now too? The way she was talking sounded so… *final*. Like she was letting me go.

I swore for a second I could hear Brianna's laughter in the middle school cafeteria, high and joyous, but the laughter wasn't for me anymore—it was for her new, better friends. I could see the text—the *text*—from Dan, telling me it was over. I could feel the world shift, violently, as I crouched behind the second-floor banister, listening to Mom tell Dad she just needed a little time away. Time to think.

I pushed that memory down, like I always did.

I could apologize and fix this, right? And yet I couldn't seem to make myself give her another apology. The words wouldn't come. But I didn't need to be sorry if I was interesting enough. Wasn't that how Sara herself operated?

I knew stealing those fireworks was a good idea.

"If I tell you a secret, will you tell me what's up with Finn?"

"Maaayyybe."

She was listening. It was promising.

"I stole something."

"What?" she screeched, turning fully around. Her oar popped out and water sprayed all over my face and torso. "When? What? Tell me right now."

Our kayak slowed, barely gliding along the surface as I stopped paddling too.

There was no one close enough to hear us, but I lowered my voice anyway.

"Fireworks."

Her eyes shot wide. "How?"

"The shed over by the third hole wasn't locked, and they were sitting there. I stuffed a bunch in my bag and walked out. I thought this random old lady saw me, but...I guess not. I've got them stashed in the back of my closet."

Her eyes sparkled and she balanced her oar across her lap.

"We'll set them off tonight. I'll tell Alex and Finn. It'll be great. Good work, Mandy," she said, and gave my calf a quick pinch.

My smile slipped. We were definitely going to get caught if we set off a bunch of fireworks.

"You can't tell anyone *I* took them."

Her expression darkened.

"Why?"

My chest knotted at the suspicion in her voice, and I couldn't get the answer out.

"I see," she said, her hands tightening around her paddle. "It's fine for *me* to steal, but not you?"

I looked away, out over the shimmering water, as guilt flooded my cheeks.

She pinched me again, harder. "Sure, Mandy. I'll tell them I got us the fireworks. No one would expect something like that from you, anyway."

I knew she meant it as an insult, and I had to swallow it because I asked her to lie for me. I sighed.

"Thank you." It must've sounded sincere enough, because this time instead of pinching me, she grinned.

"What would you do without me?"

"I seriously don't know." For better or worse, I didn't. "Now tell me about Finn. What's the secret?"

She didn't answer.

"Sara!"

"What? I said maybe. And *maybe* I still don't trust you."

"Fine." I gritted my teeth.

But things were very much not fine.

Not at *all* fine.

We were falling apart, and I hated it.

I just didn't know how to stop it.

33

NOW

MONDAY NIGHT. ONE YEAR AFTER.

The door to the cottage creaks when I open it, and an audible "What was that?" comes from the shared bedroom, behind the closed door. Mom and Dad's bedroom is dark. They're probably still at the lounge.

I hesitate, embarrassment tickling my scalp at having failed on my promise so quickly. My mission to talk to Finn hadn't gone well at all. I should have tried harder, but he was talking to someone about *me*. Which might mean—

Something thuds to the floor and my feet fly across the thin carpet. I jiggle the handle but it doesn't budge. The door's locked.

"Kelsey?" I call, my lips hovering above the dark wood.

The door muffles their frantic exchange.

"Over there. It was over there." Kelsey's voice carries. She never was good at whispering.

My cheeks flame and my fingers curl into fists. Is this why

Natalie was so quick to agree to let me talk to Finn? Which I didn't do. But still. Brats! They wanted me out of the cottage.

"Open the door, Kelsey, I swear to—"

There's a click and Natalie stands before me like we're two friends running into each other between classes. Unbothered. Friendly.

Over Natalie's shoulder, Kelsey cowers beside my bed, looking guilty as hell.

In their obvious haste to put my stuff back where it all was before, they missed a pair of socks that rolled under the edge of the bed.

"Hi, Mandy. We were just going to go down to the lounge and…" Natalie trails off under the withering glare I shoot her direction. On the dresser beside us, even Kelsey's betta fish stops swimming.

"Kelsey"—the warning rumbles in my voice—"why were you going through my stuff?"

"What?" She fidgets. "I mean, we weren't."

I sidestep Natalie and walk slowly to the bedside and to my suitcase that's been haphazardly closed. A pant leg hangs out the side. Kelsey flinches when I squat and retrieve the socks.

"What were you looking for?"

She shakes her head, hair flying, and backs away from me. I'm all out of patience. All out of tact, or kindness, or any number of traits that keep people from behaving terribly. I snatch her upper arm and pull her forward. She stumbles at first, and then her heels dig in, fear rampaging across her face.

God help me, but we're doing this. With my free hand I shove my hands in my pockets and brush the necklace chain, squished into the bottom. I roll the links between my thumb and forefinger, and draw out the necklace. "Were you, perhaps," I hiss, "looking for this?"

She licks her lips. "No." She corrects course, but not fast enough. "I—what is that?"

"Stop lying. You know what this is."

Suddenly that guilt and fear disappears, like a switch being thrown, and fire fills her eyes. Fire and something I'm afraid might be close to hate. Natalie says Kelsey's name, but my sister doesn't seem to hear her friend.

"Lying?" Her voice shakes, climbing higher as she continues. "You're accusing *me* of lying?"

"Yes. Why would you do something like this? It's sick. Honestly even after I realized it was just a look-alike it was still a really shitty thing to do. How could you?"

I swear, her eye twitches, and an absolutely feral look swarms across her face. This isn't the little sister I know. This is someone different. Someone more on edge maybe even than me.

My stomach sinks.

"Fake? You think it's fake?" Her laugh sounds like it's strangling her. She steps into me, and I keep hold of her arm because I can't seem to let go. Like a deer in the headlights, I can't move at all. "I can't believe you. I can't trust you. You—you—you." She's shouting in full, her voice breaking into ragged pieces. "Monster!"

MURDERER. I see the word in my head again, spelled out in red.

She jerks her arm free with so much force I lose my footing, falling backward. My shoulders thump into the dresser. Natalie gasps, and Kelsey yelps. The fishbowl tips off the edge.

The bowl shatters, and glass glitters in the water soaking the thin carpet. Shimmering blue scales and a fanned red tail flop pathetically.

"Shit," I whisper.

Hands shove me out of the way with enough force I almost face-plant.

"Move," Kelsey says, after the shoving.

Oh God. Don't let me have killed her pet. Oh God, oh God.

"Kelsey, I'm—"

"Just *shut up*. Natalie, get the cup out of the bathroom." She tenderly scoops the fish from the flood. The faucet runs, and Natalie reappears. "No! No tap water will kill him. Mandy, get the unopened water bottle from the sunroom."

I do as I'm told. Please don't let her fish die. He *can't* die. She'll never forgive me.

"What does the label say? Is it spring water?" Kelsey asks.

I scan the small writing. My chest is tight. "Yes," I force out.

"Good. Pour it in the cup."

My fingers shake. I'm too slow. I'm always too slow.

"*Now*," she snaps.

The lid cracks open and I pour the water into the cup. Kelsey eases her limp, twitching pet into the makeshift home.

We all stand and stare for several seconds. I can't breathe.

"He better not die," Kelsey says, and bursts into tears.

Fear and fury warp her soft, familiar features into those of a stranger. Natalie moves to stand behind her like a wall, ready to prop her up against the world.

Against me.

Kelsey balls her fists at her side and I tense, expecting an actual blow, but the next words out of my sister's mouth hit deeper than any fist.

"I hate you."

I've been expecting it since I arrived, and yet it hurts. It hurts so, so much. I swallow and look away before she can see my eyes go glassy. "Okay." I can't think of anything more eloquent to say.

"Okay?" Kelsey's voice is more a wail than anything else. "That's all? God, you don't even care that I said I hate you? What is *wrong* with you?"

"I care, but I don't know what to say." Honesty. Honesty because everything already hurts and it can't possibly get worse. "I cut you out of my life and it was such a terrible thing to do, I can't believe that person was really me. *Is* really me. I'm so sorry."

"Don't you care about anyone?" she whispers. "Did you care about her? Before—"A violent, shoulder-shaking sob rips through her, like yanking a piece of her soul out with each raw gasp.

She continues sobbing and stares at me like she's

drowning, and I'm watching from the shore, clutching a life preserver to my chest while she sinks. Selfish.

Selfish little monster, still hurting everyone I love.

I tear my gaze away and stare at the necklace pooled in my palm. Slowly, her words from earlier crystallize, and an awful suspicion emerges. *You think it's fake.* "Kelsey… where did you get this necklace?"

She can't get a full word out between wet gasps. Natalie hugs my sister and rests her chin on Kelsey's shoulder. Kelsey nods frantically.

"She dug it up that night," Natalie says.

The room tilts. Sweat prickles my palms and it feels like someone's punched me in the stomach. I might throw up. When I can get my head to stop swimming with shock, I look at Kelsey and Kelsey only. "That's why this is so clean? You've had it this *entire time*." My throat tightens. "How?" Oh God, *how?*

Her shoulders are still shaking in sudden, erratic bursts, but the tears have slowed.

"I followed you. You were drunk, and…I don't know… in shock? I thought you'd hear me. Turn around and catch me. I really did. But…" Her lip quivers and a fresh bout of sobs breaks out.

I'm frozen, like I could slip out of time and away from this cursed place if I could just make myself hold still enough. Gradually, a thought so terrible slides into my mind that I want to stop existing all together. "When did you start following me, Kelsey?"

I'm shocked she can make out the words, they're so soft.

But she does, and I wish to God she didn't, because then maybe I wouldn't have to hear the answer.

"I saw you kill her."

34

NOW

MONDAY NIGHT. ONE YEAR AFTER.

The three of us stand in silence that feels like it could stretch until the end of time, and probably a while after.

"You what?"

She lowers her voice, but somehow the words come out steadier than before. "I saw you attack her." Kelsey's lips are slick and shining with tears, and her cheeks are splotchy. "And all...*all* I wanted from this trip was for you to tell me that it wasn't true! Or to tell me what I saw wasn't,"— she hiccups—"wasn't what it looked like. Natalie promised she'd help, since you wouldn't talk to me. Maybe we could force you into telling *her* that there was some good reason for—for—for..."

She makes a strange choking sound. She's falling apart, and I want to hug her. I have to hug her.

I have to tell her.

There's a second heartbeat in my neck. How do I—

Kelsey keeps going. "I was so scared. How could you? She was your friend. So I ran. But I panicked. I didn't know what to do, and I eventually went back. I had to talk to you and ask why you just attacked your friend." The words are choppy, like she's held them so tight she doesn't know how to let them out in a coherent fashion.

I hate that I did this to her.

She lets out a breath that sounds like a death rattle. "By the time I came back, you were stumbling off through the woods. I followed you. I didn't even realize you'd—"

Is she going to throw up? Her skin is too pale, and she presses her fingers to her lips.

"I didn't even know about the firework until later. And after a while, I started telling myself I must've been wrong... somehow. You didn't get arrested. You couldn't have killed her, because then you'd be in jail. I must have seen wrong. Remembered wrong. But this whole trip you *still* won't explain what happened. I thought with Natalie putting Sara's story out there you'd defend yourself. But you haven't." Her face crumples again.

"Kelsey..."

"Why? Why did you kill her? What did she do?"

I can't get a full breath, and Sara's face, perfect and washed in moonlight one second, gruesome and bloodied the next, swims in my vision. Hands around my neck, laughing, the weight of the rock, so much hate I thought my chest would explode but it was a different explosion I should've been worried about and—

Carnations, zinnias, mums, roses, camelias, violets, inhale, exhale.

Shit.

Okay. I take a shuddering breath and go to the sunroom to lock the cottage door. The dead bolt thunks home with a certain finality. I'm doing this.

Kelsey and Natalie trail me at a distance. When I face them, Kelsey's eyes show far too much white. Fear. Naked, confused fear.

"Sit down," I say.

Neither of them moves at first, so I take the large chair, and I wait.

"I'm going to tell you about that night, and then we're never going to talk about it again. Understand? Natalie, give me that phone or so help me God."

She huffs but hands over the phone. I double-check that the camera is off and then set the screen face down on the end table. A quick glance at the door, but no one is coming. No Mom and Dad to give me an excuse to change the subject.

I tell them what happened.

Or.

I tell them a version of what happened.

One where I'm not a monster.

35

THEN

WEDNESDAY NIGHT. THE DAY OF.

Sara promised everything would be fine.

We'd go past the Snack Shack. Past the golf courses. Past the honeymoon cottage sitting all alone at the edge of the resort. Across the bridge at the far edge of the resort and down the lake trail.

Tucked around the curve of land and invisible from the main property was an old abandoned dock. Even if someone noticed the flashes of light from the fireworks, no one was going to come investigate. She promised.

My nerves hummed. I didn't want to do this, but I hadn't *refused*. I should have refused. The concession, the submission by silence, needled at me.

We were going to get caught.

I could feel it.

But I didn't want to be left out, and she *would* leave

me, if I insisted on turning back. The knowledge was heavy. Gnawing. Angry.

Finn walked a few paces ahead, my canvas bag stuffed with fireworks swinging from his hand with each step. He hadn't said more than a word or two to Alex, and nothing at all to Sara, but the lure of lighting things on fire and watching them explode had been too big a temptation to resist.

"Stop it," Sara giggled, and I turned in time to see her give Alex a playful shove.

I fought a scowl. Alex was too forgiving for his own good. She'd *used* him, and here he was laughing like it didn't bother him. But at least they weren't making out, so maybe that was over, at least.

I knew the lilt in her voice, though. She would win him back over. Sara always got what she wanted. Well…not *everything*. We were still at odds over the whole Finn situation.

A low, nagging voice in my head whispered, *What if she's more pissed off than you think? What if she leaves you behind for this?*

I tripped on a raised mound of gravel and staggered a step before regaining my balance.

"Don't face-plant," Alex called.

I forced a tight smile when they drew up beside me. Sara on my left, Alex on my right. Sara pinched my hip, getting a chunk of skin and tank top between her thumb and forefinger. I hissed through my teeth, but held my tongue.

She frowned.

"Nothing's going to happen," Sara said, an edge of

annoyance creeping in as she shimmed up to me and squinted at my face. "I'm the one that stole the fireworks anyway. You're just...here."

Rude. But... I'd asked her to tell them she took the fireworks, not me. I couldn't even blame her for stealing the spotlight this time.

Alex nudged my shoulder.

"Yeah, you're athletic, right, Mandy?" He chuckled. "As long as you can run fast, you'll be fine."

"Alex, don't say that. She's not going to have to run." After a significant pause she added, "Probably."

I groaned. "Probably?"

"Well, it's not like we're going off the property. Someone might come looking when they see flashes from around the bend." She shrugged. "But you *are* fast, and everything *will* be fine. I don't want to talk about it anymore. You're taking all the fun out of this."

I'd literally said one word.

36

NOW

MONDAY NIGHT. ONE YEAR AFTER.

"I was following you," Kelsey says.

"Obviously I know that now."

"But you didn't that night?"

"Of course not."

She frowns.

"What?"

"I wish I'd been less sneaky. Maybe all this could have been—" Her lips tremble.

"Don't go there, Kelsey. There's no point. Things turned out...the way they turned out. It's not your fault." I wish the same were true for me, but I had chance after chance to change the course of that night, and every time I chose wrong.

I let her die ~~on purpose.~~

"But—"

I shake my head. "Anyway..."

37

THEN

WEDNESDAY NIGHT. THE DAY OF.

Sara tipped back another airplane bottle of cinnamon whiskey and tossed the empty to the ground next to the sack with the remaining selections. Also in the mix was a half-full plastic water bottle full of vodka that Alex brought, and a half-empty bottle of tequila that Finn had swiped from his parents' bar back home. The idea of drinking straight tequila was only slightly better than the idea of drinking straight vodka. I pulled the tequila out of the sack and screwed off the top.

One sip, and I was coughing.

"Absolutely terrible," I choked out.

"It's tequila," Finn said, laughing as he laid the fireworks out in a row on the ground. "What were you expecting?"

I stuck out my tongue but resisted the urge to attempt wiping the taste away.

Alex had dragged a log to the edge where the overgrown

dirt path bled into the old forgotten dock, and was out scavenging for another. On one side, the trees blotted out much of the star-speckled sky. On the other, the dock jutted out over the moonlit lake. Clouds gathered in the distance.

From here, the Snack Shack and the lifeguard stand, the swimming area and the floating dock, the main lodge with its glowing yellow lights were all hidden by the curve of the woods along the shoreline. They were a solid twenty-minute walk away. Would they notice when we added our fireworks to theirs? Would they come all the way out here if they did?

I scuffed the toe of my sandal in the dirt, kicking at one of the many rocks littering the ground. "What else is in the bag?" I asked. I needed more to drink. Preferably something better. Had no one thought to grab sodas?

Sara dragged the bag across the dirt in front of her and let the mouth sag open at my feet. "None of it is great," she said, "but the Fireball isn't...bad."

I snatched one out and cracked the plastic top.

Her face screwed up. "Is that the last Fireball?"

"Yes."

"Get a different one. You don't even like whiskey."

"But I like cinnamon."

She exhaled slowly.

I held my breath.

"Sure, but that's not really the same as liking whiskey, and I actually *like* whiskey," she said.

I watched her eyes widen as I cracked the top and tipped the contents into my mouth.

Her nostrils flared.

Silence.

Alex crunched his way into the clearing empty-handed. "It's way too dark. I'm going to sit on the dock."

I eyed the warped boards.

He laughed. "Don't make that face. You realize we're not setting off fireworks beneath this thick canopy of trees, right? Do you want to burn down the forest? We're going out on the dock anyway."

"I know."

"It's not going to collapse."

I was fairly convinced those boards were far too rotted to support our weight, but everyone was acting like I was the one being unreasonable. Whatever, we could all swim. Or maybe Sara would fall in and she could get a taste of what it felt like to drown.

Oof. No. What an awful thing to think. Stop it.

"I know," I repeated. The tension in my shoulders twisted tighter, and I could feel Sara staring at me. I ignored her.

"Then come on," Alex said, still smiling.

A small groan slipped out before I could stifle the sound of protest.

Sara made a soft sucking noise between her teeth, and that flicker of annoyance flared hot, lashing down my spine and drawing me up stiffly. I twisted toward her.

What is your problem? The words were crystal clear in my head, but I couldn't get my lips to cooperate, my lungs to breathe the words to life. I didn't want to be the one to make the fighting start again. If she and I started, started for real, it would probably set off her and Finn, and then the whole night would be ruined. It wasn't worth the fallout.

The moment passed, and I unclenched my jaw to take another warm swig of whiskey, finishing the airplane bottle.

38

NOW

MONDAY NIGHT. ONE YEAR AFTER.

"I almost left that first half hour," Kelsey says. "I was bored. And you didn't want me anyway."

Ouch. Straight to the heart. But I was sorry she hadn't left. I was sorry she'd stayed to see me as a monster: angry and afraid and not so sorry at all, in that moment.

"Why didn't you?"

"I got scared one of you would see me when I tried to creep out of the woods. And you were drinking. I'd never seen you drunk. It was so weird. Besides, why couldn't I hang out with y'all? It wasn't fair." She locks her hands together in her lap. "I was so mad at you, but I definitely should have left. After that night, I couldn't stop thinking about it. What you did. I dream about it all the time. And you're right, I *have* been sleepwalking. Since last summer. Mom and Dad think I'm stressed about school, and I just act like they're right because *duh*. I can't tell them. They have to think I'm scared of *normal* things like tests and sports...not my sister being a killer."

Guilt settles heavy around my shoulders, and I clench my hands in my lap to stop their shaking. There's more story to tell.

39

THEN

WEDNESDAY NIGHT. THE DAY OF.

A Roman candle went rogue and shot toward Alex. I gasped.

"Fuck, man!" Alex shouted, diving out of the way and falling off the dock in the process. The moon-silvered surface shattered as Alex crashed into the shallow water. He came up sputtering and hauled himself onto the rough boards.

Sara laughed. How was she not stressed about any of this?

"It's not funny," I snapped.

She whipped to face me.

"Do you *try* to be so boring?" Her exasperation grated against my raw nerves. I was already a little tipsy, and when she rounded on me with yet another insult, I wasn't ready for how much it would hurt.

"Excuse me?"

"You worry too much. There's no *point* in including you. You just get pissy and ruin things. Even when I try to tell you things, you're too much of a baby to be any fun."

"Sara…" Alex cautioned.

"No point?" I breathed. "You think *I* ruin things?"

She tipped her chin up and her eyes were hard.

"Yes," she said coldly.

My heart ached, making it hard to swallow. Hard to focus. She was just angry. She didn't mean it. I could hold us together if I said the right things.

But…

Was that really what I wanted? My jaw twitched. Of course that was what I wanted. To be Sara's friend. To be like her and be liked *by* her, because she knew the secret to holding on to people. Even now, annoyed and hurt and confused, I couldn't possibly *leave* her.

I stepped close enough to beg without Alex or Finn hearing me humiliate myself. "Is this all because I wouldn't help you with Finn?"

She leaned away from me, forcing me to come closer to hear her.

"So what if it is?" she asked.

I breathed in and out through my nose. "Okay fine. I'll help you with whatever you want, and we'll forget how weird things have been?"

Her eyes searched my face. "No."

I flinched. "What?" I hoped she couldn't hear the panic leaking into my voice. "Why not?"

"Because I handled it. I don't need your help. I don't *want* your help."

And with that, she strode away from me, across the creaking boards, and over to Alex's side.

I couldn't tell whether the stabbing feeling in my abdomen was hurt or rage.

I watched, vibrating with the urge to throttle her, as she ignored me in favor of Alex. He'd stripped out of his soaking wet clothes, down to his boxers, and she hooked a finger into the waistband and gave them a little snap.

I finished the airplane bottle of watermelon vodka I'd been holding. Awful.

God, I hated her in that moment. Even with a pile of contraband fireworks scattered about and a half-naked boy shivering in the night air, I couldn't stop staring a hole into the side of her face. Freckled cheeks and little wisps of hair curling around her temples.

I took a slow breath and swallowed the urge snatch her away from Alex's side and make her keep talking. Make her stop ignoring me.

"Let's light off the rest of them," Sara said. "And maybe don't hit Alex, Finn."

"Please," Alex said.

Finn gave Sara and Alex a long look, and guilt twisted Alex's face into a grimace. He stepped away from Sara and closer to his friend, but Sara snatched his hand back. Alex stiffened, eyes darting between Sara and her brother. I could have sworn a trace of anger flickered across his usually cheerful face.

Maybe he wasn't as quick to get over being used as I thought.

"That's all there was." Finn gestured to the charred debris on the dock. "And I'm out of here."

He hopped the step down from the dock and grabbed the mostly empty bottle of tequila from where it had tipped over in the dirt. How much of that had *I* drunk?

"I'll be taking this." He gave it a shake for good measure.

"And what do *you* have to do besides hang out here?" Sara stomped after Finn, needling him.

Alex stopped beside me with his wet clothes in a bundle beneath his arm. "I shouldn't have taken my pants off," he said.

I mumbled an agreement, but I was way more focused on Sara and Finn.

There's no point in including you.

I don't need your help.

I don't want your help.

Sara's voice was cold in my head.

I don't want *you.* That's what she really meant. I was certain.

I chewed my lip. Tried to take a deep breath, but each inhale was more unsatisfactory than the last.

Was I too boring to be her friend? To be anything to her?

Yes, that cruel voice in my head hissed. She'd basically said as much.

"It's none of your business," Finn snapped at Sara. "I'll see you in the morning. Don't you dare tell Mom and Dad I'm staying out."

"Off to see your friend?" Sara asked, and Finn whirled on her.

"No, actually. It's over, and you're already getting what you wanted; now leave—me—alone." Finn bit out each word. His voice cracked by the end, and he almost seemed... sad? Desperate?

Alex was practically vibrating with tension beside me. Water drip, drip, dripped into a small puddle forming at his feet.

"And you're telling Mom and Dad you don't want the car?" Sara asked smugly.

Finn made a sound halfway between a sigh and a snarl. "I'm done with this," he said, and left without looking back.

I stared, open-mouthed.

After a minute of awkward silence, Alex said, "I should go too. Since I now have no clothes. And I have to work again in the morning." He gave his hair a thorough shake, sending water droplets flying. A few landed on my cheek.

I didn't wipe them away, but my skin was dry by the time Alex finished searching for an airplane bottle for the walk back.

"Y'all sure you want to stay out?" he asked.

Sara ignored him completely as she chewed her lip, and I nodded even though what I meant to do was ask him to stay. I didn't want to be alone with Sara. His wet flip-flops squelched with each step faded away.

What just happened? How did we go from four to two? Now Sara was even angrier, and my head was too fuzzy for figuring out what to do, so instead I just stared at her. She reclaimed her seat on the log and downed another shot. A quick lick of her lips, moonlight illuminating her face, and she said, "Are you going to sit?"

I hesitated. I was definitely drunk and pissed off. Way too annoyed for dealing with Sara and her moods. She was meaner than usual tonight.

I could be mean too.

"Actually, I'm going back to the resort," I said. Let her sit out here alone, with the spent fireworks and the empty bottles. Let her have her own *exciting* night here all by herself, if I wasn't good enough company for her.

Her mouth twisted, lips pulling into a sneer. "Why? Because *Alex* is gone, or because you're still scared?"

"It's not weird that I'm scared of getting caught." I threw my hands up. "Just because your parents don't give a shit what you do doesn't mean I won't get in trouble."

The arch of her brow held the weight of so many perfect summers. But also of judgment and control and each of us fighting to carve out just a little more space inside the other.

I backed up a step.

The prickling at the base of my neck screamed, "Mistake! Mistake!" The night pressed closer, as if drawing nearer for the show.

I licked my lips. "I didn't mean to imply your parents don't care about you..." I should have known better, especially after all the drama this year with her brother, the golden boy.

Her skin was flushed with dabs of pink, spread like misshapen butterflies over her neck and chest. Her eyes glittered with tears.

"Maybe your parents love you," her voice wavered, "but that's *all* you have. You think I'd want to hang out with you if I had any of my real friends here every year?" She laughed, and the laugh was a thousand tiny slaps.

She put my worst fears into words and laid them between us like a challenge.

"You don't mean that." My chest caved in, pressing against my ribs so it was hard to get a deep breath.

Sara stepped closer. Close enough I could've fixed the strap of her tank where it slipped down her shoulder. I could have plucked the leaf from her hair.

I could have scratched her eyes out.

"Yes. I do. So why don't you go run off after *Alex*? You might as well. I'm done with him. Take your shot." Her voice was a blade, but the kind that cut both ways. Her eyes glittered. "Maybe he'll want you, but I doubt it."

I slapped her for real.

Hard across the face.

Pain burst over my palm. A fistful of beestings and a bitter satisfaction swelling hot in my chest.

Sara gasped, hand flying to her cheek, and then she lunged at me. Her torso crashed into me with more force than I expected. Nothing holding her back. No thought for falling. My feet slipped in the dirt, and when my tailbone hit the ground, I yelped.

"Sara!" I screamed her name because I couldn't think of anything else except the girl struggling to get the leverage she needed to…to what? I tried to scramble away—dirt beneath my nails—but her legs pinned me on either side, and she clawed at me like she could flay six years of friendship from my bones if only she could get that first nail under the skin.

I struggled, catching one of her wrists, but she jerked free.

I fought to get air, but the breaths came too fast, and my heartbeat ricocheted around my rib cage.

Sara's hands closed around my neck.

40

NOW

MONDAY NIGHT. ONE YEAR AFTER.

"Oh my God," Kelsey gasps. "I didn't even... I didn't realize she was choking you! It didn't look like that from how far away I was."

I nod because I don't trust myself with words.

"I should have stopped y'all," Kelsey says softly.

I purse my lips together. She doesn't need to explain herself. Not to me. Especially not when I'm only giving her half-truths.

"I was too surprised. And confused," she says.

"It's okay."

"It was over so quickly..." She looks afraid, like she doesn't want to hear the rest.

I don't want to *tell* her the rest, not even this version, where I make myself sound better. Less monstrous. Where I twist the past into gentler lies because the truth is too sharp-edged.

But we've come this far and even though I'd rather stop, we can't.

Some things can't be stopped.

41

THEN

WEDNESDAY NIGHT. THE DAY OF.

Sara ignored my gurgled plea for her to stop. I didn't understand, and yet...

I understood perfectly.

We couldn't quite seem to simply exist in each other's world anymore, and we couldn't, or wouldn't, break apart. Doomed to this moment. Or doomed *for* this moment.

Doomed.

My lungs burned.

"Help," I gurgled, lips moving, but no real sound came out. There was no one here to help me, anyway.

"Help me, help me," Sara said, mocking me. "Help yourself, if you want away from me so badly."

I reached for her, but all my fist closed around was the chain hanging from her neck. My necklace, warm from her skin and shining silver in the moonlight. I yanked, and she jerked forward as the chain snapped. Her arm buckled, and her forehead smacked against mine.

She came up laughing.

Laughing, laughing, *laughing*.

She leaned in, lips parted. "Fight me, Mandy." Maybe she was whispering, or maybe the blood rushing in my ears was simply too loud for anything else. My fingers fumbled in the dirt. Searching.

There.

Rough and cool. I grabbed the rock in my left hand.

Sara's eyes widened, and I smashed the stone into the side of her face.

42

NOW

MONDAY NIGHT. ONE YEAR AFTER.

Sometimes I think I missed a word, there in the dirt with my heart pounding and Sara's face dark above mine.

It could so easily have been, "Fight *for* me, Mandy."

I'd always thought Sara was perfectly capable of fighting for herself, but that night I was wrong. I was wrong about so many things.

I can't bring myself to look Kelsey in the eye. "You saw that part, I guess."

A beat of silence.

"Yes."

43

THEN

WEDNESDAY NIGHT. THE DAY OF.

Sara wasn't moving. Was she breathing? Flecks of dirt that had fallen into my contact lenses made my eyes water. I blinked against my blurred vision, hissing as the grit only made things worse. Surely, she was okay, I just wasn't seeing straight. I slipped the ruined lenses out and shoved them into my pocket along with Sara's necklace, but couldn't bring myself to look back to Sara.

My chest and head pounded like either might explode at any second.

Part of me *wanted* to explode.

Implode.

Explode.

Inhale.

Exhale.

A high whine snaked up my throat. I clapped my hands over my lips.

Out of the corner of my eye I could've sworn I saw a blurry flash of light coming down the trail, but then it disappeared. Sara wasn't moving, and blood pooled in the dirt around her head. Where the blood was coming from? Her cheek? No, her temple. Oh God. My stomach rolled, and the earth bucked around me. Adrenaline and alcohol and terror frothing like a violent sea.

Again that flash of light.

Someone was coming.

I threw myself toward the cover of trees on unsteady legs. The thick bushes that crowded the clearing swallowed me with a soft rustle, but I kept running. I had to get farther away. I couldn't let them see me.

My knees buckled. I sunk my hands into the dirt to steady myself, but it didn't help. Every breath was like trying to cram a fist into a teacup—not enough space, on the verge of shattering.

A twig poked into the soft space between my fingers and I bit my lip against the whine.

Sara was—

I had—

She'd made me—

Motionless and bleeding and oh God what had I—

Get up. Please, God, get up.

A spark of hope flared in my too-tight chest. Maybe she *had* gotten up. On my hands and knees, and quietly as I could, I turned back toward the clearing. I couldn't see Sara anymore—I was too far and the woods too thick—but a new figure stood in the clearing. Only bits and pieces were visible from where I crouched in the dirt—a small torso, brown hair...maybe? A girl, I was pretty sure.

I squinted, inching forward in hopes of a better view through the leaves and branches and trunks. If only I hadn't had to take out the contacts. The girl turned, and I froze. Could she see me, even though I could barely see her? Fear pulsed through me so strong my vision grayed.

Don't come over here, don't come over here, don't come over here.

She paced the clearing, searching for whoever had attacked Sara, surely.

I was a statue. I would never move again. Never breathe again.

The flood of panic beating through my skull made every sound muffled, like it was filtering through cotton, and crickets kept a steady trill. Stop. I needed them to stop. I couldn't *hear*. Was Sara telling this girl how I'd hit her? But she'd attacked me first; it wasn't my fault. Right?

I shifted and caught a glimpse of Sara, still lying very, very still.

I killed her. Oh my God, I really killed her.

The girl made a noise, or spoke, but I couldn't make out what she said. She wasn't speaking loud enough. This was it. She was going to go get help and everyone would discover what I'd done.

My vision slid in and out of focus from the strain of trying to see more detail. Sara: a dark shape. The other girl:

her legs, part of her shoulders, half a face that I couldn't make out.

Her foot struck out. I might not be able to see details, but I could see movement.

Did she just *kick* Sara?

"Get up," she said, louder this time, but the distance and the wind made it impossible to recognize the voice.

I shivered. Hot tears raced down my cheeks.

How could I have—

Sara sat up.

44

NOW

MONDAY NIGHT. ONE YEAR AFTER.

"What?" Kelsey screeches.

"I didn't kill her." ~~Liar.~~ It's truth adjacent. Sort of.

I push the guilt down and focus on reassuring Kelsey. That's what matters now. Reassuring my sister, and rebuilding a relationship with her. One where she's not walking around thinking I killed Sara.

"But I thought..." Kelsey trails off, staring at her hands in her lap.

My brow wrinkles, and my gaze jumps between my sister and Natalie. They thought I'd done it. They'd been so sure. I take a slow, shallow breath. If we're airing secrets, maybe they can clear something up for me in return.

"Were y'all the ones who spray-painted the walkway? Honestly. The ones who wrote 'murderer' that morning?"

"No. No, I swear. That wasn't us. Right, Natalie? Tell her." Kelsey shakes her head so fast her hair flies around her face.

"We didn't."

If they're telling the truth...shit. Shit, shit, shit. Who else at Highmark would be committed to making sure people blame me for Sara's death?

Whoever killed her.

I killed her. Not on my own, ~~maybe~~ not on purpose, but I had so, so many opportunities to keep Sara from dying. Before. During. ~~After...no, shh, I wasn't telling Kelsey that part.~~

What I'd done was the same as killing her, really.

Or, that was what the insidious little voice in my head had insisted all year, worming its way in every time I lapsed on my avoidance rituals. After she died, no one else had come forward to add their side of the story, or make the story make sense, and all I had left—with any certainty—was *my* story, my *own* role.

I didn't know who else to blame, so I had to blame myself, and that had been far too terrible to bear.

So I'd shoved down the memories of what happened that night, for fear that remembering would make things worse, but I'm dragging them out now.

And eventually, I'll have to *do something* about them.

I chew my lip. Whoever wrote MURDERER is probably the person who lit the firework. After the initial terror passed, and the girl I'd seen that night never went to the cops, I'd assumed she would stay quiet forever. I'd put her out of my mind. I'd been so caught up in my own guilt, obsessing over what *I'd* done, that it was easier than expected. But with

Kelsey and Natalie stirring Sara's story up all over again, maybe the mystery girl is here, and getting proactive.

Or, it was some bored kid who talked to Natalie and decided to mess with me. Which would mean if I start asking around, I might make things worse. Ugh.

"If it wasn't y'all, do you know who might've done it? You've been talking to people at the resort. Have you found anything?" I ask.

"Oh, you want to be involved now?" Natalie asks.

"Nat," Kelsey says, pleading.

Natalie sighs. "No. No one's said they had anything to do with that."

Frustration wars with the relief, but I shove the frustration aside because if I can get my sister back, the rest doesn't matter. I have a chance now that I didn't have before. I'm not going to ruin it.

"You really didn't recognize the person's voice?" Natalie asks, leaning forward.

"No. Like I said. I was too far away, and too disoriented, to hear clearly. I could barely make out the words." That part, at least, is true. I might be keeping a lot of information from them, but I don't know who the girl was.

"When I saw you hit her and she didn't get up, I ran," Kelsey says. "I just...I ran. I couldn't believe what you'd done and I was so scared. I ran but then... Well, what was I going to do? Who was I going to tell? You'd go to jail. I couldn't..." Her face contorts. "I couldn't let anyone see me crying, so eventually I went back to the dock. You were all I had that night."

"And you found me again as I took off down the trail to bury Sara's necklace," I finish for her as realization sets in. She saw me hit Sara, she saw Sara go down, and she saw me run. She never saw what happened in between.

"But why did you run, if she wasn't dead?"

"We'd all been drinking. And I'd just bashed her face with a rock. When she sat up, I was scared she was going to tell the girl everything." Lies, all lies. But believable lies. "Honestly I just needed to get away. I wasn't thinking straight."

"I guess I get it. I ran too." Uncertainty flickers across her face, but she settles on a tentative smile. One that I could easily snatch away. "If I'd just…turned right and gone into the clearing instead of chasing after you, I would've seen who really did it. I'd have known it wasn't you."

I don't want to be the one to kill the hope in her eyes.

She doesn't need to hear the rest.

No one does.

45

NOW

TUESDAY MORNING. ONE YEAR AFTER.

The morning sun hasn't quite burned off the dew from the lawn, and I dodge a gnat cloud hovering in the middle of the walkway between our cottage and the lodge.

Kelsey and Natalie were gone from the cottage before I got up, which is probably not a great sign. I'd hoped telling them my side of the story, or a version of it. would be enough to satisfy them, but the creeping feeling at the back of my neck says it's done the opposite.

I'm going to have to get more involved. Kelsey and Natalie are going to end up in serious danger. Whoever *else* was responsible for Sara's death may have killed her for very personal reasons, but that doesn't mean they can't be pushed into more violence if Kelsey and Natalie don't stop digging up the past.

I might hate myself for my own part in Sara's death, but I'd hate myself way more if I let anything happen to my sister.

And now that I've forced myself to say at least *some* of what happened out loud, it's easier to counter the vicious voice in my head that insists it was all my fault. Easier…but not easy. Especially because of what I learned after—

No. Jonquils, jacaranda, jasmine.

I swallow. I need a solution. One that ends this, for real. And doesn't land me in jail.

I wish I had a clue how to make that happen.

Two figures on the main lodge's wraparound porch look my direction as I approach. Ugh. I should've stayed in bed. It's only ten; I could have slept longer.

Mrs. Ellis waves me over to her and Mrs. Miller. They're seated in identical rocker chairs on the porch, with white porcelain cups of coffee on the table between them. A half-eaten fruit bowl sits closest to Mrs. Ellis on the table. Mrs. Miller has an untouched muffin.

"Mandy," Mrs. Ellis says. It takes her a couple tries to blink away the pain that's always in her eyes when she looks at me. I know she's trying to be kind, and to not blame me for leaving Sara out there, but it has to be hard. "We're working out some last details for tomorrow's memorial."

Every muscle in my body wants to turn and walk the other direction, but it's far too late to escape. Mrs. Miller gives me a look that I think is pity, but maybe she's just disappointed that I'm butting in on her conversation with Sara's mom. She gets so few opportunities to be included in things here. It must be awful, knowing everyone liked the first wife better.

I understand not feeling good enough.

I glance at the open glass doors leading into the lodge. I can *see* the coffee cart from here. If I just…

"Finn asked me to give you something," Mrs. Ellis says.

The blood rushes from my head, leaving me momentarily unsteady. What could Finn possibly want me to have? Has he told anyone what Alex said? Is this some "gotcha" moment?

"*Temporarily,*" Mrs. Ellis clarifies. She sounds nervous. She leans down and retrieves a shoebox I hadn't noticed. "They're photos from Sara's room. He said you, well, it's not important what he said. I think they might help you with your part of the memorial speech. I wish there were more…" She trails off for a few seconds and her eyes seem to drift. She shakes her head.

She half lifts the box, but I can't seem to move my hands from my side to accept this horrible, horrible gift. She lets the photos sink to rest in her lap, and an uncomfortable silence settles across the porch. Is Finn trying to torture me? Or trick me somehow?

Mrs. Miller's eyes shift between Mrs. Ellis and me, and God bless her, she fills the silence.

"You have such a considerate son, Charlotte," Mrs. Miller says, sucking up to Mrs. Ellis. She shakes her head. "Nothing like my—nothing like Leigh." Her mouth does a strange little dance as she fights the scowl, unsuccessfully.

What are they fighting about *now*? For a second, I feel guilty about Sara and me eavesdropping on them last year.

"You haven't seen her around this morning, have you,

dear?" Mrs. Miller asks, and I fight the reflexive cringe. It's weird to be called "dear" by someone who's maybeeee fifteen years older than me, but she's trying to be nice.

"No, sorry."

Her mouth purses like she's tasted something bad. "She's been extra difficult this year. I swear, that kid is—" She cuts herself off and looks nervously to Mrs. Ellis. Probably wishing she could take back any mention of problems in the family. Everyone here wants so badly to be perfect, and Mrs. Miller tries harder at it than anyone else.

Mrs. Ellis holds the box out again. "Here, take them. Hopefully...hopefully they'll...inspire you." The words are dragged out in pieces, like she wishes she didn't have to involve me, but can't pass up the chance to hear just one more new story about her daughter.

"Are you sure?"

She blinks tired blue eyes over a brittle smile. "Yes. Bring them back when you're done."

There's nothing friendly about the last part. *Bring them back safe, unlike my daughter,* she means.

I barely feel my fingers when they curl around the cardboard.

46

NOW

TUESDAY AFTERNOON. ONE YEAR AFTER.

"Virginia! Hi!" I call. I can't seem to make myself take the lid off the shoebox, which I've pushed as far down the bench from me as possible. Maybe she can talk me into being brave, or at least less of a coward.

She grins and ambles across the grass to join me by the firepit overlooking the lake.

She walks slowly, favoring her left side, but despite her limp there's a confidence to the way she moves. A peace. I envy her. I can't remember what peace feels like.

She sits in the Adirondack chair and props an elbow on the arm. Her bird-watching binoculars hang from her neck, and her fanny pack bunches around her waist.

"How are you?" she asks.

The usual lie, *I'm fine,* is on the tip of my tongue before I swallow the words. Why did I call her over? Didn't I want to talk to someone who wasn't related to me, or related to Sara, or trying to turn our story into a true-crime series?

"I don't know," I say.

I wait. I don't know how to move this forward. I'm trying, but I've been bottling too much up for too long. Releasing a little pressure without exploding is nearly impossible.

"Well, that's all right," she says, gently. She tips her head toward the opposite end of the bench. "New shoes?"

"They're some of Sara's pictures. Mrs. Ellis gave them to me this morning." God, how long have I been sitting here? I remember sitting down, pushing the box to arm's length, and then…things blurred.

Virginia nods, and there's something so soft and sad about her smile that the first hint of tears pricks my eyes. I blink and look down.

"And have you found any good memories in there?"

I shake my head. "I haven't looked at them yet."

"You'll look when you're ready." She sounds so impossibly sure.

Would I ever be ready? Could I face Sara, frozen in time and glossy paper?

"I'll have to go through them soon. I'm supposed to talk tomorrow, and I have no idea what I'm going to say."

Virginia makes a small thoughtful noise.

"Jamie always loved this view," she says, smiling.

"Jamie?" I ask.

Virginia nods and smiles. "My wife. We came here for ten years together before she passed away. But I keep coming, and I make a point to enjoy the things that used to bring her joy."

I fight the way my mouth turns down at the corners. Virginia doesn't sound sad, so what right do I have to be sad for her? Or for myself? I swallow.

"Virginia?"

"Yes?"

"How can you stand being here without her? How can you talk about her and...?"

"And be happy?"

I nod because speaking is hard.

She drums her fingers on the wooden arm of the chair. "You're asking because of Sara, yes?"

I nod again, my throat too tight to speak.

"Okay." She's quiet, and in between my own heartbeats, birds call to each other and kids squeal down by the docks. "Well first, I don't want you to think that your friend losing her life so young, so abruptly, is the same as my experience. Jamie and I had a long life together, and she got sick, and I had time to prepare for our goodbyes. Not much, not enough... because really is there ever enough time to say goodbye to someone you love? But Sara was a child, and what happened to her was tragic. There's a difference between sad and tragic, even though both can break your heart for a long time."

Heartbroken.

The word vibrates in my chest. Is that what this is? Heartbroken? I know I'd loved Sara, though never romantically. There hadn't been room left between us for those feelings even if I'd known then what I figured out later—that I was into girls and boys. But I'd loved her as the friend I so desperately wanted to be like.

Or am I heartbroken for the good person I thought I was? For the days when I wasn't working so hard to shut down the pieces of me that were angry and disgusted and disappointed?

But I'd walled off the good pieces too.

I used to know how to be a good sister, friend, daughter. I used to smile without wondering if it looked like a grimace.

Virginia continues. "Time helps the most, but only if you aren't actively holding on to the misery. You can't live your life torturing yourself with the past."

She gazes steadily at me, and I realize I've curled in around myself: shoulders hunched, arms tucked across my stomach. Holding myself together so nothing escapes. With gritted teeth, I force myself to straighten. Relax, as best I can.

"I don't know how to stop," I whisper, and my voice wobbles. I have to blink furiously to keep from crying.

"Start by doing what you can about *today*. You can't undo what happened to your friend. You can't say goodbye, or hug her one more time, or prevent the," she clears her throat, "the accident. That hurts, I know. But you can find things that make you happy, and try to hold on to that feeling when you think about Sara. It doesn't mean every memory has to be perfect. It just means maybe they don't have to hurt as much. You'll find balance, eventually."

The weight on my chest is heavy.

Each breath, in and out, is slow and deliberate. I hear her, I do. I want to find balance and not hurt so much when I think about Sara.

Part of moving on is fixing my relationship with Kelsey, but I have a terrible suspicion that the other part means confronting what happened last year. All of it.

I take a risk.

"Hey, Virginia? You must see a lot with those binoculars?"

Her brows lift. "I do."

I shift, digging the heels of my boots into the ground. My fingers curl around the wooden slats of the bench. If she brings up seeing me steal the fireworks, so be it. I've learned enough about her to be able to silence the voice in my head that insists she's secretly judging me for that part of my role in Sara's death.

"Did you see who spray-painted 'murderer' on our walkway? Anyone over by our cottage early that morning?" Her cottage was only one down from ours. Our cottage, one of several that was currently being renovated, Virginia's, the Ellises', and then the Millers'.

She looks away.

Anxiety flares. I shouldn't have asked. What do I say now?

"Sorry, I can't help you there. I didn't see anyone." She smiles and reaches over to pat my hand. "I know that was a rotten thing for someone to do to you and your family, but it was probably harmless. Try not to let it eat you up, okay?"

Dang.

"Thanks anyway," I say, trying hard not to sound too disappointed. It wasn't her fault.

Her smile wavers, only for a second, but it's enough to make me wonder how much she *really* believes the message was harmless.

Or whether she thinks the vandal is right about me.

47

THEN

SUNDAY AFTERNOON. THREE DAYS BEFORE.

Sara's voice carried from the second floor of the Ellis cottage. She wasn't happy, but despite the volume, I could only catch a few words at a time. I hesitated at the bottom of the stairs. She'd texted me to come meet her to work on the scavenger hunt list, but I didn't want to get caught in the middle of an argument.

A one-sided argument. Sara's voice was the only one I could hear all the way down here. She shouted a name—her best friend back home, I thought. I frowned. Sara hadn't said anything about fighting with Mary, but from the sound of it, Sara was *pissed*.

"Jesus," Finn said from behind me, and I jumped, back-pedaling from the stairs.

He stopped and tipped his head to stare at the second-story windows. A breeze picked up, stirring the sweet smell of lilies and what I assumed was Finn's bodywash, probably something called "Energize," with a picture of an orange on the label.

After a second, he sighed. "She's making everything worse."

I bristled. I might be annoyed with her still, but she was my friend. "What's that supposed to mean?"

He glanced at me, his right eyebrow arching. "My sister isn't as chill as she pretends she is. It's why she can't keep friends. She's always fighting with anyone who doesn't do what she wants."

"You *would* think that. You're her brother. Siblings fight. That doesn't mean she's a bad friend to people she actually likes." The defense was reflexive, but it was followed by a soft voice in my head saying, *Maybe he's right.*

From above, the shouting stopped and my shoulders relaxed.

He evaluated me. "Hmm. Maybe that's why you don't know what I'm talking about."

"What? Why?"

"Because you do whatever she wants."

I had to bite my tongue, hard, to keep from telling him that I didn't do everything she wanted. I wasn't helping her frame him for stealing from the resort. But even though I might not be helping Sara with her childish plan, I also wasn't going to rat her out to her brother.

"Ass," I grumbled and brushed past him, but he called out as I climbed the stairs.

"Watch out for her, Mandy."

I couldn't place the tone of his voice. Regret? Disappointment? Pity?

"Why?"

"Because you're her friend, and I'm worried about her."

I stared, unsure what to do with that information.

"Is that why you told your parents she was flunking classes?"

A faint flush climbed Finn's cheeks. "I didn't mean for it to be such a big deal. Please tell her to let it go. It's not worth…it's just not worth all this."

The last spark of anger faded. "I tried. She won't listen."

The door to the Millers' cottage banged open, and Finn and I both turned to see Leigh storm out.

"God," I winced. "At least your family isn't as dysfunctional as the Millers."

Finn frowned, his gaze trailing after Leigh. "I guess. Well, thanks for trying. I'm glad she has you still." He flashed a tight, awkward smile.

He backpedaled before pivoting and striding off down the path, leaving me confused at the foot of the stairs.

Sara had me, but did she want me? Lately it was hard to tell.

48

NOW

TUESDAY NIGHT. ONE YEAR AFTER.

The illumination of the porch light reaches over the rail and halfway across the stretch of water running past our cabin, but drops away into darkness before it can reach the trees on the opposite bank. The brush of moonlight adds texture to the woods, casting silver highlights over the leaves. This should be peaceful, but instead all I feel is loneliness.

It's almost midnight, and I have next to nothing written for tomorrow's memorial. My mind keeps drifting to Kelsey and Natalie. They're avoiding me. They hardly said anything through dinner, and when they came back to the cottage a couple hours ago, they hurried past me, whispering.

Not a good sign. I told them what happened to Sara—sort of—and it doesn't seem to have improved things between Kelsey and me. I have to fix things with my sister.

I have to write a speech. *I have to figure out the identity of the mystery girl*.

No. Focus, Mandy. I can't handle that right now.

I sigh and return to the electronic glow of my phone screen, rereading what I've painstakingly typed out into my notes app. Two little sentences are all I've managed to salvage from the unusable bits, and those that remain are shit. They could be about anybody.

Sara wasn't just anybody. We were... What were we? My finger hovers over what I've written.

Sara was an amazing friend *when she wanted to be. It's possible I was never a good friend*. *Deleted*. We spent two weeks every summer for the past six years at Highmark together, *and then I failed her so badly that there was no coming back from it*. *Deleted*. It's still hard for me to believe we won't have any more years of sitting by the lake, *or scratching and clawing at each other in the dirt*. *Deleted*. Or...

Or what? What can I say about Sara that isn't a superficial slap in the face to everyone listening? Every time I try to come up with a touching story to share, my brain short-circuits. The good memories hurt worse than the bad. They hurt so much I can't get a single one started.

All I have left is the pain.

Help me.

How does this help anyone?

My fingers curled in the mud and water seeped into my jeans.

I couldn't even tell my own sister the true story. The whole story.

"Mandy?"

I didn't hear the cottage door open, but Kelsey hovers with her hand on the knob.

"Can I sit?" she asks.

"Sure." My skin crawls with discomfort. Every detail I spilled to Kelsey is scorched into the space between us. Sure, she hadn't really watched me kill Sara, but I didn't exactly come off great in the recounting of my version either. What a disappointment for her, to finally get the explanation she was after and find out it still sucks.

Kelsey picks up the shoebox in the rocker next to me and sits. "What's this?" she asks, pulling the lid off without waiting for an answer.

I swallow a sigh. "Pictures from Sara's mom."

Kelsey picks up a stack and flips through them, and I hold my breath.

"Huh." Kelsey says. "Where are all the pictures of people?"

"What?"

She holds up a selfie of Sara and me standing by the firepit, with the lake and mountains in the background. Sara's face is half-turned toward mine, her tongue out and her nose scrunched. That was three years ago, but I can practically feel her arm draped across my sunburned shoulders. A breeze has lifted our hair to blow across us both, strawberry blond and honey-brown, and I'm smiling like I'll never frown again.

Wow, was I wrong.

"Are there any other photos with people in them? It seems like it's all nature shots and some pics of a puppy."

"There are other people in there," I say, frowning. Aren't there?

She shrugs. "Okay."

"That's weird," I mutter, more to myself than to Kelsey. No photos of her and all her friends from school? *She can't keep friends.* That's what Finn had said last summer. But that wasn't true, was it? Finn was just being a jerk.

Kelsey shuffles the pictures together and places them back in the box. "Well, you made the cut, at least," she says.

That is the *worst* thing she could've said. My stomach drops.

She sets the box on the porch and pulls her legs up into the chair with her. Her face gets terribly serious and I brace myself.

"I wish you'd told me about that night sooner," Kelsey blurts out, voice rising only a fraction above a whisper. "I wish you'd talked to me at all."

Oh. *Oh.* Somehow, even in trying to open up to her, I've misunderstood the heart of the problem.

"I should have paid more attention to you after last summer. Then I might've noticed how freaked out you were and realized you—you saw things you shouldn't have had to see. I don't have a good excuse. I wish I did." I chew at my lip for a while before saying softly, "You kept reaching out, even when you thought I killed her." Half question, half astonished statement.

"I knew there had to be more. There *had* to be." She says it with such ferocity the night crackles. "You wouldn't have killed her just because y'all were in a fight."

Her words are hauntingly familiar. I'd thought the same thing, the morning after. There had to be more. The mystery girl would come forward. She had to.

But she didn't, and I wasn't brave enough to go to the cops with my own version. It would've meant facing what I'd done, and going over it in detail that I didn't know if I could handle.

It's becoming increasingly obvious I can't handle the path I chose either, but I don't know how to undo it without making everything worse.

"I still shouldn't have hit her."

"But she choked you."

She did. But...

"True." ~~False~~. I look away to the trees.

"So it wasn't really your fault."

Oh, but it was, at least in part. My jaw clenches.

"Anyway, now that we know there was someone else there, Natalie's even more excited about the story. Did the other girl kill Sara on purpose? Why? And who is she? Or maybe it really was like the cops said... Maybe Sara was messing with the firework and did it herself, after you ran away." Her brow furrows. "But I doubt it. We're going to keep talking to people and see what else we can find."

"That's a terrible idea." A *dangerous* one. So why does a small terrified part of me perk up?

"There could be a killer out there who wasn't caught, and it wasn't *you*. We can't stop now."

"No," I say shortly. Every muscle in my body tenses for a fight, even if the fighting will be verbal. They can't do this. She can't do this. "Kelsey, this isn't some decades-old true crime. Sara's killer is out there, and what if it *is* someone still at Highmark? It has to be, right? A guest? A staff member? How do you think they're going to react to you and Natalie asking a ton of questions? With Natalie's videos getting more attention, it's too dangerous. You're going to get hurt." Or worse.

"I'm not afraid."

"You should be."

We stare at each other, caught on opposing sides of disaster's precipice. I'm not wrong, and I don't look away. I have to do better for Kelsey than I did for Sara.

Kelsey scowls and turns her gaze out over the water. When she stands to go inside, I catch her hand.

"Promise," I say. "You have to promise. I—you can't end up like Sara. You just *can't*, okay?"

"I'll talk to Natalie."

She notably didn't actually promise they'd stop, but I tell myself they will because otherwise worry will gnaw straight through my bones. I'll keep an eye on them, though, until I can figure out how to put a permanent stop to this.

Before I give up and go to bed I look once more at my notes app, and then delete everything. In place of the lackluster sentences, I punch out, SHE'S DEAD.

Because that's the truth, and everything else I could

say—anything about friendship or good times or love—feels too much like lying.

I should at least start being honest with myself.

Starting with what really happened that night.

49

THEN

WEDNESDAY NIGHT. THE DAY OF.

Sara loomed over me, her legs pinning me on either side. Her right hand captured my wrist, pinning it beside my head. I swiped at her face with my left. She dodged, but my fingers snagged on the necklace, and the chain broke with a snap and landed high on my belly. She put her forearm against my throat. I gagged and coughed, my eyes instantly watering. What the *fuck*?

"You're choking me," I wheezed, the words broken and incomplete.

She didn't let up.

She... Was she trying to kill me *again*?

I grabbed her hair and pulled. She gasped and eased up on my throat. She wasn't choking me anymore. I dragged in a ragged breath, relief washing through me, but she quickly caught my free hand and drove it into the dirt.

Her mouth curved. She'd better not laugh. It wasn't funny. It was cruel. She was cruel, and I hated her.

"Get off me," I snapped.

"Or what?"

I squirmed and pushed my lower body against her weight, but she didn't budge. A strangled, frustrated sound slipped out.

"Ooo help me, help me," Sara mocked, voice tinged with laughter. "Come on, Mandy. Fight me. I know you want to."

Her laughter carved angry lines through my skull. Hit her. Hit her.

But I couldn't, she had me pinned.

I took a breath and gritted out, "I'm sorry."

She rolled her eyes.

Bitch.

She let go of my wrists and sat back so that her weight settled on my hips. She pinched my stomach, but this time there was no pretense of playfulness. Pain rippled across my belly as my skin twisted. I gasped.

"You're supposed to be my friend," she said. "You're supposed to care if I'm fighting with my brother. And you're not supposed to go off to college a year early for some boy who, turns out, didn't even like you very much." She paused. "I don't think we should hang out anymore."

My face flushed hot with anger. She was dumping me—discarding our friendship like it meant *nothing*, because of Finn? Because of Dan? I mattered that little to her if I wasn't doing exactly what she wanted? I had to get away from her. *Now.*

I glared at her while my fingers curled around the rock. I glared at her while I said, "I hate you."

I glared at her while I smashed the rock into the side of her face.

Dirt rained down, bits landing in my mouth as I gulped in ragged breaths.

Her eyelids fluttered. She sagged to the side, and I scrambled out from under her, letting the rock slide out of my grasp. The necklace fell to the ground, beside the rock.

I blinked. My eyes stung with every movement—too many flecks of dirt in my contacts. I gritted my teeth.

Everything was one buzzing, sloshing swirl of alcohol and rage and shock. Had I really just hit her? She'd be fine. I wished she wouldn't be fine. Goddamn. No. I didn't wish that. Did I?

I sat and stared and waited for the fear and guilt to hit me.

She'd wake up soon.

What if she didn't?

She wasn't moving. Shit. Was that blood? Was she breathing? My eyes watered so badly it was hard to tell. Hissing, I removed my contacts and tucked them in my pocket. Better, but they still burned, and I still had to force myself to look at what I'd done. She was fine. Right?

My head and chest pounded, like either might explode at any second.

Part of me wanted to explode.

Implode.

Explode.

Inhale.

Exhale.

A high whine snaked up my throat. I clapped my hands over my lips.

I should call for help, shouldn't I? What if she needed a doctor? Of course she needed a doctor, her head was *bleeding*.

Out of the corner of my eye I could've sworn I saw a flash of light coming down the trail, but it disappeared.

I leaned closer to Sara. In the dark, with my contacts ruined and removed, I couldn't make out exactly where the blood was coming from. Her cheek? Her temple? Oh God. I was so screwed. What had I done?

My fingers brushed something cool and hard in the dirt beside us. The necklace.

Again, that flash of light.

Someone was coming.

The trees were too far away, and too dense. I'd make so much noise trying to hide in them, and then I'd be caught. No, oh shit, no that couldn't happen.

I snatched the necklace up and shoved it into my pocket as I ran to the lake, crawling with my hands sunk into the mud until I was hidden beneath the dock. My entire lower half was immediately soaked, my jeans clinging to my legs and fluffy mud sliding between my feet and my sandals. Twigs poked at my fingers. Tiny snail shells dug into my skin. I swallowed every gasp and held still.

The dock sat low over the water, with a small step up onto the boards. Through the narrow lumpy space between the wood and the earth, I could make out where Sara was sprawled several paces away.

I flattened myself, sinking deeper into the lake.

This was bad. Really, really bad. But she was fine. Sara was always fine. She'd sit up and blame me when it was her fault too, and then she'd laugh about how much trouble we'd be in for all this.

Somewhere not far away, a frog croaked loudly..

A figure appeared in the clearing, but the dock cut off everything above their midsection. I couldn't squeeze myself close enough to the opening to see any more. I squinted, but the angle was all wrong and my unaided vision was even worse than normal in the dark. Mud squished deeper into the crescent moons beneath my nails.

The new person made a sound, but with the lake water lapping at my earlobes and my pulse pounding inside my skull, the cramped space beneath the dock made it hard to tell anything about the voice. A girl? Maybe? The frog continued to drone on.

As they got closer to Sara, they stopped to pick something up off the ground. Okay. The newcomer was a girl, but she was facing away from me. Did she have brown hair? Dark blond? Was it short, or had it just been pulled up in a ponytail? Who *was* this intruder?

She nudged Sara with her foot.

"Get up," she said, but Sara didn't move.

Panic throbbed against the side of my neck, and my eyes watered. Why wasn't she getting up?

I couldn't see the source, but a pool of light flicked on and off. A lighter? She circled Sara. On and off.

What had Sara been doing without me? Who was this person that she apparently had a whole history with that I didn't know about?

A hot tear spilled down my cheek and dropped from my chin into the cool waters of the lake.

How could she—

Wait, *what*?

Sara sat up.

I could come out now, but an angry, petty, curious part of me refused to cooperate.

I stayed put.

Waiting.

50

NOW

WEDNESDAY AFTERNOON. ONE YEAR AFTER.

There are thirty or so people gathered on the side lawn for Sara's memorial. A wooden podium and the modest flower arrangements are set up in front of the firepit, and the sky is bright and clear.

A beautiful day for belated goodbyes.

I said goodbye once before, all alone and terrified.

Mrs. Ellis finishes speaking, and Finn takes her place at the podium.

Finn looks…rough. I can see why Mrs. Ellis would be worried about him. His hair, although trimmed, is wild, and his eyes skim over the crowd as if he's not seeing us.

When they land on me, though, they sharpen.

He clears his throat and I hold my breath.

"I can't believe I'm standing here to talk about Sara." His voice rasps, and he swallows. "I keep thinking she's going to pop up to tell me how I *should* be giving this speech. She always has an opinion—had an opinion—and was never afraid to share it. Not with anyone. It made her strong, and passionate, and honestly pretty annoying as a little sister." He laughs, but his face is terribly sad. Soft chuckles and one quiet sob ripple through the small crowd.

"But even when we were fighting over who had to take out the trash, or who got the last waffle, or…" He takes a long, deep breath. "Or fighting over bigger, more important things, I knew we'd get over it. And I knew she wanted the best for me, just like I wanted that for her. She was there to tell me things I didn't want to hear, but maybe needed to, and I never would've imagined that I'd be here without her."

He goes silent again, for long enough that there's anxious fidgeting rippling through the crowd. His gaze settles on me again, and he grips the sides of the podium. His forearms strain and his knuckles jut out sharply.

"A memorial feels like she's in the past, but she's not. And neither is what happened to her. Her killer was never caught, and there's someone out there who knows more than they're saying."

Several people gasp, and Mr. Ellis flinches. Mrs. Ellis takes a tentative step toward her son, as if she can ease him away from the spotlight and everyone will quietly forget what he just said.

Why isn't he looking away from me? My stomach drops as a few other faces cut toward me. They try to be subtle, but the shift is obvious.

They'd all seen the spray-painted message: MURDERER.

How many of them believe it?

Could Finn have done it? The message was left before Finn arrived, but what if he'd been here longer than I knew? I grind my teeth together. I'm getting paranoid. But if not Finn, who else besides Kelsey and Natalie wants to guilt me into ~~admitting confessing~~ saying I killed Sara?

Finn shakes his head. "My sister should be alive today, and it's unfair that she's not." Anger bleeds into his voice, thick and choking. "So unfair. That's it. That's all I've got."

He moves as if he's going to step away from the podium, but he pivots back to say one more thing.

"But I hear Mandy is speaking next, so maybe *she* can enlighten us."

Shit.

51

NOW

WEDNESDAY AFTERNOON. ONE YEAR AFTER.

If I could've crumbled into a pile of dirt and let the grass bury me, I would have. My cheeks flame. Mom's fingers brush my arm, and I think she might have said my name, but it's like I'm losing time. I'm supposed to be headed up to the podium right now.

Now.

Now!

But my feet won't move. Mr. and Mrs. Ellis can't really want me to get up in front of everyone after what Finn said, right? Ah, yes. Good. Mrs. Ellis takes Finn's place and smiles at everyone. She'll say something to smooth things over and close out the memorial, and I'll be spared.

"I know Sara would've been so touched at how much her brother misses her. It's hard to be here without our sweet, smart, passionate Sara with us. It's hard for all of us."

Oh no. She's glossing right over Finn's final

sentiment—pretending nothing happened. I glance around at the shifting crowd and discover there's a widening circle of space around me. Only Mom and Dad and Kelsey and Natalie are still within arm's reach.

Sara's brother, eyes glassy with anger, had insisted I might know how Sara died.

He's not wrong, but still.

I should never have agreed to come to this, much less speak.

"Mandy?" Mrs. Ellis waves me forward.

"You're okay, honey," Mom murmurs and gives my arm a squeeze that ends with a small nudge.

The crowd parts, and I drag myself to the front, like moving through thick mud. A lot of faces turn toward me without actually looking directly at me. Their eyes dart to Finn. Or flick down to their shoes. Or stare just slightly off-center.

My legs could go out from under me at any moment. This is hell, and the only way out is forward.

I clear my throat and nudge my glasses up the bridge of my nose. Get it over with and get out. I can do this.

"Hello," I rasp, shriveled and shaky. I try again. "I'm Mandy, for those who don't know me, and Sara was a good friend of mine." Mom and Dad stare at me: Mom with her hands clutched to her chest and Dad with pity creeping onto his face.

Kelsey stands with her head resting against Natalie's shoulder. There's a small amount of comfort in the fact that neither of them appears to have a phone out. Maybe Kelsey really did manage to convince Natalie to stop her crusade to share Sara's story.

Toward the back of the crowd, Alex and Hannah stand with a few of the other people who work here. Even Leigh has showed up, sitting on the retaining wall of the bar patio. She doesn't look impressed. If anything she looks bored, and as stuck-up as always.

This is absurd. Tomorrow we'll barbecue and kayak and watch fireworks like Sara wasn't found dead with half her face mangled a year ago.

People shift uncomfortably. I haven't spoken in too long. I have to get through this. Say the words. Show my parents I'm fine and can be mature about a tragedy I helped cause. Everything else can wait.

"I've thought a lot about what we lost when Sara died." Murdered. She was murdered and I know that, and it sounds like Finn's convinced he knows that too. "We lost a bright light who made everything more exciting, more special. I was so lucky to be her friend."

52

THEN

TWO YEARS AGO.

Laid out on the floating dock at the edge of the roped-off portion of the lake, Sara nudged my foot with hers. "Hey."

I cracked an eye and turned my head enough to squint at her. Our wet hair fanned around us, a few strands tangling in the middle. "Hm?"

"Who's your best friend?"

I frowned. "Like, at home?"

She hesitates.

"Sure. Yeah."

I shrugged, my shoulder blades jutting against the wooden planks. "I don't really have one best friend. Why?"

Her eyelids fluttered, like the sun was in her eyes, but a passing cloud shadowed us. "But none of them would…" She pauses and her mouth twists. "They don't act one way around you in a situation and then different in another? Like you're just friends, always. Right?"

It was such an odd question. My answer came out strangely high-pitched. "What? I mean, yes. My friends are... normal."

Her cheek twitched and she rolled her head to stare up at the sky.

I nudged her foot, like she'd done to me a moment before. "Did something happen? Do I need to tell you all the ways you're awesome and don't have to put up with shitty friends?" I ventured a grin, hoping to lighten the mood even though I was dead serious.

The sound of water slapping against the underside of the dock filled the quiet until she sat up, propping herself on her hands to stare down at me. A smile replaced the worried pinch, and she said, "Nothing happened. I don't know why I asked. But yes, please, tell me all the ways I'm amazing."

I rattled off a long list. It was easy.

53

NOW

WEDNESDAY AFTERNOON. ONE YEAR AFTER.

I blink into the expectant faces of the memorial-goers. Two summers ago, I hadn't realized what Sara was really asking. *Was it normal for your friends to gaslight you? To betray you? To cut you out when it helped their social standing?* No. Or, no, it shouldn't have been. I hate that Sara had to ask, and even more, I hate that somewhere along the way I stopped thinking all those nice things and started to see her as my enemy.

I hadn't realized, hadn't asked, exactly how much she was struggling.

The shoebox full of photos but only a handful with actual people.

Finn's comments last year, about her inability to keep friends.

The boyfriend who she said she dumped, but did she, or did he break up with her?

What did I *really* know about Sara outside of Highmark?

"She brought out the best in me during our summers together." And the worst. How deftly she brought out the worst, like peeling back all the good layers to reveal the rotten core. "She showed me I could stand up for myself"—though she didn't mean to—"and encouraged me to be brave."

My throat closes. I did everything wrong.

Even if we hadn't stayed friends after last summer, I still should have saved her life.

I may have failed Sara, betrayed her in every possible way when it mattered, but I can be better now, can't I? Back then, I was too wrapped up in what she was to *me*, instead of who she was as a person, and look where that got us.

I won't keep making the same mistake with Kelsey. I have to be there for her, the way *she* needs.

And I have to *protect* her.

"I'll always treasure the memories of scavenger hunts and kayak races, ice cream from the Snack Shack and card games in the lounge." She really did want so much out of life but she's dead now. Murdered.

And someone wants to make sure the whole resort is looking at me for the crime. MURDERER, spray-painted where it couldn't be ignored.

Who are you?

I scan the faces of the crowd.

Where are you?

54

THEN

THREE YEARS AGO.

"You're killing me, Mandy," Sara groaned.

I shoved her shoulder, but I shoved harder than I meant to, and she went staggering sideways with a shrill cry.

"Eek! Hey, not cool," she said, laughing as she regained her balance.

"You brought it on yourself."

"By asking whether you finally hooked up with Dan yet? You could have, you know, answered me instead." She waggled her eyebrows. "Come on, spill. Did you get with him or not?"

I was deeply regretting texting her to hype me up before the house party two weeks ago. I'd figured her enthusiasm would be enough to push me to make a move. I'd been right. But…

"We made out."

"I hear a *but* in there?" She eyed me suspiciously.

I shrugged. "We've been texting, but we're not like... together."

"Why not? Do you want to be together, or are you just having fun?" She'd stopped walking to give me her full attention, and I blushed under the intensity of her stare. "Well?" she pressed when I didn't answer.

I grinned. "I definitely want to make out with him again."

"And dating?"

"Maybe."

She nodded. "Well then text him. Right now. Something flirty. That way you can see how you feel while you're here and do whatever you want when you get home."

"I—"

"Don't overthink it, Mandy." She stepped close and slung her arm around my shoulders. She gave a soft, playful pinch on my upper arm. "You're gorgeous and smart, and *anyone* would be lucky for even a *crumb* of your interest."

I blushed even harder.

"Come on, you can do it. I believe in you," she said.

I leaned into her side and bumped her hip with mine. She was so good at getting me outside my comfort zone. "I'll text him tonight. And what about you? How's Matt?"

Her smile wilted. "He's fine. Okay, now tell me *exactly* what you're going to text Dan."

55

NOW

WEDNESDAY AFTERNOON. ONE YEAR AFTER.

She'd been broken up with Matt and *then* Nathan by the following year. She never told me what happened between her and Nathan, and I hadn't asked.

My eyes burn and my nose prickles as my brain gets caught in a loop. I grit my teeth and force the inner monologue to shut up. "I wish Sara was still here with me for all the little things, and the big things that she'll miss out on. I was lucky to have a friend like her for as long as I did, and I hope somewhere out there, she knows that."

I do. I really, really do. But it's probably just wishful thinking.

I step away from the podium and spot Alex, still hovering at the edge of the crowd with Hannah. Leigh has disappeared. Alex waves at me, but she whispers something in his ear, and the sympathetic tilt of his mouth disappears. A spark of anger, and fear, coils in my chest. What is she saying to him?

As Mr. and Mrs. Ellis reclaim the podium, Finn appears at Alex's side. Hannah moves to put herself closer to Finn. They draw close, obviously in conversation, and a horrified voice in my head insists they're talking about me. They probably *are* talking about me. Hannah's been rude as hell since I got here, and Finn is clearly suspicious of me.

Alex shakes his head and gives me a strange look, but Finn grabs his arm and leads him away, with Hannah trailing behind.

My stomach hurts as sadness spills through me. They'll turn Alex against me. Make him hate me too.

How do I keep that from happening? There has to be something I can do.

Because I'm done losing people.

56

THEN

WEDNESDAY NIGHT. THE DAY OF.

Water kissed my chin, and dampness settled in my lungs with each shallow breath. The faint scent of decay wafted from the muddy banks. A sharp pain pierced the place between my shoulders. But none of that was important.

Watching Sara squirm was all that mattered. A bitter, jealous, eager spark fixed my eyes on her and the girl. If there was no point in including me—if I *ruined* things—then fine. She didn't think we should be friends anymore, so let's see how this would turn out for her.

I would watch Sara's perfect summer crumble.

Sara sat forward, her arms hanging over her bent knees, and looked up at the other girl. I wished I could see higher than the girl's waist, but I'd have to come out from under the dock for a clear view, and…no. Then this would stop, whatever *this* was, and I had to know how it would end.

I kept my breathing quiet and listened.

"What—hell happened—you?" The girl's voice was barely loud enough, but if I concentrated really hard, I could get the gist.

What the hell happened to you. Shit. Here it was. Sara would tell her that I bashed her face with a rock. And she'd tell her parents too. I was going to be in so much trouble, and Sara would just love that. She could hold this over my head for ages.

Nearby, thunder rolled.

Sara groaned and wiped her hand across her cheek. Her hand came away dark with blood. Wet, matted hair clung limp to her shoulders.

I'd bloodied her, and with a pang of revulsion I found I *still* wasn't sorry. Not like I should have been. I was worried, but not sorry. She'd picked at me like I was a scab she could peel off, discard, and then repeat the process all over again when my need to be with her regrew. Always thicker, wider, and the wound got deeper every time.

But you can't pick a scab without bleeding too.

I watched, and I tried to hear, but I was too afraid of—

Of—

Interrupting—

To come out from where I hid beneath the dock.

"Hellooo?" the girl demanded, louder. "Sara—face?"

Who the hell was she? It was so hard to make out the voice, with the echo of the water swirling around my head and all the freakin' wildlife. Freakin' frog. Freakin' thunder.

"Oh," Sara said, slowly, like she'd forgotten about the question. She swayed. "Nothing.–fine."

Sara was facing my direction. It made her easier to hear, but barely.

"Whatever. I don't—about that.—need to undo—you told Finn. Tonight. You—everything—and you are going to *fix*. *It*."

The person's voice raised at the end, ragged with anger. I blinked hard, piecing together the fragments. Sara and Finn and this girl were fighting about something. Ha! I knew I'd been right not to get more involved in Sara's arguments with her brother. The fighting was spreading. To Alex. To me. To this mystery girl.

And Sara was the poison at the center of it all.

That wasn't fair.

I didn't care.

I swallowed and shifted carefully in the shallow water, but with each minute that passed, the liquor we'd been drinking made it harder to keep my vision clear and things were… sliding. The harder I tried to hold still, the dizzier I got.

The croaking frog wasn't helping.

Water sloshed into my ears again. Ugh.

"No," Sara said. "That's not my problem—me alone."

"It's your fault," the new girl said, harsher. The voice still seemed familiar, but it was so muffled that I couldn't place it.

Sara tilted her head and the movement made the blood-painted side of her face gleam. She hadn't gotten up from the ground yet. Maybe she couldn't. Maybe she was dizzy too. She was definitely losing blood. I swallowed.

"What's my fault?" When Sara spoke, the words were

tinged with confusion, like she wasn't quite following the conversation. Concussion? No...no I hadn't...no. She was just drunk.

"—broke up—me. He said you were—and harassing him—us, but that you might be right,—needed to—"

The wind picked up, whistling as it rushed beneath the dock and bringing with it the scent of pine and the oncoming storm. The rustle of the trees and the lap of the lake along the shore ate away at her words, until there wasn't enough left for me to guess at. I caught, "You got in his head," at the end.

Sara's head dipped, then snapped back up. She was drunk, that was why. Definitely not the head wound or the blood loss. "—don't give a shit. Y'all were never going to work anyway. I just—Finn see what a joke you and him were."

"No we aren't!" she shouted. So, so shrill. No human was supposed to sound *that* screechy.

Again, that burst of light, on and off, adding faint illumination to the dark ground in a pool.

"*Weren't*," Sara corrected.

In a tight voice, like the girl was snarling through clenched teeth, she said, "You—what you're—about—turned him against me—you're selfish and jealous of him—you have nothing. He tells me when—together—how much more your parents expect of him—he's going places, and you're— And—feels bad—because no one likes—"

You. I was sure she'd said *you.* I swallowed the guilt. Sara brought this on herself.

"You're not better than me. You're gross," Sara snapped.

My skin prickled, and a small quiet voice at the back of my head said to give it up and come out. Sara would mock me for hiding, and I'd be caught in the middle of this mess, but something was wrong.

Several things were wrong, and they were getting worse, fast.

The faint light flickered over the ground, and disappeared with a snap.

On, off.

There one second, gone the next.

I didn't come out. I stayed beneath the rotting boards, watching through the small gap and falling deeper into the unfolding argument as surely as I was sinking into the mud.

57

NOW

WEDNESDAY AFTERNOON. ONE YEAR AFTER.

There are a few other people in the lounge after the memorial—an older couple with matching snowy white hair, a man sitting at the bar sipping a coffee, two women chatting in the corner—but everyone seems to be giving the Ellises space.

Even Kelsey and Natalie ran off, which is suspicious in a way I can't quite pinpoint. Then again, I might've run off too, but Mom had tucked her arm through mine and practically dragged me along. I'd been in an armchair, blinking at Mr. and Mrs. Miller sitting on the couch across from me before I'd had a chance to consider protesting.

"That was nice," Mom says, handing Mrs. Ellis a glass of wine.

Mrs. Ellis nods, but I catch the brief flick of her eyes in my direction. Searching. I recoil.

"I'm glad we were able to put it together. Thank you,

Eric. You didn't have to do that, and we really appreciate it. The flowers were beautiful," Mrs. Ellis says.

Mrs. Miller, sitting right next to her husband, forces her scowl into a smile. The effect is…unpleasant. How much of the memorial did Mr. Miller actually handle, and how much was eager-to-please wife number two?

"It was my pleasure," Mr. Miller says.

There was nothing pleasant about the memorial. My skin still crawls from the memory of all those eyes on me. What were he and Alex talking about? Our ruined alibi? Were they telling Hannah now too?

"It was no problem," Mrs. Miller cuts in. "Anything to help. And is Finn all right? I saw him leave with a couple of our off-duty staff. I hope they didn't drag him away when he should've stayed here with family." Mrs. Miller shakes her head. "I can text Hannah and let her know his parents are looking for him, if you'd like."

Her need to be helpful is so uncomfortable. I shrink as deep into the armchair as possible.

Mrs. Ellis frowns—a soft, delicately displeased pout. "No. No that's all right. He's fine."

Sara's dad stares off toward the patio doors. His frown is tired. Lost. Finn had always been their perfect kid. I'm not sure the Ellises know how to cope with him being anything else. But then, what was it Virginia said? It's okay to be sad, and Finn has every reason to be a mess.

"Wine, anyone? Red?" Dad asks, rising from his chair.

"Please," Mr. Ellis says.

"Me too," Mrs. Miller adds.

If only. I reach for my phone since no one is paying attention to me anyway. What have Kelsey and Natalie gotten up to? I should text—

"Ah! Leigh, come sit," Mr. Miller calls, and I twist in my seat to see her frozen, halfway through the door exiting into the rest of the lodge.

She looks like a deer in the headlights, if that deer were very, very annoyed at the oncoming car. Her dad scoots on the couch to make room for her between him and her stepmom. If Leigh is making any effort at all to hide her feelings on the invitation, then she's a terrible actress. She wears a deep scowl as she settles between Mr. and Mrs. Miller and whips out her phone.

Dad returns with the promised glasses just as Leigh looks at me and says, "You know if Sara hadn't saved you from that whole drowning thing last year, it might've been your memorial going viral instead. Although, you're pretty much the focus anyway."

I blink, but no words form. Why am *I* the focus? What have they done now? Should I run? I could run.

"What are you talking about, Leigh?" Mr. Miller asks, leaning over to peer at her phone.

"Natalie's posted a video of uhhh…part of Finn's speech. It's getting tons of views and comments." She grimaces at me.

"Let me see," her dad growls.

My mom's face has gone very, very pale.

"Sure, *Dad*," Leigh says pointedly, turning to block her

stepmom's view as she shows Mr. Miller the screen. Mrs. Miller makes a sound like someone's strangling a gull, but she clears her throat and paints a decent attempt at neutral on her face.

"Leigh, I can't see," she says.

Leigh ignores her, and Mrs. Miller stands to see the phone now clutched in her husband's hand. My parents and Sara's all draw closer.

I don't need to see. *"Mandy is speaking next, so maybe she can enlighten us."* That'll be the part Natalie posted, for sure.

Leigh kicks her feet up on the coffee table, tapping the toes of her canvas sneakers together.

"I can't hear anything. How do we hear?" Mr. Miller asks. Annoyance saturates every word as his volume climbs.

Leigh presses the volume button and Finn's voice fades in, *"enlighten us."*

Called it.

"And Finn's not totally wrong," Natalie's voice comes on. *"Because I finally got Mandy to open up, and let's just say soon, we'll have an eyewitness account of what really happened to Sara that night. The true story. Or, the true-crime story. Get ready. The next CrimeChatWithNat will be wild."*

Mom screeches. Honest-to-God screeches. "Mandy?" She shouts my name even though I don't think she means to. "What is she talking about? What does she mean by 'eyewitness'?"

I shake my head so hard my vision wobbles. "I don't

know!" Liar, liar, my life's on fire. "I swear. I never said anything like that. I swear!"

"If you know something—"

"I don't!" My voice breaks.

"Mandy…" Dad warns, but all I can do is keep shaking my head.

Mom clutches her hands together as if she can crush the terrible thoughts that way. "Did you know what they were doing? You can't encourage dangerous rumors like that. You never know what the internet will do with lies. And it's just cruel. I didn't think you would—after everything—" she can't even get a full sentence out by the end.

How could Kelsey and Natalie do this? Did they really not think eventually people here would find out?

Mom bends to rub Mrs. Ellis's knee. Sara's mom shakes her head silently, with her fingers pressed to her lips. Mr. Miller seems to be barely resisting the urge to throw the phone, and his wife's wide-eyed gaze is bouncing from one person to the next, unsuccessfully searching for a safe place to look. She settles on her lap.

Leigh is the only one who seems unbothered. Is that a hint of a sneer tugging at Leigh's lips? Is she *enjoying* this? *How* is she enjoying this?

Dad's face reddens, and the muscles in his neck jump. "Shit," he grits out. "I don't know what the girls were thinking. Charlotte, James, we are so sorry. You too, Eric. We'll talk to them. This won't happen again."

Leigh continues tapping her feet. A faint smudge of

red—paint?—coats the hexagonal rubber sole of her left shoe.

MURDERER, like aerosolized blood on slate.

She reaches over and plucks her phone out of her dad's hand. "Gotta go," she says into the stunned, awkward silence that's settling over our little group.

MURDERER, the message left in the dark so I couldn't face my accuser.

I slide out of my chair and follow her through the patio doors.

I can face her now.

58

NOW

Leigh climbs the three steps up from the sunken patio onto the gravel path. In front of her, the firepit and grassy yard overlook the water. She turns right.

Where's she going?

"Hey!" I call, storming after her.

She jumps and turns around, a moment of fear flashing across her face.

"You off to find more *spray paint*?" I hiss.

"I don't know what you're talking about," she says and turns, veering toward her family's cottage.

I quicken my pace and catch up with her.

"I saw the paint stain on your shoe."

She slows, and after a harsh exhale she turns.

"And? I spray-painted your walkway. So what?"

"Why?" I ask. I knew Leigh never liked Sara or me very much, but I didn't realize she hated me enough to call me a murderer for the whole resort to see. I try to remember instances where I'd misread our interactions, but all I can come up with are snippets of her showing up when Sara and I were hanging out, not saying much, and leaving—often mid-conversation. We'd decided *years* ago that it was better to let her do her own thing, since she so clearly wanted nothing to do with us.

Leigh throws her hands up and inches away from me. "I don't know. I was high, okay? And your sister and her friend started bugging me from the minute they got here. I wanted to embarrass my dad and that woman. And your sister's friend, talking about Sara on her channel was too perfect."

"Really? You threw me under the bus to piss off your parents?" My voice is a cringe-inducing pitch. Squeaky. Breathy. Not maintaining my cool *at all*.

"Not my parents. My dad, and his wife." She nearly gags on the last word.

An inarticulate, frustrated sound slips out of my mouth. Leigh snorts.

"Did you always hate us this much?" I ask.

Her brows lift, and her voice is heavy with skepticism. "Really?"

"Yes."

"Of course not. I tried to be y'all's friend. The summer I started coming here instead of camp I actually hung out with you *several* times."

She waits, as if I'll suddenly remember all the good times, but nothing comes.

She laughs. "Typical. Well the two of you ignored me, so I gave up. Guess it's a good thing I did…"

"I didn't kill her."

Leigh's eyes widen.

"I didn't say you did. Oh. Okay, yes I did, with the spray paint, but not just now. Look, I'm sorry you're mad but it was just a note on a path," she says, sarcasm thick and chin tipped up so she's looking slightly down her ski-slope nose at me. Short dark hair haloes her face. "You're not going to *die* over a word."

There's a loud, wordless scream pressing against my chest. If I open my mouth, it will burst, and I'm not sure I'll ever stop.

I turn on my heels and storm back to the cottage, slamming every door in my path until I'm safe in my room.

I let Sara die over and over, and deep down everyone knows it. Leigh. Kelsey and Natalie. Alex? Mr. and Mrs. Ellis. The Millers. Finn. Hannah.

I bury my face in my pillow and scream, but I swear I can feel sharp, swift pinches roaming over my exposed arms.

Sara knows it too.

59

NOW

WEDNESDAY AFTERNOON. ONE YEAR AFTER.

Mom and Dad are *deep* into chewing Kelsey and Natalie out over the video, explaining all the possible ways what they did was inappropriate. Well, Mom's doing most of the explaining. Dad's running backup.

Do they realize I'm in here, eavesdropping? The door is shut, but these walls aren't thick, and Mom's voice carries. Also, I'm pressed up against the door, listening at the crack.

"It's great to have hobbies," Mom says, "but it's not fair to put those interests over how the people directly affected feel. Do you understand?"

Kelsey and Natalie's murmured acknowledgments filter in from the other room.

Dad's voice is gruff, like he'd rather be yelling. "James isn't okay with the idea of seeing Sara back in the news, and Charlotte is worried that this isn't good for Finn. Or for you girls either—"

"But Mom," Kelsey protests, drawing the words out into a whine. "Natalie isn't—"

"Kelsey, stop it," Dad cuts her off. "This is serious. You two implied Mandy witnessed what happened to Sara. Do you understand how bad that is? That would mean she lied to the cops, or worse, that—" He cuts himself off. "It's dangerous."

My fingers go numb where they're braced against the door.

"It was just for more views," Kelsey says, softly.

I exhale a sharp breath of relief. She's not going to tell our parents what I said. The tiniest of silver linings.

"That's not an excuse for saying something like that online," Mom says. "You and Natalie could get Mandy in serious trouble. And the Ellises are really hurt seeing Finn and the memorial used for attention. How do you think Finn would feel seeing that?"

I chewed my lip. How would Finn feel? He probably did see it, but he wasn't exactly hiding his feelings on his sister's death or that I knew more than I'd said. Would he be upset that Natalie put part of his speech online, or would he be glad?

"You girls need to be more careful, and respectful. Imagine someday there's a case, and a killer, and you go advertising all this information and your location. Can you tell me why that might be dangerous?"

Oof. Mom has entered the vaguely condescending phase of guilt-tripping. I don't envy Kelsey and Natalie, though they brought this on themselves. Mom's right. I'd told them someone else was with Sara when she died and they still thought it was a good idea to poke that murderous wasp nest with a stick. Horrible plan.

But as much as Mom presses them, and as much as they murmur reluctant agreement, I've learned better than to trust them.

"Natalie, we need you to remove the video," Mom says. "It's not acceptable to leave up."

"Mommm," Kelsey pleads.

"Absolutely not, Kelsey," Dad says. "The video comes down, or we'll cut this vacation short."

"I'm sorry, Mr. and Mrs. Jenkins." Natalie's voice trembles. "I'll take it down. I didn't know how mad it would make everyone."

She might take down that video temporarily, but Mom and Dad are clueless if they think Natalie's going to permanently delete it.

"Good. Thank you," Dad says.

"Can we go?" Kelsey is definitely pouting.

"Yes, you can go," he says.

I backpedal from the door, but the external door slams a moment later.

They've left.

Good.

That gives me the time I need.

60

NOW

WEDNESDAY AFTERNOON. ONE YEAR AFTER.

It doesn't take me long to find the notebook I'd discovered that first afternoon, before I knew anything about Natalie or her true-crime obsession, or the fact that Kelsey was convinced she'd watched me kill Sara.

The first page has a few additional notes added. Virginia has been added to the list as "neighbor," and "old bird-watching lady." There are a couple names I recognize from the staff party.

Interesting, but not helpful. I need to know who Natalie and Kelsey have been talking to and figure out how to get them to let me in. Let me help. Whether or not they have to hide the channel from Mom and Dad, I'd bet almost anything they're not going to stop investigating. Which means I have to get ahead of them. Whoever else was there in the clearing that night, she's not going to be happy with all the questions and social media attention.

And what if she believes what Natalie said, about me being a witness?

Oh. Oh, *God*. Are we all in danger if she's here and thinks I've said too much to Kelsey and Natalie? Killers aren't generally big fans of leaving witnesses. Kelsey and Natalie are in way over their heads.

I'm in way over my head.

The next several pages are on Sara's case and the initial news coverage. There are lots of notes, and I'm sure there are more in Natalie's phone. She is *thorough*. I pore through them, morbidly fascinated and hating myself for every single line I read. I *know* all this. I tortured myself with it in the months following her death.

But I can't keep letting my sister put herself in danger. I let Sara die ~~I caused her death~~, and I can't live with watching it unfold all over again. I have to piece together what I saw and what I heard that night, and figure out who else was there, fast. If I can tell Kelsey and Natalie that I know who lit the firework and offer them a full interview with me after we leave Highmark, that might keep them safe while we're here. As long as they don't post anything else, or ask any more questions, we might be okay.

My legs, folded beneath me, fall asleep, and I untuck one leg at a time until I'm sitting V-style. I also kind of have to pee, but they could come back at any moment. I need to keep reading.

Wait.

This page is different. I lean closer, as if pressing my

face directly into the ink and paper will enable me to absorb Natalie's scratchy handwriting instantly.

Finn's name is scribbled across the top, and below, Natalie has written several bulleted notes.

- Was at college in Georgia. Dropped out, living at home. Get more info about what he's doing now. Wouldn't say much at first. After I told him we thought there was more to Sara's death than a "firework accident," he was into it. Wanted to know what we knew, who we were asking questions. Really wanted to know if Mandy had said anything to us yet.

I blink, my mouth hanging open. Finn dropped out of school? A fresh pang of guilt and sadness for Sara's brother tightens my chest. He'd been so excited about college, but then so had I, before everything went wrong. Before *I* made everything go wrong.

I keep reading.

- Getting here Tuesday. Maybe Monday.
- Account Sara_0078. Check for any DMs.
- Wants to talk to Mandy himself but agreed to wait. We can figure out what she knows. Seems like he blames Mandy, or is suspicious? idk if he knows more, like Kelsey. Super sad about Sara, supports channel. Will talk to us once here. Maybe vid. Need to convince.

A dull throb forms in the center of my forehead as I frown harder than I've ever frowned in my entire life. Has Finn been *working* with them? At least in part?

Suddenly it clicks—how Natalie seemingly bypassed her rule not to cover cases without family support. Finn agreed.

There's a gross, crawling sensation moving down my arms, and I want to fling the notebook away and shake off the feeling of having been…manipulated? Deceived? I don't know, but it feels weird knowing that they've been in contact with Finn. And if he knew about the false alibi from Alex, why didn't he tell Natalie?

I flip to the next page, but it's not about Finn. My breaths come shallower and shorter with each second as I scan the remainder of the notebook, searching for more. There. Finn's name in a nearly full page of comments, and then again on the next.

They've been meeting with him here. Maybe more than once. I chew my lip. They didn't tell me any of this, which means Kelsey still doesn't trust me. And the more my sister talks to someone like Finn, or Hannah, the harder it's going to be to convince her to let me back into her life.

I return my attention to the page to see what he's said, but the front door opens, and I only have a couple seconds to jam the notebook back into Natalie's bag and scramble to my feet before Kelsey and Natalie storm into the room.

Their scowls tell me they're still mad about Mom and Dad's scolding.

Kelsey strides to her bed and flings herself face down onto the freshly remade bed's cotton quilt.

A garbled "arghhhh" spills from my sister.

Natalie leans against the dresser, face caught somewhere between a pout and a frown. She's got a half-drunk bottle of Sprite in one hand and a cookie in the other. I guess they went for snacks to fuel their scheming.

Kelsey flops onto her back and swings her feet, rattling the bed frame.

"What now?" she asks, staring at the ceiling.

"I don't know. Honestly, we can keep digging, and I'll wait to post until we leave."

I *knew* it.

And that option still means they'll be running around asking questions about a murderer who could be anyone that might've been hooking up with Finn last summer. Who? I should know this. I would know this, if I'd been paying attention to anyone except Sara.

Or if I'd agreed to help Sara with getting back at her brother.

Who was Finn hanging around with last summer? Me and Sara, Alex, but we're off the list. I already know my role, and I know it wasn't Alex. Hannah was with us a lot last year, hanging out around the firepit together. Could've been her, though she'd had a serious boyfriend. Whatever happened to him? Leigh's next door, so it would've been easy for them to sneak around. And she did spray-paint "murderer" on our walkway. But it's a big jump from vandalism to spite your parents to killing someone. Still…

Who else? There was a girl that worked the front desk of the main lodge, who I saw him talking to once or twice, but he never stayed at the desk *too* long. Not that I knew of.

I can't ask Finn, because I'm probably the last person he'd tell about his personal business. He'd be a lot more likely to interrogate *me* instead. And I can't tell Finn why I'm asking without admitting I watched his sister die and then stayed silent about it all year. But Alex might know. I could ask him, unless he's with Finn.

I run my hands over the backs of my thighs and clear my throat.

"I think I know who killed Sara." Sort of. I have a place to start.

Natalie whips her head around to face me, and Kelsey rises like a damn zombie from her reclined position.

"I knew it!" Natalie shouts, before clamping her fingers over her mouth. When she lowers her hand, she hisses, "I *knew* it."

Kelsey stares, but I can't read the look on her face. "So… you've been lying to me. Again." She frowns. "Still."

I'm literally lying right now. This exact second. Because I don't actually know who killed Sara, but I have to let her believe I do, until I can find out for sure.

"I'm sorry, Kelsey. But you and Natalie posted a whole video claiming I was going to be some big eyewitness on her channel without even talking to me first, so, we're all not great in this situation, okay? Besides, I really wasn't sure, but I think I know now, and if y'all will please, please just let me talk to a couple people, I can get the answer. But I'm only going to do it if you two promise not to talk to anyone else in the meantime. I'm serious. It's not safe, and Mom and Dad are right, you could get hurt. Or killed."

Natalie goes to the closet. After rummaging through a bag, she turns around with something cradled in her hands. It takes my brain several seconds to make sense of what she's holding, and when I do, my breath catches.

She's holding a gun.

61

NOW

WEDNESDAY AFTERNOON. ONE YEAR AFTER.

"Holy shit! Is that a gun?" I ask. An absolutely ridiculous question. Although…maybe not so ridiculous. It's a burnt red color, not metallic black. "Where did you get a *gun*?"

"It's not a real gun," Natalie says. "It's a flare gun. We found it in the storage at the back of the Snack Shack while we were looking for scavenger hunt items. So don't worry about us. We can protect ourself with this if we have to. You thought it was real. Should be good enough."

Highmark needs to do a better job of locking doors.

"But it's a real flare gun. It could still hurt someone, or hurt y'all. And also…no! No, oh my God, you can't be serious? If you need that type of protection, things are very, very bad." What am I supposed to do about this? The previously dull headache grows sharper, spreading through my skull.

Kelsey's mouth thins. "Are you going to tell Mom and Dad?"

I should. But also…if I tell our parents, Kelsey is going to be pissed at me all over again. I can't be the crappy big sister who shows up only to snitch. There's no way she'd trust me after that, and I need her to trust me, or the deal I want to make won't work.

"No. But swear you'll leave it here. You won't need it if you let me find out who killed Sara for you. Stay out of it, and I'll get us answers."

Natalie puts the flare gun back in the closet.

"And what happens when you get that answer?" Natalie challenges.

I glance back and forth between them, Natalie with her eager eyes and Kelsey with her hurt ones.

"I'll tell you what I find out on Saturday, right before we leave."

Natalie scowls, clearly having already abandoned her resolution not to post more videos while at Highmark.

"And?" Kelsey asks.

My brows raise. "And what?"

"And if you find out who killed Sara, are you going to go to the police?"

Cold unfurls in my stomach and a shiver jolts up my spine. The thought of actually going to the police and admitting all the lies that I thought kept me safe—but really just let a different kind of nightmare devour me—is too big. Too permanent.

What if they reopen the case, and I end up taking the blame? There was evidence of me, me and Sara and violence, *everywhere.* The ease of blaming it on reckless teens and a partying accident, combined with Sara's parents not wanting to endure the pain of fighting with the cops to keep the case open, saved me once. How would an investigation play out now, if they were pushed into calling it what it was: a murder? Even if I find the mystery girl from that night, who's going to trust the girl that already lied *so much*?

"I don't know," I said. "But I promise to tell you. And when we're away from this place and *safe*, I'll do that video Natalie promised on her channel, for real." If the cops take it seriously and come around asking questions, I'll deal with the fallout then.

There's a pause—please take the deal, please—and then Kelsey says, "Done."

"Awesome," Natalie adds, grinning so broadly her eyes crinkle.

Justice for Sara, who I failed. Closure for Kelsey, who I abandoned. All for the unsavory price of confronting what I'd worked so hard to repress all year. Great.

62

NOW

THURSDAY AFTERNOON. ONE YEAR AFTER.

"Here," I wave Kelsey and Natalie over to one of the yellow kayaks lined up along the muddy launch area behind the Snack Shack. A few friends and family members mill around the shaded grassy area, but most guests who are down to watch the race are laid out on the sandy beach or watching from the dock in front of the Shack.

Natalie hops up front, while Kelsey slides into the seat behind her. The boats are old, with dinged-up plastic curving over the front and back ends. Kelsey plucks several dead leaves out from around her seat as she gets situated.

"Thanks," Kelsey says. She smiles like she means it, and I grin back, giving the nose of the kayak a shove.

"Gooo Kelsey! Go Natalie," I holler, which causes everyone gathered to jump and stare at me.

"Ignoring you," Kelsey groans.

"Good luck," I shout back as their paddles slice into the still waters.

The boat glides out over the shallow murky green lake, and they paddle their way to the starter buoy. One by one, the other racers gather around the small red ball.

I walk around the Snack Shack and have to pass the lifeguard stand to join Mom and Dad at the end of the dock. Alex, shirtless and tan and just the person I need to talk to, sits on the stand. His classic red swim trunks are so freakin' cute. But I don't need to talk to him about how good he looks; I need to ask him about Finn, and who Finn was with last summer. But I also can't jump straight into grilling him about Finn.

I shield my eyes and squint at his face, framed by unruly brown curls. The lighter coppery highlights gleam in the sun. "I saw you at the memorial yesterday," I say. "Sorry I didn't say hi."

What I mean is, *Sorry you ran off so quick.*

He grimaces. "Yeah, that was…rough. I can't believe Finn said that. I would've come over but he…"

Alex trails off.

"Yeah. I get it. But…are you and I good?" This is incredibly uncomfortable, but I told Kelsey and Natalie I would do this, and I can't give up at the very first hurdle.

He nods. "We're good. Finn is confused, but it's just because he's having such a hard time. I don't think he can accept that it was all such a random accident. But he knows it's not your fault."

Even though Alex is wrong, the words are comforting coming from him. At least I have Alex.

"Good." Should I go for it now? Just ask him? "Hey, uh, do you know—"

Hannah appears at my elbow, and I choke on a gasp.

"Hey Alex," she says, ignoring me. "Finn says check your phone."

His brows lift. "You know Mr. and Mrs. Miller are wandering around today. I can't be checking my phone on the stand. I don't even have it with me. Why didn't Finn come tell me himself?"

She shrugs. "I don't know, but I went to drop off some of the leftover flowers from the memorial and he insisted I come all the way down here. I'm just the messenger. Trust me, I didn't voluntarily choose to come interrupt you."

She eyes me, a slow up-and-down.

Screw this.

"Alex, can we talk later?" I ask.

"Sure."

"I'll text you tonight when I can get away from my family. Probably after the fireworks, but maybe before."

"The staff will be hanging out around the firepit by the cabins tonight, so text and come over whenever."

Hannah doesn't even try to stifle her groan, but I ignore her. Was she with Finn last summer? Did *she* kill Sara? She can act as judgy as she wants, but if Alex says she and Finn were together, then I'll know she's a bigger monster than me.

I stride away from maybe-murderer Hannah, grateful

that Alex will still talk to me, and join my parents at the edge of the dock overlooking the rest of the lake.

Yellow kayaks dot the surface of the water, some moving more efficiently than others. A few teams seem like they've never been in a kayak in their entire lives. ~~Sara was so good at~~ I crush the thought. I don't want to tear up.

Dad asks Mom if the two young boys spinning in a wobbly circle are giving her flashbacks to her own attempt at kayaking, to which she points out that he was the problem, not her.

I smile, scanning the water for Kelsey and Natalie, but they must be around the bend already, toward the flag arch. If they went a little farther up the river, they'd pass the old abandoned dock. I haven't gone back to that cursed, miserable place, but suddenly a twisted part of me wants to see the warped boards and muddy ground. I want to see the blood washed away and imagine what life would've been like if the blood had never been spilled at all.

But I don't want to see *that* badly. Not badly enough to face the memories that might drown me. I can figure out who Sara's murderer was without reliving the worst night of my life. I can—

A high-pitched scream cuts across the water.

63

THEN

SUNDAY NIGHT. THREE DAYS BEFORE.

"You could at least do the kayak race with her. You don't have to spend every second of vacation with Sara." Mom's tone dipped dangerously close to anger.

Kelsey looked down at her plate and pushed a bite of green beans toward her mashed potatoes, never actually eating any of it. Dad sawed at his pork and left the guilting to Mom.

"Why does it matter if I'm Sara's partner? Kelsey doesn't even like kayaking."

My sister's head snapped up and her brows pinched toward the bridge of her nose. "That's not true. I want to do the race this year."

"See?" Mom leaned back, squaring her shoulders against the chair.

"But you've never wanted to before?" I made it a question. If it mattered to Kelsey, and Sara kept making out with people I liked, maybe I really would do the kayak race with my sister next year.

She shifted in her seat and gave me pitiful doe eyes that tugged, obnoxiously, at my heart. "Yes I did, you were just always *Sara's* partner. You're *always* with Sara."

Mom raises her brows at me. Defensiveness sparks. "I'm not always with Sara. I'm not with her right now. I wasn't with her this morning on our hike."

Kelsey's eyes drop, and again there's that annoying tug deep in my chest. She's fourteen, but she's not a *baby*. When we're not here, when I'm not keeping up with Sara, we're close. And yet all this time I never knew she was upset about the kayak race.

It's not fair, I know, and I'll make it up to her.

Just…not right now.

64

NOW

THURSDAY AFTERNOON. ONE YEAR AFTER.

I freeze. Chatter quiets, and in that empty space the rushing of blood in my ears mingles with the rustle of trees. The breeze lifts the hair off the back of my neck, and I shiver. Whose scream was that? Not Kelsey. It can't be Kelsey, because Kelsey has to be fine. I can't lose *her* too. Come on, Kelsey, where are you? Sara's dead because I did everything wrong, and I'm doing everything wrong all over again.

I'm wrong. Something's wrong with *me*.

My mind slips, as easy as diving into the water. Down, down, down.

You wouldn't.

But she'd been horribly wrong.

A loud bang and a scream cut short.

Dad's hand touches my arm, and I nearly jump out of my skin. The gasp that drags through my lungs is rough and thready.

"Whoa now," Dad says, withdrawing his hand. "I asked if you wanted anything to eat."

I shake my head and Dad walks to the Snack Shack. It takes me a couple seconds to refocus, but when I do, it's clear everyone else has gone back to their conversations. No one panicked. No one had a memory breathing down their neck, waiting to pounce.

I scan the water, and near the opposite side of the lake two kids try desperately to clamber into their overturned kayak. The sounds of splashing and laughter have replaced the momentary quiet.

There was no life-threatening crisis. A kayak flipped over. Completely normal.

What isn't normal is the way my heart still patters erratically and the way Sara's short, final scream lingers in my mind like a nightmare after waking.

I fold my arms over my stomach and hug myself, doing my best to relax as warm sunshine kisses my shoulders. I squint when Kelsey and Natalie's kayak comes around the bend of the lake.

They're going to win—they're easily the first headed to shore. I can't believe they managed to get to the arch and find their flag so quickly. Who knew they could paddle so fast?

But they aren't going very fast at all. I frown. As they get closer, it's obvious Kelsey is the only one rowing.

"Uh-oh," Dad says, wandering over with an already sweating beer can. He pops the lid with a hissing release of pressure. "All the paddling get the better of Natalie?"

"Maybe," Mom says, but there's worry tugging at the corner of her mouth.

Natalie hurls herself out of the kayak the instant they're out of the lake and lands on her butt in the dirt. She scoots farther away before stopping to look at something on her calf.

Kelsey scrambles out behind her. She breathes heavily, sweat dripping down the sides of her face.

"She thinks she got bit by a black widow. It was in our boat," Kelsey says.

Mom gives Kelsey's hand a squeeze as she goes to Natalie, who's frantically tugging at her skin.

"I saw it," Natalie says. "It crawled over my knee and got away. It's somewhere in the front. Under the plastic." Her eyes dart to the covered, shadowy part of the bow.

I inch closer, and there's a red, splotchy patch on Natalie's leg where she must've swatted at the spider.

"What…what do I do?" Natalie asks, her voice sounding smaller than I've heard the entire trip. "Do I elevate it? Am I supposed to move? Will that make it worse?" She seems to shrink. "Am I going to die?"

"Aw, sweetheart, no. No, of course not. Black widows aren't that venomous. You're going to be fine." Mom twists. "Mandy, go grab some napkins from the Shack."

It takes me a beat too long to realize she wants them for Natalie, whose cheeks shine with tear tracks.

"Right," I mutter and run around to get the napkins, but not before pausing by Kelsey. She bends over, her chest heaving. Kelsey has never handled spiders well. "Hey, you okay?"

She swallows and her eyes dart to Natalie. She squeezes them shut. "I'm fine."

I know that line. Liar.

"Come with me?" I ask, hoping to break her panic cycle.

She takes several shuddering breaths and follows me around to the Snack Shack, but she won't look at me. By the time we return, Mrs. Miller and a couple of Highmark staffers are with my parents and Natalie. Dad has his phone held up near his nose; he doesn't have his reading glasses. I know he's looking up black widow bites.

"Here you go." I pass a handful of napkins to Natalie, who blows her nose into the whole wad. Beside me, Kelsey grits her teeth and bounces from foot to foot.

"Come have a seat over here, Natalie. Out of the dirt," Mrs. Miller says. "We've got someone on the way with an ice pack and wrap for you."

Mom and Dad help Natalie over to the wooden porch lip that extends from the rear of the Shack. Dad taps his phone. "She should be fine, but I'll call telehealth and see what they say. Just to be safe."

"Good. That's good. You'll feel better with some ice," Mom tells Natalie.

Kelsey looks at me and motions with a nod to follow her. My stomach sinks. I don't like the look on her face.

I join her over by the trees, away from everyone else. "What's up?" I ask, trying hard for casual.

There's a beat of hesitation, and then all that's left in her eyes is accusation. Just like Finn. Just like the police. Just like Hannah and Mr. and Mrs. Miller and even once or twice, Sara's parents. Everyone's eyes slip, sometimes, and say what their mouths won't. *Why did you leave her? What did you do? What did you see? Can we trust you?*

"You picked our kayak."

"Yeah, so?"

Her eyes narrow. "You didn't give us one with a spider in it on purpose, did you?"

Her words don't make sense. I hear them, but they're ridiculous. "Are you asking if I tried to…what…kill Natalie with a spider? That's absurd. And *why*?"

Kelsey ducks her head. "Natalie posted that video about you witnessing Sara's death, and what Finn said at the memorial. You were mad."

Heat rises, flushing my chest and neck. "Really, Kelsey? How would I have seen inside the body of the kayak in the first place? Or under the seat? Spiders hide. It's what they do!" I cling to anger and disbelief, because the hurt will bury me.

"Okay. Whatever. It was an accident. I don't know why I asked." Her shoulders hunch as she folds herself away from me.

"I don't believe you. You think I gave you a boat with a spider in it on purpose. Jesus Christ, Kels, who would do that?"

When she looks at me again, I wish I hadn't asked.

Me. She thinks someone like *me* would do something like *that*. Deep down, she thinks I'm still lying.

And she's right. No wonder she doesn't trust me. But I *am* trying to help.

"I'm working on…the thing we talked about," I say, lowering my voice. "I'll know soon, and I'll tell you right away. Please. Trust me." Even a little.

She nods, and returns to Natalie.

I can do this. I'll find out who killed Sara *and* get my sister back. Alex is busy until tonight, but there's one other person I could ask.

Virginia.

65

THEN

THURSDAY MORNING. HOURS AFTER.

I was dying. I had to be dying. I'd been hit by a truck, and that was why my skull throbbed and my chest ached when I tried to roll over. A loud pounding wedged itself deep in my already shattered skull. What the hell was Kelsey *doing*?

Oh. Someone was knocking at the door.

I groaned and forced my eyes open, sucking a gasp through my teeth at the burning when air met my dry, puffy eyes. I'd been crying. All night.

Sara was dead.

A burst of light and the world-breaking explosion of the firework replayed itself. Sara crumpling to the ground. Oh my God, I could have saved her and I hadn't. Oh God, oh my God. I couldn't breathe. That other girl, who was she? I didn't imagine her, right? No. No, that was too far a stretch. Someone else had been there, but how the eff did we get to the point of Sara being *dead*? Maybe she isn't dead! Maybe I was wrong and the mystery girl went for help, but Sara was awfully still...

Dirt beneath my nails, water soaking my jeans. I didn't get up and save her I let her die I watched her die she's dead because I let her die it's my fault oh God all my fault so much dirt on my hands dirt and blood washing down the sink, pretty blue flowers and—

Stop, I have to stop, hydrangeas, roses, tulips, lilies oh right someone's at the door but Sara's dead someone murdered her shit where's her necklace shit shit shit okay I buried it God stop it, Mandy, think of anything else, anything at all, okay back to the flowers, keep thinking of flowers—

Sunflowers, roses, daffodils, dandelions, what other flowers are there, violets, ummm, um, um Sara's dead her neck and jaw were so were so torn up and I also smashed her face with a rock first shit and I was the last one with her I'm going to be sick.

Shit.

A sound between a whimper and a sob oozed up my throat, and I curled into the tightest, smallest ball my body would allow.

Thud, thud, thud. "Mandy? Mandy, honey, are you up?"

I stopped breathing. Pretend to be asleep. Look natural. I uncurled from the fetal position, and turned my face into the pillow, wincing as my skin met cotton crusted by dried snot and tears.

The door creaked open and light footsteps approached my bed. A hand rested on my shoulder.

"Mandy?" Mom's voice.

Breathe in, breathe out. I couldn't face anyone. Not yet. Someone—whoever that was last night—must have called 911. I wanted to ignore reality a little longer.

Mom gave me enough of a shake I couldn't pretend to stay asleep. Groaning, I stirred slowly and blinked at her worried face. My stomach swooped. Here it came. The news.

"You can go back to sleep in a minute," she assured me. "Sara's parents stopped by because Sara wasn't in their cottage this morning and they were wondering if you know where she might've gone?"

Oh *no*. No one knew yet. She was still out there. Somehow this was worse. I couldn't tell Mom what I knew. What I'd done—and not done. I needed to wait. I couldn't be the one to tell the whole story.

I needed to look confused. I frowned and yawned, shaking my head in hopes she'd let me lie down again. Anything to buy time. What the hell was I supposed to tell her? Sara's dead?

But what happened? A girl. Fighting. But *I'd* been fighting with Sara too. Was I remembering right? She was hurt. Shit. She was hurt, because I hit her with that rock. But then what? A firework...hit her? No. God, *no*.

The panic must've showed on my face because Mom tucked wild hair behind my ear. "They're not mad. It's okay if she..." Mom wrung her hands together and dropped them. "Well, they want to make sure she's all right. If she stayed the night with a boy..."

She let the sentence trail off. A question. A cracked window to let in hope.

I sat up and pulled the covers to my lap, hiding the way my hands shook. "I haven't seen her since I left with Alex last night."

The lie spilled out, and there was no taking it back. Crap. Now I'd need to get to Alex before anyone else talked to him. The blood drained from my head so fast the room dipped and I sagged against the headboard. Breathe. I had to keep breathing.

Mom nodded. "Where were you all hanging out when you left her?"

"The dock." The words cracked, barely passing my lips. Please, let her assume I meant the docks on the main property.

"Okay. I'll let them know. You can go back to sleep." She straightened. "Actually, would you mind texting Sara first? Maybe she'll answer you. I know you girls are more likely to answer your friends than parents."

She patted my blanket-covered foot on the way out the door.

Slow motion, like I was back in the mud, struggling out from beneath the dock, I turned to my phone resting on the bedside table. I stared. There was something cold and breathless and lonely spreading through me. I had to text my friend, knowing she was dead. Knowing I'd abandoned her. I clenched my fists until my nails bit into the skin.

"Are you going to text her?"

I jumped and a scream squeaked out. "Shit! Kelsey."

She stared at me from her bed on the other side of the room, her own eyes puffy and red. She looked sad? Or confused? Or maybe tired, because she just woke up and I was projecting. I shook my head and picked up my phone to text my dead friend.

Hey your parents are looking for you. Where are you?

Dead. Beside the lake. In the dirt. Alone.
Murdered.

66

NOW

THURSDAY AFTERNOON. ONE YEAR AFTER.

Water drips to the carpet in slow, *pat, pat, pats*. The ice bag, wrapped in a white cloth napkin, has almost completely melted. Natalie's propped-up leg rests on the coffee table, and when she shifts, the ice clunks together.

"How's the leg?" Dad asks. Swirling his whiskey.

"Not bad," Natalie says.

Kelsey leans into her friend's shoulder, tucking her head into the bend of Natalie's neck. "Sorry you got attacked by nature. Now you can tell your mom that you were better off hanging out with your friends online. The outdoors hates you."

Natalie rolls her eyes. "You want me to tell my mom you tried to feed me to the spiders? After I promised her I'd be safe while they were in Italy?" The teasing now is the complete reverse of her initial panic by the lake.

You didn't give us one with a spider in it on purpose, did you?

The words ooze through me like mud between toes.

Have I done my part in the show of sympathy for Natalie? I don't want to seem insensitive, especially after Kelsey's suspicions, but I also want to go talk to Virginia before the barbecue and fireworks start. Between her and Alex, I'm sure I can figure out who killed Sara. Maybe I wasn't interested in risking a confrontation before, but I am now, and I don't want to wait.

"I'll go get more ice for Natalie," I say. If it takes me a little longer to return, no one will notice. I can stop by Virginia's cottage and see if she'll talk to me.

I round the edge of the porch and crash into an eye-level bundle of cellophane and wicker. A screech comes from behind the basket as the bearer staggers backward, and the basket spills to the ground.

There's crunch and a crack, and Hannah gives me wide, annoyed eyes.

"Way to go," she mutters, kneeling.

Candles and oranges and a pair of spa cloth slippers tumble out of their decorative wicker and press against the cellophane. A breeze blows off the river, crinkling the thin gift-wrap. I squat beside her, fumbling awkwardly to help her right the basket.

"Sorry."

She sighs as she checks the damage. "Doesn't matter, the basket is for your sister's friend, anyway. Mrs. Miller made me bring it over."

Knowing Mrs. Miller, Hannah is probably supposed to

say something nice and apologetic to Natalie on behalf of her and her husband. I'm not holding my breath for anything nice out of Hannah's mouth.

"Well, it is what it is." Hannah says, pushing to her feet and bringing the slightly lopsided gifts with her.

The movement and another soft breeze off the water sends a pleasant floral scent swirling between us. Notes of lemon and…lilies? Familiar, almost.

I stand but don't reach to take the package. I need to get to Virginia and back before my family expects me for the start of dinner on the lawn.

She sidesteps me, but pauses, half-turned. "I hope your sister's friend is okay. After…" Her expression darkens and she shakes her head. "After Sara, I think everyone's just really touchy about…accidents."

She walks toward the door, but her scent lingers and again I swear I know that perfume.

I chew my lip as I walk through the grass between our cottage and Virginia's. Kelsey is going to love rifling through those goodies. She'll probably try to steal the slippers from Natalie. Mr. and Mrs. Miller must've been panicked to hear about the spider bite; they sent that basket *quick*.

What a nice gesture.

What a nice scent.

What am I forgetting?

———

Virginia sips a mint julep, with large sprigs of fresh mint. She swirls her straw and pushes back and forth in her rocker. As the first hint of twilight approaches, the shadows beneath the trees across the water darken. The soft burbling of the water flowing below Virginia's raised porch is peaceful.

It's the start of a beautiful evening, but I feel sick.

I press the heels of my feet into the porch boards to keep my feet from tapping.

"What was it you wanted to talk about?" she asks.

Be cool. Be normal.

Be quick so I can make an appearance at the barbecue and go to Alex.

"Did you notice Finn hanging out with anyone last year?"

A small wrinkle forms between her eyes. "Well, sure."

"And?"

The wrinkle deepens.

"Are things all right between you two? I know he said what he said at the memorial, and he's wanting a better answer than the one he got for why he lost his sister, but sometimes there is no better answer. It's a shame how hurtful grief can make us, when what we need is support."

"Yeah, everything's fine between me and Finn. I'm just trying to remember something, it's nothing bad." It's very, very bad.

"I only really saw him with your little group. You know. You and Sara. Alex and…oh, what's the girl's name? The one who cleans this row of cottages…Helen?"

Realization surges through me, like someone's brushed a sparkler through my insides. Tingling and hot and unbearable.

Finn is where I smelled Hannah's perfume before. The day I ran into him on my way to the kayak race. He'd brushed past me, angry, and I swear Hannah was standing in the group he'd been leaving.

"Hannah," I croak. "Her name's Hannah."

67

NOW

A loud pop joins the chatter around the fire as a log splits and sends a spray of embers up to the dark sky. My breath catches. Frozen at the edge of the tree line, I watch the dancing orange flecks.

Low crackling, a flash of light, Sara's body dropping to the ground.

I blink. Hannah and Alex sit next to each other on one of the benches. Hannah sees me first, the smile sliding off her face.

"Mandy! Hey," Alex says, waving.

The firelight wavers across his beautiful, warm face, and I hate that I've come here to ask about betrayal and murder. There are so many more enjoyable things we could do tonight.

I walk over, careful not to stare at Hannah. My skin prickles, and my pulse jumps against my neck.

"Hey." My voice comes out raspy. "Can we talk now?"

"Sure, sit down. Want a drink?"

Hannah's eyes narrow, flitting between Alex and me.

I lift the corners of my mouth and let my gaze move slowly across Alex's face. Those thick coppery lashes. Those soft—I assume—lips. Better Hannah think I'm stealing him away for a hookup than to ask about how she was involved in a murder.

"Can we talk alone?" I jerk my head toward his cabin. "In there?"

His brows lift, and there's a moment where I let myself believe he's excited by the prospect, instead of confused.

Hannah gives a disgruntled snort, but Alex ignores her.

"Yeah, let's go."

I follow behind him, close enough I could've reached forward and grabbed his hand. Twined our fingers together and let the warmth of his skin distract me from the dread building in my stomach. But instead, I look over my shoulder, expecting to see Hannah behind me, a thick log in hand, ready to bash me over the head and leave me bleeding to death just like Sara.

~~Two of us left her bleeding to death.~~

Alex takes the short set of stairs in two bounds. I'm so nervous I trip on the second step, my foot sliding off the front end. I land with a smack.

I yelp as my palms slap the porch.

"Are you—"

"I'm okay." I scramble to my feet, wiping my stinging palms against my hip to relieve the pain.

He catches my right hand in his and rubs his thumb across the underside of my knuckles. It tickles. And it's amazing. And I don't want him to stop.

"What was it you wanted to talk about?" he asks, voice low.

"Inside," I say, reluctantly taking my hand back.

Worry wrinkles his forehead. "Okayyy," he says slowly, gesturing me through the door.

The living space is empty. Everyone else is either out by the fire or in another cabin.

"Do you want to sit?"

"Sure." My legs are wobbly. Sitting sounds better than collapsing.

I take the corner seat on the couch, and he sits next to me.

He drums his fingers against his knee. "Your parents let you bail on watching the fireworks with them?"

"Mom made this face." I purse my lips and scrunch my brow. "But they didn't explicitly say no, so I ran off before Mom could roll out the full guilt trip."

Alex chuckles at my exaggerated mom-face.

"I'm glad you came. What did you want to talk about?"

My mouth goes desert-dry. I have to ask about Finn and Hannah, but the longer I leave the question unsaid, the longer I can continue as I have for the last twelve months. The less I know, the less real all this is. Like if I tried hard enough, she could still be alive. No killer to be held accountable, no friend gone forever.

Also, I'm just plain scared of having to explain myself to Alex.

What if he hates me?

He shifts closer, his T-shirt pulling across his chest. I *know* the thin fabric hides some excellent abs. His eyes catch on my lips.

His face is wonderfully, terrifyingly close.

"We don't *have* to talk, if that's not what you want," he says. He lets the offer hang—tempting. *Very* tempting.

Maybe just…one nice thing…before everything blows up.

I lean in and brush my lips against his. The worry and guilt pulling me apart don't go away under the touch of his fingers curling over my jaw and trailing down my neck, but they do quiet beneath the pulse that runs down through my core.

Alex's thumb brushes my cheek, and my lips part even more. A sigh slips from my mouth to his at the movement of his tongue, proving he's a good kisser. I knew it. I find the hem of his shirt and slip my hand beneath, hooking my fingers along the top of his jeans. The delicate touch draws a small sound from Alex, and I'm drowning in how badly I want to crash my body against his.

As long as I keep kissing him, I don't have to think about—

Hannah.

Hannah and Finn.

Hannah and Sara.

Sara and me.

Sara.

A chill washes over me, dousing the fire until there's nothing left but a sad, dying ember.

Alex pulls away, his eyes vaguely out of focus. He blinks. "What's wrong?" His voice is rough.

I drop my face into my hands. Hiding. Why am I *always* hiding?

"Hey," he says softly. "Hey, it's okay. We don't have to do anything you don't want. Want to go back outside?"

If I don't ask, I'm going to chicken out again.

"Were Hannah and Finn hooking up last year?" I spit the question out in a rush.

Silence.

More silence.

I lift my head and find him staring at me, open-mouthed.

Finally, he shakes himself, straightening enough to put distance between us. "Mandy...I...I'm not telling you how to live your life, but generally it's considered a little weird to admit to thinking about, well, *several* other people while you're making out with someone."

I laugh. I can't help myself. "Trust me, I would way rather have continued kissing you."

"Why are you asking?" The first hint of suspicion creeps in.

I hate that I've made him sound that way almost as much as I hate the way he's pulled his arms into his lap, careful not to touch me anymore.

I'd hoped to avoid telling Alex why I need to know. Miraculously, he believes Sara's death was accidental, and I don't want to be the one to dump the truth in his lap. Besides, how do I explain how I know she was murdered without admitting to all my own lies?

I open my mouth, ready to dodge the question, and pause.

Why am I here? To find out who killed Sara. To stop keeping all my secrets so close to my chest. To stop letting my own fear leave Sara's murder unsolved, my friend blamed for her own death while her killer walks free.

"Sara's death wasn't an accident."

He doesn't react at first. Then his eyes widen and his forehead bunches. Horrified. He looks horrified.

"Mandy…what do you mean?"

My head spins, like I'm floating, and all the words I want to say burn in my chest. My gaze darts to the cabin door. The three other doors that lead into staff bedrooms are open, and dark. The living space is silent as Alex waits for me to respond, but my throat is so tight.

"She was killed," I squeeze out.

He shakes his head and scoots away from me. "Why would you say that?" He's disgusted…or afraid.

"Because it's the truth."

"And how would you know that?"

There's a challenge in the question.

Did you kill her? That's what he wants to know.

Yes, and no.

"I was there by the dock. I saw it."

His face crumples, and his eyes dart back and forth across my face, like he's trying to pick answers out of my head.

"Shit. That's why you were so eager to alibi me. You weren't doing me a favor; you were covering for *yourself*."

I flinch. "Yes." There's no point in splitting hairs. He's right, and he deserves the truth.

He launches up from the couch, stalking around the low, beat-up coffee table. He stops in front of me.

"Well?" He's practically shouting.

"I didn't kill her. I… We'd gotten into an argument." I won't get into exactly what that fight entailed. I can't. "A fight, really. She had me pinned on the ground, both of us saying terrible things. And I hit her, but I didn't kill her. Not… not really. I ran and hid when I heard someone else coming. Whoever the girl was, she's the one who lit the firework that killed Sara. I just couldn't see who she was from where I was hiding under the dock."

His eyes narrow and from the way his mouth works, I'm pretty sure he's biting his tongue to keep from shouting at me.

"But I could *hear* them. Bits and pieces. The sound was muffled pretty badly by the water, and the cramped space beneath the dock. And I was way too drunk by that point, but I heard enough. Sara and the new girl were fighting over Finn. Sara broke them up, or Finn dumped her because of Sara. The other girl was mad about it. Really mad. She started demanding Sara fix things and, well, you know Sara. She didn't exactly dial back the situation. And then…"

Alex knows the *then*. Everyone does.

She died. ~~Eventually.~~

And the cops called it an accident, and I let the lie warp and grow and derail what was left of Sara's story.

He sinks down, sitting with a thud on the coffee table.

His hands hang down between his knees, and he looks at me like he wishes he could turn away.

"You watched."

I nod, my throat aching as the guilty knot swells.

He's quiet for several seconds. "Jesus, Mandy."

"I know."

"So you think Hannah killed Sara because Hannah and Finn were together last summer, and Sara messed that up?"

I nod again.

He shakes his head. "No. No, I don't think Finn was hooking up with Hannah. She, uh." He falters. "She tried, even though she was with that other guy at the time, but Finn actually shut her down pretty hard. I was kind of surprised."

That can't be right. I *know* I smelled Hannah's perfume on Finn last year. It took me a while to remember, but I'm certain.

"But—"

The door swings open, banging into the wall.

The dark silhouettes Hannah in the doorframe, and I swear my heart stops beating.

68

NOW

THURSDAY NIGHT.

Hannah crosses her arms over her chest. "Nice, Mandy. Real nice."

Alex stands, but he doesn't move away from me. Thank God. I resist the urge to shrink behind him.

"What? Nothing to say now?" she snaps, stepping into the cabin and slamming the door behind her.

"Were you listening from the porch?" Alex asks.

Hannah scowls and stalks farther into the cabin, slamming the door behind her. "Oh, right. I'm the creep here." She points at me. "She accused me of murdering a girl and you're worried about me being nosy. You actually believe her? That she conveniently witnessed Sara's murder, but oh noooo, she had nothinggggg to do with it. She just *watched* her best friend get murdered, and then kept it a secret. And now is conveniently blaming me? Wake up, Alex."

I scramble up from the couch. Alex tenses.

I glare right back at Hannah. "Whoever was hooking up with Finn last summer killed Sara, and I know it was you. *You* killed her."

She shoves me in the chest.

A choked gasp gets lodged in my throat and the room tilts as I spill backward. I'm falling, my stomach lurching into my chest, and then Alex's arms hook beneath mine. He catches me right before I topple to the floor.

"Hannah!" he shouts. "Stop!"

She fumes, her eyes blazing as she clenches her fists at her side. "I didn't kill Sara. I don't have to stand here and listen to her lie about me."

She spins around.

"Wait. The perfume you're wearing…I smelled it on Finn last summer when he was acting so weird."

She pauses and turns, keeping her eyes downcast.

"Oh," she says.

"Oh?" Alex's voice climbs an octave.

Holy shit, I was right.

She's a murderer. I start to reach my phone in my back pocket but freeze. Do I need to call the police? What am I supposed to do? I've never *done* anything besides lie about my own role ~~and leave when I should have stayed~~.

"About that," Hannah says, rubbing her neck. "I think I know what perfume you mean, but I wasn't wearing it at the start of last summer. I uhhh. You know how I said I like to move stuff around, sometimes swipe little things from guest rooms when I go in to drop off towels and shit?"

"Yeah," Alex says.

I keep frowning.

"I took it out of a wastebasket last year. I'm pretty sure it was *after* Sara died." She shrugs. "It smells amazing, but it's not cheap, so I don't wear it that often. Just a little bit of it every now and then."

She seems like she's telling the truth. Goddamnit.

"Which wastebasket did you say you got it out of?" I ask.

She hesitates.

"Which wastebasket, Hannah." It comes out flat: a demand instead of a question.

"I took it out of a bathroom in the Millers' cottage. They throw away such random stuff, but a half-full bottle of fancy perfume was a new one. I couldn't resist."

The three of us stand in heavy silence.

Leigh.

Freakin' *Leigh*. I can't believe I bought her bullshit about spray-painting MURDERER on my walkway. *Ohhhh I just wanted to piss off my parents.* Ha! She must have seen Natalie's teaser videos about investigating Sara's story and decided to make sure the focus landed on me, as one of the last *known* people to see Sara alive.

She won't fool me again.

"I'm going to talk to Leigh," I say, shivering a little at the way my voice sounds.

"Uh?" Alex makes a strangled sound around the word. "You don't really think…"

"I do."

He shakes his head. "That's—it's—*no*."

I bite my lip to keep from shouting.

"I don't have time for this. I'm sorry. I have to go talk to her, *now*." And if Leigh killed Sara, I need to keep Kelsey and Natalie and their questions *far* away from her.

"I'll come with you," Alex says. The worry is as plain on his face as the doubt.

"Don't be ridiculous," Hannah cuts in with a voice that perfectly matches her eye roll. "You're not going to go harass the owner's daughter over a *hunch*. Especially when Mandy's probably still lying anyway. Be smarter."

I shake my head. I refuse to say the words *Hannah's right,* but...

"You really shouldn't be there when I accuse your boss's daughter of murder."

His tan face pales, but after a second his jaw clenches and he nods, almost to himself. "I'm not so worried about this job that I'd put you in danger over keeping it. If you think she did it, I'll go with you."

I grab his hand and squeeze. "She's not going to attack me in the middle of the resort."

"Y'all are on your own," Hannah says. Her face says plainly exactly how little she thinks of the whole plan.

I ignore her.

"Just...keep your phone on you. I'll text you if I need you," I say to Alex.

He pulls out his phone and turns the volume on. He gives

the phone a little shake and says, "All the way up. If you need me don't hesitate. It's not worth getting hurt."

"Thanks." If it had been Alex out there with Sara last year, he wouldn't have left her when she needed him most.

I'd been all she had, and I messed up as badly as any friend ever could, but I can at least get some justice for her memory.

Time to find Leigh.

69

NOW

THURSDAY NIGHT.

The lawn running between the main lodge and the row of waterfront cottages is mostly empty. Dark blankets the sky, but there's a softness as the last of the daylight bleeds out. Crickets trill and their song seems to hum beneath my skin.

Or maybe that's just the adrenaline.

I take the Millers' stairs two at a time. If I hesitate, I might think about whether this is a good idea or not, and honestly, I don't want to know the answer.

I want to watch Leigh's face crumple when she realizes I know. Even if it means me having to tell the police the truth, the *whole* truth, to ensure she pays for what she did, I'm not backing out.

I knock on the door, hard and fast. Pain jolts through my knuckles and up my hand.

No answer.

My phone buzzes in my back pocket. While I wait, I check the message. It's from Kelsey.

Meet us at the honeymoon cabin for filming. Got someone to interview.

Anxiety flows down the back of my neck. She promised they would wait for me. Ugh.

I smack my palm against the door. "Leigh?" I call. "Hello?"

Come on. *Answer.*

"Mandy? What's wrong? What's going on?" Virginia calls from her porch. Her porch light casts sharp shadows in the deep worry lines rippling across her face.

"Have you seen Leigh?"

My chest is so tight.

"Sure. But it was a while ago. During the fireworks. She was with your sister and your sister's friend. Is everything all right?"

Yes. No. Maybe? God, I don't know.

"Thanks, I've got to go!" I shout and fly down the stairs.

She says something that I don't hear. All I can hear is a voice in my head screaming, *Hurry! Hurry!*

70

THEN

WEDNESDAY NIGHT. THE DAY OF.

I held my breath, listening to their distorted argument.

"I. Am. Not. Gross," the girl said.

The words are garbled, but I can make them out.

Sara ignored her and climbed unsteadily—either from the alcohol or the blow to the head—to her feet. The other girl backed up a step, but stopped.

"Get out of my way," Sara said.

"Are—to talk to—?" Finn. Was Sara going to talk to Finn.

Again, the quick flick of the lighter, on and off.

Sara laughed, like the girl had just said the most absurd thing in the world.

"No. It's not—problem—finally realized—weren't worth the trouble." Sara walked past her, toward the path out of the clearing.

An enraged howl, and the girl bent to pick something up

from the ground, but her face was angled away from me. I squinted, inching closer to the gap, but a spiderweb brushed my forehead, and I stifled a gasp, freezing as I waited to feel spindly legs crawling across my face.

"Stop," she shouted at Sara.

Sara swayed a little as she turned.

"—wouldn't," Sara hissed.

Now Sara was too far away to hear clearly too.

Wouldn't what?

"I call Finn, or I—sure this looks—an accident and you won't be able—drive us apart—"

Make what look like an accident?

Get out. Stop this. It didn't matter how mad I was at Sara; this was getting *bad*. Sara would make fun of me though, for hiding. Or be pissed I watched this whole time.

The lighter flicked on, but this time it didn't go out. What the hell?

A plume of sparks erupted, red and yellow hissing through the darkness.

I thought Finn had picked up all the fireworks. He'd missed one.

There was a shuffling sound, and a laugh—Sara's, I thought.

"Yeah, right," Sara said.

The other girl yelped. For a split second, the sparking tail and the rocket fell toward the dirt and then the fuse spent, and the rocket launched up with a loud bang.

Sara gave a short harsh scream.

Oh fuck oh fuck oh fuck.

She crumpled to the ground. Dropped like a puppet with cut strings.

I stopped breathing.

White noise in my head.

...

...

...

The girl's footsteps traced a frantic circle in the clearing. Sara didn't move. Or did she? Was she moving?

I couldn't hear a thing over the whirring in my head.

What the hell just happened? I couldn't have seen what I thought I just saw. It wasn't possible. There's no way I just hid here and watched my friend get *murdered*.

Inhale.

Exhale.

Quietly, oh God she's dead keep breathing oh God.

The next inhale was a strangled gasp, and my chest burned with the pounding of my heart, burning, burning, burning like the firework that tore through Sara's neck and jaw. Hot, sour bile rose up my throat and spilled across my tongue. I spat, but it clung to my lips and dribbled down my chin.

"Shit," I whispered to myself and the quiet hollow beneath the boards. What was I supposed to do?

Maybe Sara could be alive. Maybe I was wrong and she was unconscious. Maybe I was dreaming and this could all be undone. I squinted through the gap between the dock and the dirt.

The girl was gone. I'd lost time.

I had to go look at Sara.

Look at what I did.

She'd be alive if I hadn't hit her with that rock first.

She hadn't realized how much danger she was in.

She might've ducked in time if it weren't for me.

She'd be alive if I'd said something. Anything.

Coward.

I'd wanted to see her suffer.

Monster.

71

NOW

THURSDAY NIGHT.

When I reach the cabin, all alone tucked into the woods at the edge of the golf course, the door is unlocked. Darkness collects like a pool, filling the basin of the first floor. I wheeze, drawing distinctly stale and dusty air into my lungs. The stitch in my side tearing up my ribs has me clutching the doorway. I grit my teeth and straighten.

Plastic tarps drape over one half of the room with paint cans clustered near the wall, where moonlight through the window reflects off the metal lids. The stillness of the shadows is a special kind of terrifying.

What if I'm too late?

But no. The second-story loft is a beacon in the dark. Voices. I bolt for the stairs.

"Kelsey," I shout. "Kelsey!" Answer me, come on. "Leigh?"

I cough as my voice breaks.

When I hit the landing, Natalie and Mrs. Miller are sitting across from each other: Natalie in a chair and Mrs. Miller on the couch, both leaned forward in conversation. They turn to face me, and Natalie smiles.

"Hey, Mandy."

My gaze darts between the two of them, before bouncing around the rest of the loft. Everything seems normal, but where is Leigh? Where is my sister? And what the hell is Mrs. Miller doing here?

"Where's Kelsey? Where's Leigh?"

Natalie cocks her head to the side. "What do you mean? Leigh was with us at the fireworks, but I don't know where she is now. Mrs. Miller offered to let us interview her, and it was too good to miss. She said I could get some filler video while we waited for Kelsey to find you. She's not with you?"

She cranes her neck, as if she expects to see Kelsey trudge up the stairs.

I shake my head. That's not right. "No. She texted me to meet y'all here." I step deeper into the room, peering into the corners as if somehow I might've missed my sister crouching behind a chair, waiting to jump out and scare me. I would scream, and she would squeal with laughter, just like when we were kids.

As I reach the chair where Natalie sits, Mrs. Miller stands.

"Kelsey's not coming."

72

NOW

THURSDAY NIGHT.

It's like my brain fails to load—one glitching thought after another.

"I don't understand."

"Natalie tells me you witnessed Sara's death. That she's very excited to do a tell-all interview with you," Mrs. Miller says, ignoring any mention of Kelsey.

Am I breathing? I'm not breathing.

"I can't have that," she says.

Natalie shifts forward, toward her phone on the coffee table between them. I glance down, and dropped in a heap beside Natalie's chair is her purse, with the dark red of the flare gun peeking out. I should have taken it away from them. Maybe they wouldn't have been so confident that they could take care of themselves. What was a flare gun supposed to do?

Mrs. Miller's head swivels and her eyes drop to the table.

She lunges to her feet and snatches the phone. I backpedal away from her.

"Hey," Natalie shouts.

Mrs. Miller pushes her glossy bangs from her face.

Leigh's not here. She's not here because Hannah said she took the perfume out of the trash at the Miller cottage, and I *assumed* that meant it was Leigh's. But no. It belonged to the new wife in her thirties who can't seem to make people like the Ellises and my parents accept her.

Ew. Oh my God, Sara saying their relationship was "gross" suddenly makes a lot more sense. Finn was barely eighteen last summer. Was it just last year, or had it been going on for longer?

Mrs. Miller's eyes narrow.

"Don't make that face," she snaps.

The thoughts whirring in my head are so loud, and so jumbled, but I need to stay focused on Mrs. Miller. I need to find my sister.

"Where's Kelsey?" That's the most important thing.

"I'll tell you where your sister is…"

She pauses like a villain in a predictable movie, and I bite off a scream. *Tell me where she is, you monster!*

"If you do one thing first."

I could strangle her. No, that's risky. I could stab her. I don't have a knife. Also, I don't know where Kelsey is and I need her to tell me.

"What do you want?"

The last of her usual, eager-to-please shine drains away.

"You're going to give Natalie and her ridiculous follow-ers what they want: an answer to how Sara died." Her stare is dark, and chilling. "Give them your confession, and I tell you where your sister is."

I stare. Natalie lifts a hand to her mouth. Anger rises hot through my core, tinged with only a flicker of the guilt that used to overwhelm everything else when I thought of Sara's death. I hurt her. I was cruel. I failed her. But that didn't make me the same as Mrs. Miller.

She'd murdered Sara.

"I'm not taking the blame for you," I say, lifting my chin. It's hard not to scream the words at her. I hate her. She took Sara from me, and I spent a whole year feeling like it was all my fault. It took me a long time to want answers, and longer still to actually get them, but I know now.

Mrs. Miller stalks closer. I retreat, putting myself in the middle of the room.

"But are you really innocent? You watched it all, and you didn't do anything to help her? You let her die, and then you didn't tell the police. You didn't even correct them when they said she accidentally killed herself. And you knew she'd been murdered. I can't believe people thought you ever *really* cared about Sara."

"Wow," Natalie says, drawing out the word.

"Shut up." Mrs. Miller waves Natalie off.

"You shut up," Natalie says.

Mrs. Miller sighs, shaking her head. "No. No I am not going to get into this with a child."

How do I get us out of this and find Kelsey? There must be a way to fix this. I just need to keep her talking. Maybe if I make her mad enough, she'll slip. "At least Natalie's not a murderer."

She pushes her hair back from her face again, harsher this time, making it worse instead of better. "I don't care what you think," she snaps.

"Why?" I ask. "So what if Sara didn't like you being with Finn, so what? She was one girl. You didn't have to kill her."

Her chin jerks to the side, almost a twitch. "Exactly. So what? Who cares what she thought? Except Finn. Finn cared so much about his annoying little sister and what she thought. He adored her. *Shocking*, for how much they fought. She was blackmailing him and threatening to tell their parents. She got in his head, and he left me. I can't have *anything* here. Everyone's always judging me. But Finn was nice, and hot, and whenever he'd see me crying over whatever my step-daughter said on a given day, he didn't automatically take her side like everyone else."

My stomach turns. Every word out of her mouth is hor-rific. Disgusting. As if living at your husband's expensive resort and having to be nice to a teenage stepdaughter is the most impossible task and totally justifies cheating with an eighteen-year-old. It's disturbing.

And this creep is keeping Kelsey from me.

Mrs. Miller gives herself a shake. "And Sara ruined that for me. And what happened at the dock that night...it's not like I planned it, but I saw an opportunity, and I took it. And now, you've provided me with another opportunity."

That's not reassuring. Not at all.

"I'm not doing *anything* for you," I snap. The tremor in my voice betrays me.

Her brows arch. "Finn's been preoccupied with finding out what you know and how his sister died since he got here. Ever since *apparently* Alex blew your alibi. And now Finn's finally confiding in me again—talking to me again—and I won't lose that. So you'll do this confession—"

A sound that's too strangled to be a scoff escapes me, and Mrs. Miller's face contorts. She continues, louder now.

"*You'll do this confession*, and once the video of you saying you killed Sara is all over the internet, Finn will stop obsessing over what really happened to his sister. And *I* won't have to worry about this shit anymore."

I gasp as a dark possibility surfaces.

"He's helping you, isn't he? He has Kelsey?" I can't believe after all my fear that Kelsey was putting herself in danger, that Finn could be the one who might harm her. No matter how angry he was with me, or what he thought he knew...he wouldn't. He couldn't...

Her lips draw down. "After. After you make the video, I'll tell you where to find your sister."

Liar. She definitely means to kill me. Because there's no way she thinks I'm going to confess and then maintain the lie when the cops haul me in. As soon as the confession video is posted, I'm dead, and Natalie probably is too.

Maybe if I can keep her talking and make her follow me farther away from the stairs, Natalie can slip past and get away. She can get help. I try to catch Natalie's eye, but I can't mouth even the word *run* with Mrs. Miller staring at me.

I take a pace farther from the stairs, forcing myself to look away from her and gaze out the windows at the rear of the room, as if I'm lost in thought.

"You're going to tell your husband, then? About you and Finn?" I ask. "You are, right? You wouldn't do all this just to stay married."

Her face contorts and she takes several steps after me, leaving a narrow path between Natalie and escape. Please, let her notice.

"Mind your own business," Mrs. Miller says.

"Why? Don't want to think about what would happen if your husband found out you were a murderous cheater?"

She stops directly in front of me. I glare right back at her. I can't believe it took me this long to fight for Sara and her memory. Fight for myself. Fight for my sister.

Mrs. Miller's face is red. "I'm going to k—"

I cock my fist and hit her in the face.

"Run, Natalie!" I scream.

Mrs. Miller shrieks and staggers, dropping Natalie's phone. It skitters across the wood floor. I pivot, but her fingers curl around the hem of my shirt, and she jerks me backward. I stumble, barely catching myself before I crack my chin on the boards, and my glasses go flying.

I kick out, hoping to connect with Mrs. Miller, but she's gone. I stagger upright and see Natalie scrambling for her phone instead of the stairs. Shit.

Mrs. Miller digs through the couch cushions.

No time to wonder about that. I head for the only way out of this loft that doesn't involve a bone-breaking jump.

Out of the corner of my eye, Natalie scoops up her phone and stands.

"Come on," I yell, but don't stop.

There's the sound of two sets of fast, heavy footsteps behind me, and then a scream.

73

NOW

THURSDAY NIGHT.

Mrs. Miller holds a huge knife that looks like she swiped it from the kitchen, except it's covered in blood.

Natalie sags to the floor, clutching her side where a red stain blossoms over her yellow sundress. Tears spill from her wide eyes.

Mrs. Miller looks shocked, but only for a second, and then her mouth sets in a thin, determined line.

"Come here," she says.

I don't move.

"Come here, or I'll *kill her*."

Every muscle in my body hums. I don't want to get stabbed, but I can't run away and let her kill Natalie. Not without a fight. What do I *do*?

Natalie folds in on herself, hunching over her knees and breathing heavily.

The flare gun!

I sprint for Natalie's bag, lying where she left it beside the chair.

"Hey! What the hell are you doing? Did you hear me? I. Will. Kill her."

Maybe, but if I can't stop Mrs. Miller, we're both dead anyway. There's no way she lets us go now that she's stabbed a kid. I have to save us.

I drop to my knees, shoving my hand into the bag and retrieving the flare gun. How do I fire this?

She's coming.

"Stay away," I shout over my shoulder, still fumbling with the gun as my voice shakes. There's a trigger but...ah! The hammer.

The heavy footsteps don't slow.

I press back on the little plastic lever and turn. No time to stand.

My glasses crunch beneath Mrs. Miller's shoes.

She's too close. I bring the gun up, point in her general direction, and fire.

The recoil jerks my arms up and the sound rips through the cottage—a bang followed by the crackle and whir of the flare as it shoots toward her.

There's light and noise everywhere, and my ears are roaring. The flare hits her high on the abdomen and—oh *God*—it *sticks.*

Mrs. Miller shrieks, dropping the knife.

She stumbles backward, cursing as her shirt catches fire and the smell of smoke fills the air. For a second I'm sure the flare will go out, or drop to the floor, but then the cursing turns to screams. I don't have enough air in my lungs to scream with her. She claws at her chest, trying to tear away the burning fabric and get to the flare, but her breath comes faster and faster.

My stomach turns, and I forget to move, run, escape while she's distracted. I can't look away from the horror. She's…she's on *fire*.

Mrs. Miller turns to run, but she either trips or doesn't see the first stair in her panic, and she falls.

Thump, scream, thump, crack, thump thump thump.

Like a fleshy tennis ball, bouncing all the way down.

I reach the top of the staircase just in time to see her hit the bottom with a heavy crunch.

Silence.

74

NOW

THURSDAY NIGHT.

Mrs. Miller lies at the bottom of the stairs, with her chest still sparking flames. One arm is bent *very* crooked.

As is her neck.

And she's the only one who knew where to find my sister.

Natalie's crying escalates, but she manages to say my name.

Shit. Natalie. I kneel beside her and realize I'm shaking. I clench my fists until the bones ache. I can't lose it now.

"How bad is it?" I ask, as if I can't see the blood staining the left side of her torso. Her face is pale and tear-streaked, and she looks so, so young.

She sniffles and a hiss escapes her lips as she lifts her hand from the wound.

"No, no, no. I—I don't know what to do for this. Keep the pressure on." She's in trouble, but Kelsey is too. I know it. Where is she? "Natalie, I'm sorry, but where have you and Kelsey been meeting with Finn? I know you've been in contact with him since we've been here. I saw your notebook. Pages from Finn."

She winces and more tears squeeze out. She opens her mouth, but doesn't manage a response.

Where would they have been meeting in private? "The old dock?" I ask, nearly breathless.

She nods and manages, "Yes."

"Natalie I've got to go find Kelsey." Her phone lies forgotten on the floor. "Here. Call 911. You'll be okay, I promise. Do you need me to dial for you?"

Natalie gives me a look, like I've just asked an incredibly silly question, and says, "Go get Kelsey. I'll even live stream this while I wait for the ambulance." She grimaces and nods. "Yeah. My followers will totally love that."

I stare for several seconds at the brave, bleeding, definitely a little bit frightening fifteen-year-old in front of me before finding my voice. "Great idea."

At least streaming means she'll be less alone.

I stand just as a ringtone blares. It's coming from the first floor, where Mrs. Miller lies crumpled and broken.

Guilt turns my stomach, but I leave Natalie and sprint down the stairs.

In the gloomy dark, Mrs. Miller hasn't moved. Blood pools from a spot on the back of her head, and her abdomen smolders. For a second, I'm kneeling in soft, wet dirt with warm rain pelting my shoulders, saying goodbye to my friend instead of staring down at the woman who killed her.

I clap a hand over my mouth and force the rising wave of panic down. There's no time for screaming. Heat and smoke radiate from her body as I rifle through Mrs. Miller's pockets for the phone.

I take the call and stay silent.

"What the hell, Alicia? Where's the video?" he snaps. Then, uncertain, "Were we wrong?"

My heart crashes into my stomach, leaving a hollow space in my chest.

I wanted it not to be true. I wanted to be wrong.

"Finn...please," I choke out. "Please don't hurt her."

Silence.

"Hmm," low and slow.

The call ends.

75

NOW

THURSDAY NIGHT.

I pray the paramedics get to Natalie in time. I pray I get to Kelsey in time. My lungs burn, and a trickle of sweat rolls down the back of my neck. These boots were not made for sprinting through the forest, and a blister has long popped and exposed raw skin on my heel. Doesn't matter. Almost there.

The clearing is empty.

The clearing is full of Sara.

The clearing is full of failure and the ghosts of everything I did wrong.

Panic swells, threatening to cover my head, suck me down and drown me.

Finn stands on the dock beside my sister. She's sitting in a chair. I squint, missing my glasses. I need to see her. I need to know she's okay.

Branches and leaves crackle as I stride toward them. He turns at the sound, but Kelsey faces out over the lake.

"Don't come any closer," Finn warns, putting a hand on the back of the wooden chair as if he'll push her in. So what? Kelsey can swim. `

I search their forms, stark against the glassy reflection of the lake, and finally see the rope.

"Fine. Okay. I'll stay right here." I hold my hands up in submission.

Kelsey cranes her neck enough that I can see her profile and the gray duct tape across her mouth.

"Let's talk," Finn says. His voice is hoarse, and his hair sticks up in wild clumps. In the moonlight his already pale skin has a silvery-gray tint, pooling purple beneath his eyes.

"Finn, I—"

A strange, ragged laugh slips out. "After a whole year of pretending you didn't know *exactly* what happened to my sister. No." And again, quieter, "No. You saw what happened, or you did it. Which is it, Mandy?"

Kelsey whines against the tape and my heart aches. I'd sent a text to Alex and another to my mom, cast out like lifelines as I left the honeymoon cabin to get to the old dock. I don't have high hopes about Mom or Dad checking their phones, or even having them on them, but Alex will see. He has to.

Help should be on the way, but how much longer does Kelsey have? Can I take Finn? Unlikely. I'm not in as good shape as I used to be, and Finn, although seemingly not well, is still very tall and strong. I would never get through Finn in time to reach Kelsey.

"Shush," Finn says, giving the chair a shake. He glares at me.

"Finn, I'm so sorry I didn't tell the cops what I knew, but I swear I didn't kill Sara." I stop short of saying, *I would never have hurt her,* because that's painfully untrue. I did hurt her. But I didn't light the rocket.

"I always thought—everyone always thought—'*Wow, how could she have left her friend out there alone, drunk, at night?* but I didn't really believe you were more than just a bad friend.*" His face darkens. "Until Alex slipped up and told me he'd actually left by himself. And your own sister was convinced there was more to Sara's death than an accident. Why was that, I wondered. So, tell me, if you didn't kill her, who did? Because I know you were full of shit when you said you left."

I stay perfectly still, not wanting to spook him. "I didn't know for sure who I saw that night until Kelsey and Natalie forced me to confront Sara's death, and what I did. But it was Mrs. Miller—I mean, Alicia. She came to talk to Sara about you, and they fought, and I don't think she planned to kill her, but *she* lit the rocket that hit your sister."

He takes two steps forward, but stops to avoid a hole. I fight the urge to run. Tension hums through me. He could kill me. He could kill us both.

"Liar. How gullible do you think I am? You're trying to save your sister and get out of taking any responsibility *again*."

I shake my head. "Finn, please. Was this whole thing your idea, or hers? Originally."

He frowns. "Mine. No, hers. I don't know, but it doesn't matter. She only got involved because I asked for help getting a confession out of you. She listened and *believed* me when I said Sara was murdered, but she didn't do it. That's...no. That's ridiculous. People don't do shit like that over..."

I can see him trying to sort through the pieces and make them fit into a picture that won't haunt him. It's a losing battle.

His voice cracks. "I don't believe you."

I don't know what to say, how to convince him, and I can feel the situation turning with every failed attempt to make him see I didn't take his sister from him.

It's hard convincing someone of something you barely believe yourself.

"Finn, I saw her. Please, untie Kelsey and then I'll go anywhere you want. We can talk. We can go to the police."

"So you can lie to them again?" He pauses. "Where's Alicia?"

"At the honeymoon cabin."

"Alive?"

Nope. I dodge the question and change tactics. "The cops are coming, but you didn't do anything bad yet. Just let Kelsey go, and we won't say anything, yeah? I know you're mad, and I don't blame you. I'm mad at me too. And I miss her, and it hurts. But Kelsey didn't do anything wrong."

He strides back to Kelsey, and my heart lurches up my throat, forcing a small terrified sound between my lips. But he stops short of touching the chair. When he turns around, his gaze slides to the patch of dirt where Sara died. He pushes a hand through the unkempt strands of hair. His neck strains.

"Did you know those pictures my mom gave you were all that my sister had left in her room? After Sara threw away any that had her high school friends in them?"

I frown at the sudden change of subject. "No, I didn't."

He nods, almost to himself. "I messed up. I accidentally let it slip to our parents that Sara was failing some classes in school, right before a big end-of-year party. They kept her home. She said I ruined her life."

"Over one party?" His thoughts don't seem to be lining up quite right, and that's almost as frightening as the fact that he's much, much stronger than me. He's unpredictable.

"Yeah, one party. Except at that one party, her shitty boyfriend cheated on her with her friend Mary. Her best friend." Disgust—with the ex, with the friend, maybe with himself—drips heavily on his words. Suddenly the intensity of her reaction when she thought Hannah—who had a boyfriend—might be hitting on Finn makes more sense. Or her disgust with married Mrs. Miller, though that one is bad enough on its own. I can even understand her sudden interest in Alex, in a twisted way. She got to be the one doing the taking.

It doesn't make things better. It just…is.

Finn keeps talking. "Everyone betrayed her. You were the only one left. She adored you, in her own way, and you betrayed her too."

I've been punched in the stomach.

"I—I didn't know."

"Even if what you said about Alicia were true, it wouldn't make you innocent. We all know my sister didn't die right away. She lay there, bleeding. She still had a chance, if you'd tried anything at all to help her, but you didn't. You. Let. Her. Die." He grinds each word out, slowly. "You killed her. Nothing else matters."

It's too close to what I've been telling myself all year.

My hands go cold. My head swims. Don't think about it don't think about it don't think about it gardenias gladiolas gerbera daisies dahlias dandelions daffodils shit shit shit—

There it is: the truth that's turned each day into a nightmare. Tortured me with what-ifs. Twisted every memory with the terrible weight of my own responsibility.

I didn't light the firework, but I did crouch beside Sara in the dirt, take her hand in mine, stare down at her bloodied face, and walk away.

I walked away while she bled to death.

In the end, I killed her.

76

THEN

ONE MONTH AFTER.

I curled deeper into the corner of the couch, my stringy, unwashed hair lying limp against my neck. My cheek would probably fuse with the leather of the sofa soon. I tugged the blanket higher until it was tucked beneath my chin. It was July, but I was freezing.

I stared at the TV. The reporter was talking about Sara. He'd *been* talking about her, and someone probably would have run in to frantically change the channel by now, but Mom was upstairs, and Dad was picking Kelsey up from soccer camp. Or, wait… Had they gone for milkshakes? That might've been yesterday.

The reporter continued to detail everything the cops and the coroner had released about Sara's death. It had been a month, and still no sign that the other girl, the one who lit the firework, had come forward. There was no one offering a complete picture of what had happened that night, and all

I had was my own blurry one. What was I supposed to do with *that*?

I blinked my eyes and they burned. I'd cried all the moisture out. Why was I doing this to myself? I could get past this, if I'd just stand up, turn off the TV, and go take a shower.

Okay, it wouldn't be *that* easy, but it would be a start. One step at a time.

"—says that Sara died in the early morning on June twenty-third. The police medical examiner says that she did not die from her injuries immediately. Sara likely regained consciousness following the incident, and it appears she tried to stumble for help. Tragically, it was already too late. She collapsed beside the lake due to blood loss from the wound to her neck and face, combined with the alcohol and the possible concussion from hitting her head against a rock when she first fell."

I stopped breathing.

No.

No.

I'd convinced myself that I'd misremembered where she fell—that she'd been closer to the lake when the rocket struck her—and that she was already dead when I abandoned her.

But I was wrong.

I could have saved her. If I'd called 911, Sara might've been alive now.

It was my fault she died. I failed her.

I killed her.

77

NOW

THURSDAY NIGHT.

Finn laughs. It's brittle. Breaking.

I shiver at the sound and edge toward the dock. The skin at the back of my neck tightens, and my chest aches with suspended breath. I'm floating outside my body and sinking straight into hell all at once. Every step closer to Kelsey is progress. It's agonizing hope.

Finn's eyes sharpen and his mouth thins, all laughter gone. I halt with one heel raised—frozen mid-step. We're playing a nightmarish game of red light, green light, and the prize is Kelsey's life.

His fingers drum the back of the chair, and he shifts his weight from one foot to the other. I'm close enough now, nearly to the dock, that even without my glasses I can see the shine of his eyes and the ruddy, splotchy color to his cheeks. He's been crying.

"You didn't try to save my sister," he says, and "try" is

the most miserable word I've ever heard. "It doesn't matter if you lit the firework or not. In *no* version of your story did you try to save her."

His fingers toy with the rounded chairback.

"I didn't know she needed saving," I plead. He has to understand. "They were arguing, but people fight. Sara fought with people all the time."

He grips the wood tight, a muscle in his jaw jumping. I'd said the wrong thing. They'd been fighting the entire trip, and then she died. Reminding him of that definitely wasn't a good move.

"I'm sorry," I apologize, but I choke, and he can't hear. *I'm so sorry and I still can't believe I let it end the way it did.* Apologies are worthless now. Sara's death has been festering inside us both for far too long.

"I could save Kelsey..." he says.

"Finn?" My voice shakes and my knees wobble. The world is fuzzy at the edges as my vision narrows around my sister and Finn. "You haven't done anything that can't be undone. You're not a—" I can't bring myself to say the word *killer.*

Some fierce, terrible emotion splits his face. Pain, or sadness, or shame—whatever it is, it makes my insides cold.

I think I hear him say, "It doesn't matter."

"Please," I beg. "She didn't—"

He shoves the chair, and Kelsey splashes face-first into the lake.

78

NOW

THURSDAY NIGHT.

"Kelsey!" Her name tears through my chest, taking pieces of my heart with it.

Finn stumbles backward, hands flailing like he's looking for support and finding air.

"Shit," he says. The word comes rough and ragged. "Oh my God, I—oh, *shit*!"

I run at him, his body half-turned in silhouette, the rolling water rippling out behind him. Swallowing my sister down into the muck. He turns. His eyes are wide with shock, lips parted like he can't believe what he's done.

I hit the dock at a sprint. He doesn't get out of the way. Instead, he takes a step directly into my path, and I crash into him. He yelps and staggers but doesn't fall, using his larger size and strength to hurl me to the boards. I skid, and a splinter, wicked sharp and thick as a fork prong, slides into my palm. My arm goes out from under me.

I'm going to be too late.

"Help her," I beg. "Please Finn, help her." It's half a sob.

I don't hear splashing.

She's dying while I sit here surrounded by rotting wood and shallow water.

Just like last time.

Finn shakes his head rapidly. "I can't. I won't. Shit Mandy, I—"

I scream, wordless.

"Finn, what the hell," Alex's voice startles us both.

Finn jumps, twisting toward his friend.

Alex got my text.

I scramble to my feet, bolting away from Finn while he's distracted.

A sharp crack splits the night a second before pain sears my calf and I collapse sideways. A rotted patch of dock gave way beneath my right foot. Jagged wooden teeth scrape skin from my thigh and I shriek. I can't breathe through the pain for a second, but I don't need air. *Kelsey* needs air.

Footsteps come from behind me, but they're retreating. Alex gives a surprised shout, and there's a thud, like someone's landed a punch.

I blink away the tears, leverage my forearms against the dock, and pull. My leg is on fire, but I ignore the pain and grunt. I'm free!

How long has it been? A minute? A lifetime? Two minutes?

One stride, two strides, and I'm in the water where Kelsey

went under. I kick and flail. The water's not that deep here, can't be more than five feet, but enough to bury her. Enough to take her from me.

My ankle clips something hard and I spin around, brushing against the legs of the chair before finding Kelsey's arms. I dig my feet into the mud and push her toward the surface. She's so heavy, tied to the chair. This isn't going to work. I can't pull her back onto the dock. I'm not strong enough. Kelsey may be shorter than me, but she's bigger, and, unlike her, I've neglected anything even physical fitness adjacent all year.

Ignoring the burning in my lungs, I trudge toward the shore, pulling Kelsey and the chair along with me. Relief washes over me as my head clears the water and Kelsey's follows, but the relief is temporary. I'm alone, and she's not moving.

I lose my footing and water splashes around my torso as my knees hit the mud. We're almost to the patchy grass.

"Come on, Kelsey. You're okay. You're going to be okay," I wheeze, voice thick with tears.

She doesn't answer. Not even a muffled grunt.

I collapse, just for one agonizing second, and then crawl around to face Kelsey. She's on her side, one leg kicked free from the chair, but her hands are tied behind her and she's completely still. Cold storms through my veins.

The duct tape clings to her slack mouth, straining the skin outward as I rip. She doesn't flinch, or cry out, or open her eyes. I press fingers to her neck, and the pulse is there, but weak.

I look around for help. Alex is a lifeguard. He'll be able to do this right. But the clearing is empty. Alex and Finn are both gone.

"Ale—" I scream. My voice cracks. "Alex!"

I get it out this time, but I can't wait around for him to come back.

I work at the rope tying Kelsey's hands. Got it. Her arms flop to the dirt with sickening lifelessness.

Her left ankle is still bound, but I lay her flat and try to remember the basics of CPR from my junior-year health class. I check her pulse, but I can't tell if she has one or not. If she does, it's faint.

How many breaths per minute am I supposed to do? Do I do chest compressions if she has a pulse?

I pinch her nose, press my mouth over hers, and breathe.

I can hardly get enough air myself, and my pulse is so fast that the dizziness comes quickly. I can't stop. Not until Kelsey opens her eyes.

Alex runs to my side. I glance up. His chest heaves and he's bleeding from a busted lip.

"Help," I manage, barely pushing the panic down enough to speak.

His face pales, but he nods and takes over, tilting her head back before placing one hand on her forehead, pinching her nose, and breathing.

Once.

Twice.

He stops, and for a heart-stopping moment I think he's

going to tell me it's hopeless. But he shifts quickly to place the heels of his hands in the center of her chest, and starts compressions.

One, two, three, four, what was that song, staying alive, staying alive, uh uh uh uh, staying alive—

Water spews from Kelsey's mouth and dribbles down her cheeks. Her eyes fly open, and Alex turns her head to the side so she doesn't choke as she vomits.

She whimpers and sobs around the spitting, but she's breathing. She's *alive*.

I didn't fail her.

79

NOW

THURSDAY NIGHT.

I know Kelsey is here, sitting in the dirt beside me, both of us draped in the crinkly blanket from the paramedic, but I can't quite believe I saved her. My heartbeat refuses to accept that we're safe.

Or safe enough.

A paramedic and two cops came out to the dock, while others rushed Natalie to the hospital and secured the crime scene at the honeymoon cabin. Police are also searching the property for Finn, who got away when Alex turned back to help revive Kelsey.

I'm so glad Alex heard me and let Finn go.

Memories of last year pound the inside of my head, demanding more attention than they deserve. I shut them out. Right now, all that matters is Kelsey's hand in mine.

I squeeze and she squeezes back.

Kelsey rests her head on my shoulder, sniffling every few

minutes. I swallow past the lump in my throat and drag the heel of my squishy boots through the dirt. My legs are falling asleep, but I'll sit on the ground with Kelsey all night if that's what she wants to do.

Alex stands with the two cops. One of them nods and scribbles in his notebook, but both of them cast more and more frequent glances in my direction.

I'm going to have to go talk to them soon. The prospect of telling them what happened, and the *backstory* of what happened, makes it hard to keep from throwing up.

I'll do it, but I'm terrified.

At our side, Dad is on the phone with Mom. She's going to the hospital with Natalie. There was no time to wait.

"She's all right. Yes, I promise. Yes, I'll tell her. I love you too. Call when you get to the hospital. Yes, we'll follow."

Kelsey stiffens beside me.

"Natalie's going to be okay, right?" she asks me, quietly, for the third time.

"I think so." I'm trying not to lie, so I don't make promises. I can't quite shake the squirming, guilty feeling in my stomach. I left Natalie alone with a stab wound, not knowing for sure how bad it was, or how long it would take the paramedics to arrive. I wrap my arms around my sister and squeeze.

I did my best, this time. I just hope it was enough.

As the female cop breaks away and walks over, I take a deep breath and tell myself that whatever happens, Sara's true story—as best I know it—will finally be told.

80

NOW

THREE WEEKS LATER.

"Welcome to CrimeChatWithNat," I say. I clench my fist enough that my meager fingernails bite into my palm. This is scary, being in front of the camera to talk about what happened at Highmark, but I promised Natalie I would do this one—and *only* one—for her.

"I'm Mandy Jenkins, and while Natalie continues to heal from her injuries, I'll be filling in for a very specific story. My story." Technically Natalie's parents have forbidden her from doing any more true-crime content herself. She did get *stabbed* in pursuit of a story, so I don't blame them, but I'm sure Natalie will be back.

"I was Sara Ellis's friend, and yes, it's true that I was there the night she was killed. But that story is for another time." Maybe Natalie will tell it, maybe not.

I've been cleared of wrongdoing in Sara's death, and Mrs. Miller's, with the help of Natalie's statements and messages found on Mrs. Miller's phone, but I know I'm not totally innocent.

"For now, I just wanted to say hi, and tell y'all that Natalie is going to be okay, but that she was injured by Alicia Miller, the woman who killed Sara. Some of you may have seen that Sara's brother Finn was arrested, after he and Alicia tried to extort a confession out of me, and in the process, Finn tried to drown my fifteen-year-old sister. Thankfully, she's okay too." I shiver, and across my bedroom, Kelsey gives me a small anxious smile.

A text from Alex pops up at the top of my phone screen. Just checking in. He's coming to visit next weekend, since he has plenty of free time before school starts now that he's quit working at Highmark.

We talked a lot about Finn right after that night, but I know it's hard for him. Finn was his friend, and he has to reckon with the fact that Finn tried to kill someone.

We all want to see the best versions of our friends, and be the best versions of ourselves when we're with them. But what happens when instead, we bring out the worst in each other?

Being with Sara was a lot like diving into the lake. It could have been exciting and exhilarating. Instead, we dragged each other deeper into the dark, until cold rushed in and all that was left was violence.

Now, when I dream of her, water spills from her charred mouth as she asks me why I could save Kelsey, but not her.

Every time, I tell her it's because I *wanted* to save Kelsey, and I wake up crying.

The dream is messy, and obvious, and wrong, but it's also true, because dreams are about more than reality. They're memories and guilt, and even though I've started therapy, it hasn't magically erased all the times I've wondered why I didn't get out from under that dock. When Sara asks me why I saved Kelsey and not her, it's not about the bitter end. It's about a thousand choices and little mistakes I made—*we* made—along the way, where if we'd done even one thing differently, she might still be alive. But those weren't the choices we wanted to make, and now she's dead.

I talk for a while longer about the night Sara died, and how big a mistake I'd made keeping what I knew a secret for so long, and then I stop the video and sag in my chair. My bed comforter rustles, and Kelsey slides off.

"Come on, let's go get ice cream," she says. It's such a normal thing to say, and it seems out of place after talking so much about death.

Before she can get to the door, I pull her into a hug. I'm pretty sure I've hugged her more in the last week than I have in our entire lives, but she hasn't complained.

"I'm glad you're staying," she mutters into my shoulder.

I pull back. I decided—with significant input from my parents—to come home for a semester before returning to school. I'm not nearly as worried about it as I was a couple weeks ago. I'll go back when I'm ready.

"Me too."

Kelsey's smiling as she heads for the kitchen.

I follow my sister down the stairs, toying with the charm

at the dip of my collarbone. Virginia said someday thinking about Sara would hurt less, so I'll carry Sara with me until then. Moving forward hurts, but I can do it.

And I'll keep Sara close to my heart, right where she's always been.

For better or worse.

ACKNOWLEDGMENTS

When I was young, I stayed up all night reading. I read paper-backs on the sidelines before soccer games, trying to wring every last word from the page before I had to step onto the field. I read at lunch tables and by the pool, behind textbooks in class, and in front of the TV. And then I stopped. I don't know what happened. Life, work, distraction. But I clawed my way back to the joy of reading, and part of what came with that was the resurrection of a dream. I was going to be a published author. It took five years (and more than five books) for the offer on *Now She's Dead* to happen, but I wouldn't change any of it. Thank you, reader, for spending your precious time here with me. I hope you enjoy(ed) Mandy and Highmark.

It's a strange experience to be looking back over the years that made this moment possible and thinking about all the moments that still stretch between me and my debut. I'm not sure that this will ever feel real, but I know it wouldn't be real without the influence and support of so many people.

To AJ Cosgrove, who has been with me since the first book and has read each and every subsequent story after that. You and Jennifer Mandula have been there for so many words, so many milestones, and so many what-ifs. Jennifer, thank you for popping into my DMs one day and joining the ceaseless nonsense. I can't imagine this writing journey without y'all (and thankfully I don't have to).

To Paula Gleeson. Without you, *Now She's Dead* doesn't exist. I could never have done this without you, nor would I have wanted to. Thank you for patiently (but ruthlessly) grabbing my hand and dragging me through turning this book into a thriller during those months of Author-Mentor Match.

To Joly—thank you for all the years of encouragement and for truly "getting" me and my books (and always being around to scream, cry, laugh, and scream some more). To Jen, who meets me every weekend to write (or talk and eat pastries instead of writing)—thank you for being a weirdo with me. To Lauren Blackwood, for always squeezing in coffee and brunch dates with me to talk books, careers, and life. I promise someday I'll have a book where you can yell at me to add more romance (and I'll listen).

To my agent, Chelsea Hensley. The first time we talked, I knew I wanted you in my corner. Thank you for always being there with sound guidance and a sense of humor. I'm so glad to be building a career with you by my side.

To my editor, Wendy McClure—thank you for your enthusiasm for *Now She's Dead* and for me as an author. Working with you to polish this book has been so much more fun than I could've imagined, and I can't wait to work on the next one together.

To Jenny Lopez, Thea Voutiritsas, Jessica Thelander, Susan Barnett, Aimee Alker, Sarah Brody, Tara Jaggers, Erin LaPointe, Karen Masnica, Delaney Heisterkamp, and the entire Sourcebooks team—thank you for everything you've done to make this book shine and reach readers. The work you do is amazing!

To the early readers of *Now She's Dead* (and of the original, almost unrecognizable version)—thank you for helping me take this story from the messiest stages to the polished thing that now sits on shelves. A.J. Van Belle, Catherine, Crystal J. Bell, Dani Cessna, Jenny Marie, Josie Keeley, Kristin Curry, and Sonja J. Kaye, I hope you love the final version!

To Peyton, my sweet, video-game-loving husband. Our mutual love of alone time is essential to my writing career. Keep playing games and I'll keep writing, and together we'll keep traveling the world and eating all the foods.

To my parents—thank you for instilling a love of reading in me. From the nights spent curled up with you reading to me, to helping me buy and borrow countless books, to never questioning when I said I was going to get published, your support made me who I am and I wouldn't be fulfilling this dream without you. To my sister, you've always been there to cheer me on, and I can't believe I'm debuting with a book you'll want to read!

To the whole host of friends and family who've lifted

me up every step of the way—my amazing in-laws, Morgan and Greg, Annie and Alex, the Gordons, Grace, Samantha, Aisha, Jim, and Kevin, and the dear friends from the artist community—thank you!

And last but FAR from least, to the Hardins. Thank you for so many wonderful summers in the mountains. Vacations with y'all were (thankfully) the furthest thing from a thriller novel, but damn, the location and scenery sure did make for perfect setting inspiration!

ABOUT THE AUTHOR

Roselyn Clarke writes about the things that haunt us—relationships, mistakes, monsters. She studied psychology (and remains fascinated by the strange places to which the mind wanders) and lives in the DC area, where she works in communications. When she's not writing, she's buying plants that may or may not survive and daydreaming about future travels. You can connect with her online for bookish content and life updates. If you want a behind-the-curtain peek at her writing process, craft advice, or random stories, you can sign up for her newsletter on her website.

roselynclarke.com
@roselynclarkebooks

sourcebooks fire

Home of the hottest trends in YA!

Visit us online and
sign up for our newsletter at
FIREreads.com

....

Follow
@sourcebooksfire
online